The golden thread that runs through Jim Campbell's wonderful book is his vivid portrayal of the hope, strength, and courage of beautiful mountain people. Mr. Campbell's superb writing clearly flows from his own Appalachian heritage and deep understanding of the very special people he introduces to you, the fortunate reader.

Just give yourself permission to move in with Mr. Campbell's adventurous Duncan family and you, too, will be able to smell the honeysuckle, ride the winding mountain roads and make yourself dizzy from sampling the "shine!"

As a lifelong mountain person myself, I assure you that Jim Campbell's creative writing genius embodies and captures the spirit of his heartfelt message.

Dr. Bob Sutherland
Director, Learning Resources Center
Southwest Virginia Community College

Ida Mae: Moonshine, Money, and Misery is a delightful depiction of life in the coalfields and mountains of Southwest Virginia during the period following World War II. To a degree, things were difficult for most of our families, yet there was a simplicity to life that causes us to want those "good old days." Jim Campbell's story allows the reader to become immersed in this culture. I immediately identified with the people, the locale, the winding country roads, the sweat and toil of those who were considered poor, and the beautiful devotion those uncomplicated residents gave to the church. Ida Mae is an unlikely protagonist in this tale of the illegal, yet romantic life of moonshine runners. Growing up in the coalfields, every one of us knew of the moonshine still in the back woods, and we were aware that adventuresome young boys and their hot rods ran the graveled roads to evade the authorities. Jim Campbell puts a different spin on the tale, personalizing this life style with humor and grace. It is a must read for anyone who grew up in our area.

Charles Grindstaff, Principal
Tazewell High School

CHAPTER ONE

LIFE ON THE FARM

Another long hot July day was coming to an end and none too soon for Ira Duncan and his family. Working the fields on Sheriff William Baxter's farm was no easy task in normal weather, but the summer of 1949 was the hottest on record. The blades on the cornstalks were beginning to curl, the hay crop was at a standstill, and two of the three springs on the farm had already gone dry.

"Might as well get ready for another sleepless night, Granny," Ira remarked to his mother, who was sitting near him on the front porch of their old two-story farmhouse.

"Ain't had myself a good night's sleep since the middle of June, I reckon," she replied. "Was doing pretty well at catching a few winks sometime this morning when two or three bats come flying through the window screen and woke me up. They wuz fluttering around after each other like a bunch of big airplanes. Must be mating season, I figured."

"I been meaning to fix that window screen," Ira commented. "Just seems I can't ever get around to it."

"Might fix that board on the Johnny house seat, too," Granny snapped. "It's been loose for nearly two months and ever time I sit down, it pinches my behind."

It was true, a few things around the place needed repair, but Ira was happier living on Sheriff Baxter's farm than any place he had lived in all his married life. After all, the sheriff gave him free rent, allowed him to have one milk cow, a couple of hogs, and whatever space he needed to grow garden vegetables for his family. He was also paid fifty cents an hour for his farm labor. In addition, he was promised the job as deputy if the sheriff was re-elected come fall. In return, Ira was responsible for growing enough hay and grain to feed Baxter's forty or fifty head of cattle. He also took care of any fence mending that needed to be done and any other minor mishaps that might occur. Not a bad bargain, considering he was allowed to hire whatever help he needed during harvest time.

"Can't ask for much more than this," Ira reasoned, as he watched his mother fan herself with what was left of her feather duster.

In the spring of '46, Ira moved onto the Baxter farm with his wife, Mary Ellen, and their four children, Ida Mae, Mary Sue, and the twelve-year-old twin boys, Kervin and Kevin. Granny came along, too; she began living with Ira and Mary Ellen when her husband died suddenly, shortly after the outbreak of the Second World War.

There was one other offspring belonging to the Duncan's; their oldest, John Robert, but he was away in the army at the time Ira moved his family to the Baxter place. It had only been two weeks since John Robert received his discharge and he was now living and working on the farm.

The daily chores having been finished, the remainder of the family began their regular routine of gathering onto the front porch. That is, everyone except Ida Mae and John Robert. Ida Mae was putting the finishing touches on a chocolate cake, which Ira was sure she baked to impress the deacon on his visit the following day.

John Robert was busying himself out in the barn, trying to repair his old 1937 Chevrolet that had been damaged while he was away.

"Scoot that chair up to the edge of the porch, Ira," Mary Ellen scolded. "Your spittin' distance ain't what it used to be, and that tobacker juice done started rottin the end offen two or three of them planks." She seated herself in one of the chairs near her husband, as if to be close enough to make sure he did as she had said.

"Don't worry about that tobacco juice," was Ira's reply. "You know Ida Mae will have the planks scrubbed clean as a whistle before Preacher Kyle and the deacon come calling tomorrow evening. And, if you ain't noticed, my spittin' distance ain't all that's been going down hill lately."

"I've noticed," she answered blushing.

Mary Ellen knew her husband was right about Ida Mae having the porch clean. Her oldest daughter, now eighteen, was becoming more and more interested in the young deacon, Donald Hale. Lately, she made every effort to ensure the old place looked as well as age would permit before each of the deacons weekly visits.

Not a bad prospect for a husband, Mary Ellen had to admit. The Deacon Donald Hale — Dooley, as most folks called him — was a handsome specimen. He stood just over six feet tall, weighed near two hundred pounds, had wavy black hair and eyes as blue as a robin's egg. He was still behind the age of 25, as best she could determine.

"Could be the counties most eligible bachelor," Mary Ellen supposed, "if it were not for his lack of common reasoning."

Dooley did not possess a wealth of education. In fact, he'd spent his last three years of schooling in the seventh grade. He did not feel the need to acquire a great deal of book-learning because life was always easy for him. His father managed to have whatever amount of cash his family needed, with some left over. It was no secret that Mr. Hale made a larger contribution than anyone each time the church collection plate was passed. Probably how Dooley got the position as one of the church deacons, Mary Ellen surmised. His mother being the sister of Sheriff William Baxter, didn't hurt anything either.

Although Dooley's mother saw to it that he led a very sheltered life, he did manage to get into town more often than she knew. His favorite hangout was the local pool hall.

One thing Dooley had going for him was the fact that he was the best pool shot ever to darken the door of Willie's Billiard Parlor. That is, until Preacher Kyle convinced him to give up the ways of the Devil and join the local Baptist Church. "Evil will come to any man who gambles for the wages of another," Brother Kyle declared. "And will cause him to commit greater sins," he added.

Dooley did not fully understand how winning a bit of change in a friendly game of nine-ball could cause him to commit some awful wrongdoing. He at last succumbed to the preacher's persuasions and hung up his cue stick. Not counting the few times he slipped into Willie's place late at night to shoot a game or two, not for money of course.

For the most part, Dooley did try to walk the straight and narrow. He even accompanied Preacher Kyle on most of his home visits. Why, within a few weeks, he was elected deacon. Shortly thereafter, he was also elected treasurer. His mother was more proud of her son being elected to the church offices than she was her brother being elected county sheriff.

Dooley did not mind holding these two offices. As a matter of fact, he somewhat enjoyed the notoriety. Being deacon required little more than riding around with the pastor on occasional visits. Being treasurer was no trouble at all. He simply took the weekly collections home and placed the money in an empty cigar box in one of his dresser drawers. His daddy told him many times he should not trust banks.

The Reverend was so proud of what he had helped Dooley become. "Quite a step up for someone who did little else but hang around a pool hall," he was heard saying to one of the fellow church members.

Crack! It was the sound of a pebble striking the side of the house.

"You missed again," Ira heard one of the twins tease, as another stone struck the side of the dwelling. He was sure Kevin was the one who'd failed to hit the Prince Albert tobacco box target the boys had nailed to the side of the house. After all, everyone in the family knew that Kervin was second to none when it came to shooting his slingshot.

"That's 'cause it's getting too dark to see," Kevin declared, as the two younger boys came running onto the porch.

"Better teach your brother to correct his aim," Ira said to Kervin. "If he shoots any more holes in Granny's window screen, it will be owls flying into her room at night instead of them little old bats she's been complaining about."

Kevin was right; it was growing late. The shadows were becoming camouflaged by darkness. The entire family was relaxing on the front porch, enjoying the coolness of the evening. For some time no one spoke. Everyone seemed to be listening for the next call of a whippoorwill somewhere far in the distance.

At last, it was Granny who broke the silence. "Sounds like that old bird is trying to summons a mate," she declared. "I suppose one will come by soon if she keeps calling."

"Why don't you learn to sound like a whippoorwill, Ida Mae?" Mary Sue teased. "Then maybe old Dooley will come calling."

"You're just jealous," Ida Mae answered, playfully pushing her younger sister from the porch and into the yard. "What makes you think I would want anything to do with the deacon anyway?"

"Because you didn't bake that big old chocolate cake for me or the preacher. That's why!" Mary Sue answered, climbing back onto the porch.

"Time for bed ladies," Ira interrupted. "Tomorrow is going to be a busy day and I don't want you girls fighting over the deacon. I don't think Preacher Kyle would take too kindly to that."

The next day would be busy indeed. Saturdays were the only day of the week Ira had to himself. The sheriff would arrive sometime before mid-morning to pay for the number of hours he and John Robert worked the previous week. Once this was done, Ira had the remainder of the day to do as he pleased.

It would be easy to catch a ride into the nearest town; a task that would have been unnecessary, had Ida Mae's driving capabilities been a little more refined. There, he would visit with a few old friends, trade a pocket knife or two, and try to influence as many people as he could to vote for his landlord; the sheriff. He would, of course, shop for whatever grocery items his family needed and then catch another ride back to the farm by sundown. Reverend Kyle and the deacon would be paying a visit before dark.

Chapter Two

THE WEEKLY VISIT

The next day began as most weekends did. Ira's mother was the last to awaken and make her presence known. And, as usual she was somewhat grouchy when she first got out of bed.

"Just in her second childhood," Ira would answer, when anyone commented on Granny's early-morning disposition.

"Not much different from her first childhood, from all accounts I have," Mary Ellen once snapped, after becoming agitated at Ira's constant defense of his mother.

"What's all that racket?" Granny questioned, as she made her way onto the porch where her son was seated with pencil and notepad in hand. "Got so an old woman can't sleep past the crack of dawn," she added.

"It's pushing nine o'clock," Ira reminded her. "And the noise you hear is John Robert trying to get his car back into running condition."

"Shouldn't never got out of running condition in the first place, if you ask me," she snapped. "And if you're figuring how much time the sheriff owes you, better check it three or four times. He'll slice an hour or two off, if you don't keep both eyes open."

"Better go on inside to your breakfast," Ira interrupted.

His mother ambled away mumbling something about what an awful feller Baxter was, but Ira paid no mind.

Ira had to admit Granny was right about the old Chevrolet. He had used poor judgment when he decided to use John Robert's car to haul their winter supply of firewood out of the mountain instead of using the team and wagon. Not a bad idea at first, until he let Ida Mae persuade him to let her do the driving.

"But only if you help load the firewood," he told her. She agreed. Ira drove the car into the wooded area, backed it into position, set the emergency brake, and with the help of Ida Mae and the twins, had the trunk fully loaded in no time at all.

"Let me go unload Daddy," she begged.

"Just be careful," Ira warned. "Me and your two brothers will have another load cut by the time you get back."

Ida Mae jumped into the driver's seat. She moved the gearshift into the neutral position without ever starting the engine. Next, she released the brake, causing the car to roll forward. All she knew to do after that was to hold on to the steering wheel and scream.

Neither accomplished anything; the further, the faster.

Ida Mae panicked. She managed to avoid hitting one of the sheriff's prime beef cattle and a large boulder or two. She also managed to jump clear just before the Chevrolet slammed head on into a huge oak tree.

Ira and the twins rushed to where the mangled car had abruptly halted.

Ida Mae was unhurt, but the same could not be said for the car. A cloud of steam was escaping from the ruptured radiator. The front bumper was broken in half, both teardrop headlights had been dislodged, the hood was standing in an upright position and a large opening was where the windshield used to be.

Ira used the team to pull the wreck off the hillside. He dragged it into the open-ended shed beside the barn, where everyone else in the family, including Granny, came to inspect the damage.

"What do you think, Mother?" Ira asked, after she completed her third circle of the vehicle.

"I think that's a mighty small load of firewood," was her only comment.

Granny was wrong, however, about William Baxter not paying exactly what was owed. He never questioned Ira concerning the amount he said he was due. Granny had another reason for not liking him and it had nothing to do with Ira's wages.

Mary Ellen and the sheriff were a steady couple throughout her teenage years, except for the times he was seen slipping around with Lou Ella Crabtree. Lou Ella was a pretty blonde that lived about twenty miles away in the southernmost end of the county.

Everyone in the community was aware of the big argument Mary Ellen and her steady had had at one of the Saturday night square dances. They also knew what the argument was about. Mary Ellen found out about the pretty blonde. Within a week, Baxter and Lou Ella were married. A few days later, Mary Ellen persuaded Ira to meet her at the altar.

In the beginning, Ira's mother had little to say about the wedding, but when Mary Ellen had given birth after only eight months, Granny pulled down her calendar.

"A healthy-looking young lad, to have been born early," the doctor said the night John Robert came into the world. Ira's mother had her doubts about her son's first-born coming early, and she would not let go of the idea that Baxter still had eyes for Mary Ellen. In fact, she objected strenuously to Ira moving the family onto the sheriff's farm a little less than a year after the passing of Mrs. Baxter. She paid no mind to her daughter-in-law's insistence that any feelings she may have had for William Baxter were long since forgotten. Granny made no effort to hide her feelings, so Ira tried to keep her as far away from their landlord as possible. Fortunately, he had succeeded again, for she disappeared inside, just as the black-and-white came into view. It was not hard to tell the county's highest ranking police officer was in somewhat of a hurry.

"What's the rush?" Ira asked, when the car slid to a stop.

"Just got wind there's a load of shine coming out of the next county 'bout noon," the sheriff said. "The boys and I are going to be waiting when they cross the county line. With the election coming up, I sure could make myself look mighty good if I could intercept some of that white liquor that's running through."

Ira knew well what county Baxter was referring to. Buchanan County lay just to the North and the quality and quantity of white liquor made there was second only to that brewed in Eastern Kentucky. The county line was at the very top of the mountain. It was rumored that the whiskey runners moved through Russell County en route to North Carolina, with little fear of being caught. It was also rumored that the whiskey movement might cost William the election.

The sheriff handed Ira sufficient money to pay both, Ira and John Robert for their week's work and quickly sped away.

"Sure wish I had a car that would run like that," John Robert said as he came strolling up to where his father stood in the cloud of dust the sheriff had created.

"Get yourself elected sheriff and the county will buy you one," Ira said jokingly.

"Or start hauling moonshine," John Robert teased, "and then I could buy myself a faster one."

"How much longer will it take to get the old Chevrolet in running shape?" Ira asked.

"'Bout another week, I reckon."

Ira gave his son his share of the weekly wages and started walking toward the gravel road to catch a ride into town.

John Robert resumed the task of repairing his car.

Hauling white liquor into North Carolina sure would beat the heck out of working on the farm for fifty cents an hour, he thought as he reattached one of the dislodged headlights.

He spent the remainder of the day working on the old Chevrolet. It was nearing suppertime, when at last; he put away his tools and sat down on one of the running boards.

"Fifty cents an hour," he thought, as he gazed down over the ten acre parched cornfield he would have to start plowing again come Monday morning. "There has to be a better way," he thought, as he picked himself up and started toward the farmhouse, where he knew the evening meal would soon be ready.

He stepped onto the back porch, filled a pan from a bucket of cool water that had been carried from the only spring that had not yet dried up and washed the grease and oil from his hands and face. The smell of fresh baked cornbread and turnip greens reminded him that he had not stopped to eat lunch. He sat in the shade of a maple tree and watched the twins playing at the end of the long lane near the gravel road. They were waiting for their daddy to return from town, so they could help carry whatever grocery items he had purchased. His two sisters were helping prepare their evening meal and Granny sat near the kitchen door leaning back in her favorite chair, snoring.

"Little wonder Granny can't get a good night's sleep," he thought, as he watched one of the neighbor's pickup truck come to a stop, near where the twins were playing. He knew it would only be a short time now, until he would be able to soothe the hunger pains gnawing at his stomach.

"How were things in town today?" Mary Ellen asked, when everyone was seated at the dinner table.

"Not so good," Ira remarked. "I couldn't find anyone who wanted to do any fair pocket knife swapping. Coffee's gone up five cents a pound and it isn't looking real good for the sheriff in the coming election, either."

"You mean Baxter might not get re-elected and have to start doing an honest day's work," Granny chimed.

"Don't be so hard on the sheriff, Granny," Ira said, as he broke a fair size piece from one of the pones of cornbread. "And pass me them mashed taters," he added.

"Ain't hard enough, if you ask my opinion," his mother snapped, shooting a glance at her daughter-in-law, as if she were throwing a dagger.

Mary Ellen ignored her, as was always the case, whenever any subject concerning William Baxter arose.

"Why do you think the sheriff might not win the election?" John Robert wanted to know.

"Because he ain't doing nothing but riding around in the new car and drawing more money than he's worth." Granny added her two-cents worth again.

Again she was ignored.

"Seems his opponent, old man Mike Fletcher, is coming down real hard on the fact that William can't catch them boys running all that white liquor thru the county. Fletcher is telling that all the shine don't get all way thru the county anyway, judging from the bottles he seen being passed around down at the dance hall last Saturday night."

"The sheriff was out after a load of them shine runners today," Ira continued. "Bet old Mike is going to be surprised when he finds out some of those boys are over in the county jail."

"Wouldn't put a lot of stock in that happening," Granny said.

Ida Mae interrupted before anyone could answer. "Better start washing these dishes if everyone is finished."

"Yeah! And we best not waste any time in getting them done," her younger sister giggled. "It wouldn't do for you to be in here doing dishes while Dooley is sitting outside wondering where you are."

"Hush your mouth, Mary Sue," Ida Mae snapped. "What makes you think that's why I want to get the dishes done?"

"'Cause that's the same reason you spent half a day scrubbing the porch," Mary Sue answered.

Everyone in the family knew Mary Sue was right.

Ida Mae barely had time to finish the kitchen chores and join the rest of the family on the porch, when Preacher Kyle's car came into view. She watched as the car came to a stop at a gate separating the end of the lane from the gravel country road. The automobile had barely stopped rolling, when the deacon jumped from the passengers seat and opened the gate allowing the preacher to drive through.

The deacon hurriedly closed the gate and stepped onto the back bumper instead of getting back inside. The preacher shifted his car into gear and came racing up the lane towards the Duncan's home. All went well, until he reached the end of the drive, at which time he had to slam hard on the brakes in order to avoid running over a flock of Ira's chickens.

The car came to a sudden stop, but the deacon did not. He went flying over the top, slid onto the hood and rolled off the drivers' side onto the grass. When he regained enough composure to raise his head, he was looking straight at Ida Mae, who was seated on the top step.

Dooley quickly pulled himself into a sitting position and took inventory of his extremities. It did not take long to determine his body was suffering far less injury than that of his pride. Grasping the fence post, he pulled himself halfway to his feet.

Ida Mae's exquisite physique filled his vision. Stretching himself to his full height, he stood and stared for a moment at the beautiful creature that for some time had been the girl of his dreams.

Her golden blonde hair glistened in the evening sunlight. Each long strand accented her rosy cheeks as it flowed fetchingly past her face and came to rest atop a perfectly formed feminine shoulder.

Her eyes, the color of a blue winter sky, were fixed on his slightly battered frame. Her magnificent smile did little to relieve his embarrassment.

"Glad you could drop in, Dooley," Ira said, trying as best he could to control the laughter that was boiling up inside. "And it's good to see you again, too, Reverend," he added.

"Good evening to you, Mr. Duncan," Dooley remarked, picking himself up and acting as if nothing out of the ordinary had happened. He followed Preacher Kyle up to the porch, trying as best he could not to limp.

"How are you today?" Ida Mae questioned, trying to ignore the large grass stain surrounding the torn knee of Dooley's trousers.

"I'm just wonderful," Dooley answered. "But, next time, I think I'll do the driving and let the preacher open the gate."

He seated himself on the top step beside Ida Mae and a bit of small talk began.

"Pull up a chair, Reverend," Ira invited.

The preacher seated himself as Ira pulled a new plug of Brown Mule chewing tobacco from the bib pocket of his best pair of overalls. He handed the tobacco to the reverend and watched as he cut a large enough corner from the plug to cause one side of his mouth to bulge.

"Me and the three deacons been wanting to talk to you about those new Sunday school rooms the church has been planning to build. Isn't that right, Dooley?"

Dooley was so infatuated with Ida Mae; he had not heard anything the preacher said.

"Isn't that right, Dooley?" Brother Kyle was louder this time.

"That's right, Reverend," Dooley answered, having no idea what it was the preacher was asking him.

"Brother Taylor suggested at our business meeting last night that we ask you to supervise the construction. Isn't that right, Dooley?"

Again, Dooley was paying no attention.

"Isn't that right, Dooley?" Almost shouting this time.

"That's right, Reverend," Dooley answered again, without ever looking in the preacher's direction.

Ira and the preacher realized the young man was ignoring everyone around him except Ida Mae.

"Everybody you know is going to hell. Isn't that right, Dooley?"

"That's right, Reverend."

It was not until everyone in the family burst out laughing, that Dooley realized what he had said.

Mary Ellen was the first to regain her composure.

"Why don't you get our guest a piece of your chocolate cake, Ida Mae?"

Relieved to be absent from the situation, she hurried inside. A few moments later, she appeared with a large serving platter with cake for everyone; Dooley getting the larger piece, of course.

"How come Dooley gets the biggest piece?" Kervin wanted to know. "I like chocolate cake as good as he does."

Ida Mae's face turned beet red.

"Just because he's bigger than you," Mary Sue giggled, which only added to her older sister's embarrassment.

Kervin gobbled down his cake just as a large black bird perched in the maple tree at the corner of the yard. Without a word, he extracted a pebble from his pocket and placed it into his slingshot. He pulled back on the pebble and let go. The bird tumbled from the tree and lay stone cold dead on the grass.

The preacher, seeing what happened, came to his feet so fast he became strangled on his last bite of cake.

"You shouldn't have done that," he scolded, once he was able to speak. "The Good Book says the Good Lord takes note of every sparrow that falls. You shouldn't be doing that if you are planning on going to Heaven."

Kervin hung his head as if he were ashamed.

Sensing the young fellow felt bad for what he had done, Brother Kyle gave him a pat on the head and added, "But that was a mighty accurate shot, boy."

The preacher returned to his seat and replaced the chew of tobacco he had taken from his cheek when Ida Mae appeared with her chocolate cake.

"As I was saying," the preacher continued, "Dooley, I mean Brother Donald, our church treasurer, has made me aware that we at last, have the eight hundred dollars we need to build our new Sunday School rooms. Not counting labor, of course. The men of the church will do that," he added. "You being the best carpenter, we would like you to oversee the construction. Isn't that right, Dooley?"

"Yes sir, that's exactly right." This time Dooley was paying just enough attention not to be embarrassed again.

"Brother Taylor, our oldest member, will soon turn eighty-five, and you all know, he is not in good health," the reverend continued. "He is determined to see that new addition to the church before he moves out."

"Where's he moving to," Kervin spoke for the first time since being scolded.

"He'll be moving on up to Heaven, I reckon," the preacher stated.

"Oh," Kervin whispered. "Then, I guess he ain't been killing any black birds."

"I'll do it, Reverend," Ira interrupted, "if I can wait until fall. That will give those of us who are farmers' time to get the crops harvested. This weather is too hot to be doing any building now, anyway."

That wasn't the real reason Ira wanted to wait. He knew he would be busy trying to get the sheriff re-elected and would not have time to supervise the building project.

"The congregation will be pleased. I'll make the announcement right after church services tomorrow," the reverend said as he got up to leave.

The reverend started toward his car with the deacon right behind, dragging his injured leg and trying not to show any pain.

"There's plenty of room inside, but you can ride on the bumper if you wish," the preacher teased when he and Dooley arrived at the automobile. Dooley took his place in the passenger's seat and slammed the door without uttering a word.

It was almost dark when the reverend and the deacon decided it was time to leave. A full moon was already beginning to rise over the horizon.

"I thought they were going to stay all night," Mary Sue complained.

She waited until the reverend was well out of hearing distance and rushed inside.

Everyone knew where she was headed. They were right. The door barely closed behind her when the familiar voice of Roy Acuff came on the radio. "You're listening to the Grand Old Opry from WSM, Nashville, Tennessee."

Ida Mae could hardly wait for the weekends. She knew Reverend Kyle and the deacon would come by after supper, as they always did on Saturday evening. She expected Dooley to ask her out on every visit, but each time she was disappointed. For a fact, the deacon was so bashful he could hardly speak to any young lady without blushing. Bashful or not, Ida Mae was determined to get him to ask her for a date.

Her younger sister, on the other hand, was glad to see them leave. She loved country music and the Grand Old Opry was her favorite program. She knew the words to every current country song, and was very good at singing along with the recording artist.

Preacher Kyle was totally against anyone owning a radio. A sinful tool of the Devil, he called it. Therefore, Mary Sue was as happy to see them leave, as Ida Mae was to see them arrive.

All the older members of the Duncan family sat in the light of the moon watching the twin's chase lighting bugs and listening to the Opry until it signed off at midnight.

"Honky Tonkin'" by Hank Williams was the last hit of the night.

"If the preacher had heard that one, he'd have his sermons for the next three Sundays'," Ira said as everyone began filing into the house.

"Don't look like Ida Mae's ever going to get old Dooley to take her honky tonkin," Mary Sue teased, as she ran upstairs with her older sister right on her heels.

"You girls behave and get to bed," their mother scolded. "You know Preacher Kyle's going to really be upset if we aren't in church in the morning."

"He knows we'll be there," Kevin complained. "You always make sure of that."

It was true. Mary Ellen might fall short where other matters were concerned, but she made sure all her children attended church. Everyone, except John Robert, who had reached the age that she no longer felt she could tell him what to do. He attended on occasion, but most times he had other things he wanted to do, which was usually repairing his car.

Chapter Three

THE CHURCH MOUSE

The next day was not unlike any other Sunday morning since the Duncan family moved onto the Baxter farm. Everyone hurried, trying to get ready for church, doing as best they could to stay out of each other's way. Not a problem for the twins. They put on their best shirts and their Sunday-go-to-meeting overalls, combed their hair as if their mother insisted, and were ready to go. Not so with the rest of the family.

The girls took so much time getting ready that the family was usually late, although they lived only a half-mile away. Each of the young ladies made sure the other looked their best. Mary Sue hoped to catch the attention of one of the several young men and Ida Mae wanted to impress Dooley, of course.

Granny, also, did little to help the situation. She was the last to get out of bed and usually complained because she did not have time to eat breakfast. "How can anyone pay attention, thinking about having an empty stomach?" she asked.

"Don't much matter about her stomach," Mary Ellen whispered, as she straightened Ira's necktie. "She usually sleeps through the whole sermon anyway."

The family finished dressing and made their way outside to where Brother Taylor was waiting. He had never missed a Sunday, taking the Duncan family to church and back, since Ida Mae wrecked the Chevrolet. The twins walked the short distance, instead of riding with

Old Ben, as they called him. There was not sufficient room for the whole family and many times they heard Granny complain that he didn't know how to drive anyway. "Never goes more than ten miles an hour," she would say.

The congregation was already singing when Brother Taylor pulled onto the church parking lot.

"Slow Poke made us late, again," Granny mumbled under her breath as Ira helped her from the car.

"Just be thankful we didn't have to walk," Ira whispered through gritted teeth.

He ushered his family to the only empty pew near the center of the building. Granny made her way to the end near the wall. There, she would have something to lean against while she snoozed, without fear of falling out of her seat. Ira, Mary Ellen and the girls followed, leaving room for their smaller children, who would be along shortly. Brother Taylor ambled up front and seated himself in one of the large chairs behind the podium. Dooley and the other deacon sat along side him. Granny could never understand why the officers of the church sat behind the preacher, where they could keep an eye on the congregation. They should be out in the congregation where they could keep an eye on the preacher, she reasoned.

Other people filled their pew before the boys arrived. This created a circumstance to which Mary Ellen did not approve. "Boys will be boys," she always said and she wanted the twins under her immediate supervision.

They'll do fine," Ira whispered as the twins entered and took a seat on the very back pew, Kervin seated on the aisle.

Another song or two followed and the deacons passed the collection plate to receive the morning offering. Mr. Hale, who always sat in the front row, was the first to make a contribution. He slowly placed a roll of bills in the plate and cleared his throat, as if to attract attention.

"Why don't the old show-off use a check? They're all ones anyway," Granny whispered.

"Be quiet, Mother," Ira told her in a voice low enough so no one else could hear. "You've found fault with everyone today, except the preacher."

"Come to think of it, he's been a little long-winded the last couple of Sundays," she shot back.

"Ah, go to sleep, Granny," he said, turning away to avoid any further comment.

After the collection plate was passed, Reverend Kyle stood to announce the title of the message for the day. "We will explore the sins of Eve in the Garden of Eden," he stated. Regardless what topic he chose, everyone knew that before his sermon ended, he would walk on the toes of anyone who patronized the sinful establishments in the nearby town. There was the dance hall, the movie theatre and, of course, the worst of all was Willie's Billiard Parlor.

"Evil will come to any man who gambles for the wages of another, and will cause him to commit greater sins,' the preacher was saying, getting louder as he got further into his sermon.

Dooley had surely heard that phrase enough times in the past. He hung his head as if to admire the shine on his shoes. It was his toes that were being stepped on this time. Although he was sure the reverend did not know, he felt just a little guilty for slipping into the pool hall on occasion.

The preacher was well into his sermon, as was Granny her nap, when Kevin gave his brother a nudge with his elbow. He was making Kervin aware of a mouse sitting on the floor under the pew in front of them.

The boys lost all interest in whatever the preacher was saying. They were giving their full attention to the mouse. They were hoping the little creature would do something exciting like run up someone's pants leg. That was not to be the case. The mouse ran into the aisle and up near where the preacher was standing. For the next several moments, it traveled back and forth in front of the podium. It did not appear that any other member of the congregation was aware of its presence. At last, Kervin could stand it no longer. He removed his slingshot and a pebble from his hip pocket. He was glad they were on the back row.

"Mother will kill you," Kevin whispered.

"She'll never know," his brother assured him. "Just keep an eye on the preacher and them other fellers up there and tap me on the leg when you're sure they're not looking," he whispered.

Kevin agreed.

Kervin pulled back on the leather pouch containing the pebble and leaned slightly into the aisle. With both eyes fixed firmly on the mouse, he waited for his brother to let him know when it was safe to let go.

The signal was not long in coming.

The instant he felt the tap, Kervin released the stone. Bull's eye, the mouse never knew what hit him.

No one in the church knew what had transpired. No one, except the reverend, that is. He was so amazed at such an accurate shot at such a small target he completely forgot the topic of his message. He stood in silence for a few moments staring at the still form, which lay before him.

"That ends my message today about how David slew the giant," he said at last, and then stepped into the aisle.

Dooley rose to his feet, looking somewhat bewildered. "Preacher Kyle and the deacons would like to meet with the men of the church immediately after service," he announced. "We need to discuss the beginning of the construction on our new Sunday school rooms," he added.

"Amen," Brother Taylor shouted. "Maybe I will live long enough to see it completed."

"If no one else has anything to say," Dooley continued, "let's all stand and turn to page 75 in our song books."

The reverend headed to the back of the sanctuary while the congregation sang. As usual, he shook hands with each one in attendance as they departed. He was somewhat concerned why so many members inquired about how he was feeling. Maybe I don't look so good, he thought, never realizing what his last comment had been.

The meeting after church went smoothly. The men voted to postpone the building project until the middle of November. This would allow Ira ample time to get his crops harvested and be able to have the project completed before winter.

Dooley reported there was now eight hundred forty dollars in the building fund, which was more than enough to purchase the materials.

Brother Rice Thompson, one of the faithful members, owned the local lumberyard. He agreed to furnish whatever was needed at wholesale prices. "There is no need to pay for the material until the project is completed," he suggested.

Chapter Four

IDA MAE GROWS UP

The hot days of summer flew by quickly — more quickly than most folks would have liked. Those in Russell County, whose livelihood depended on farming, were suffering. Rainfall was so scarce, the entire area was parched. Every day seemed a little hotter than the one before. Most of the county's residents talked of little else.

Like most of their neighbors, the Duncan household was as busy as a beehive. Ira and John Robert tended the small amount of corn Mother Nature permitted to grow, while they watched most of the winter hay supply dry up in the fields. The twins spent a goodly portion of their summer carrying water from the only surviving spring to the family garden. A fine job they did, too. The garden vegetables were the only crop on the farm that showed signs of survival.

The two girls helped Mary Ellen with the harvesting, canning, preserving and storing whatever the garden produced. Even Granny did her part when it came to such chores as stringing beans or stripping the shucks from the ears of sweet corn. No one ever complained about the amount of labor the garden required. Every item was either eaten at the time it ripened or stored for the cold winter months. The vegetables, along with a couple of hogs Ira slaughtered each fall, were their main source of food supply.

John Robert, at last, found time to get his old Chevrolet back into running condition. The Chevy was still a far cry from where she was before Ida Mae took her first, and last, driving lesson, but at least, the family had a means of transportation.

"Now, Granny won't have to complain about Brother Taylor's driving when he takes us to church on Sunday," Mary Sue giggled.

"Don't you worry," her mother answered. "Granny can always find something else to complain about."

Ira used the car as if it were his own, except for Saturday nights, at which time it belonged to his son.

John Robert looked forward to his weekends away from the farm. He usually visited the local establishments, where he was most likely to run into some of his buddies he had not seen since going into service. A few beers at Mickey's Place, take in a movie with one of his old girl friends, and then hang out in Willie's Pool Hall until it closed at two in the morning, was his regular routine.

Each time John Robert went into town, he became unhappier with life on the farm. Oh, he would keep living with his parents until the crops were in, but he knew that before winter, he would find his own way of earning a living. He would have been content before his tour in the army, but during that time, he was subjected to much more interesting types of employment.

Having worked in the motor pool most of the time he was away, he was able to repair his Chevrolet without assistance from anyone. Building and driving fast cars was what he wanted to do.

Life for Ida Mae was far from exciting, also. Dooley had taken a job at one of the only two service stations in town. Saturdays were the busiest time for people in that type of business, so he no longer was able to accompany the reverend on his weekly visits. She only saw him at church on Sunday mornings. It was a situation she was determined to change.

Ida Mae was not allowed to date until her 18th birthday. That day was now a month into history. She had shared Sunday school picnic lunches with a fellow or two, and had been allowed to have some young man walk her from church on a couple of occasions. But, she was never permitted to share the company of the opposite sex without a chaperone. Now, things would be different. She was allowed to go out with whomever she chose, and Dooley was the man of her choosing. She was determined to get him to ask her for a date.

As summer drew to a close, the sheriffs' visits to the farm became more frequent. Not that he was concerned about the crops or his cattle for that matter. He was confident Ira was capable of handling whatever needed to be done. It was the election that Baxter was worried about.

He had not yet been able to capture a single load of the liquor being transported through the county. Fletcher was coming down on this issue like a ten-pound hammer on an anvil.

"You've got to help me figure out a way to confiscate some of the white lighting or Fletcher will be the new sheriff," Baxter told Ira.

"What happened to that load you were after a few weeks ago?" Ira wanted to know. "I figured them boys would be doing time in the calaboose as we speak."

"Slipped right past us," Baxter said. "We waited for them at the county line for half a day, in that hot sun I might add, but they never did show up. Them fellers are slick; they had an old boy driving back and forth through the roadblock. He got word to them just as soon as we gave up. I heard later, they hauled that load right across the line ten minutes after we were gone."

Ira could detect the anxiety in the sheriff's voice. "What is it you think I can do?" he questioned.

"I don't know, but we got to figure something real soon. Fletcher is already making his brags about how he is going to send me back to the farm, while he takes over the law enforcement business. He says them moonshiners are getting rich and I'm not doing one thing to stop them."

John Robert walked up to where the sheriff and his daddy were talking just in time to hear Baxter say them moonshiners were getting rich.

"How do they go about making all that money?" John Robert wanted to know.

"Simple," the sheriff began. "Some of the best corn liquor ever run through a still is made right over there in Buchanan County and the other good stuff is made in Eastern Kentucky. Everybody in the eastern United Stated knows that too. Those fellers make the shine way back in the mountains and pay big bucks to get it hauled into the Carolinas. Once they get it across the state line, it is easy sailing from there. My job is to see that they never make it through our county, but I haven't had much luck lately, as my worthy opponent keeps reminding everybody."

"You'll figure something out, Sheriff. You've still got a long time before Election Day and if you get a load of the real good stuff, save me a jug. It's too expensive down at Mickey's," he smiled as he headed toward their house.

Hauling corn sure sounds like a much easier job than growing it, he thought as he began washing up for the evening meal.

Everyone was soon sitting at the supper table, waiting for the sheriff to leave so Ira could join them. No one in the family would think of starting to eat before the head of the house took his place at the table.

"When you reckon your heartthrob is going to get up enough courage to ask you out?" Kevin directed his question to Ida Mae.

"Ain't got no heartthrob," his sister lashed back.

"Yeah, you do," Kevin continued his teasing. "I saw where you was writing his name in the dust with your big toe, while you were sitting on the side of the watering trough, watching Mommy milk the cow yesterday.

"You forgot to erase it," Kevin burst out laughing.

Ida Mae was just about to launch one of her mother's biscuits in Kevin's direction, when her Daddy entered the kitchen.

"Thought that old windbag was never going to leave," Granny snapped, as Ira seated himself at the table.

"He's got problems, Granny," Ira told her as he began filling his plate.

"He ain't nothing but a problem, if you're asking me," his mother growled, shooting a quick glance at Mary Ellen.

Ira's mother had never gotten up the nerve to say anything to her daughter-in-law about her suspicions, but she was well aware that she could make her turn red every time she criticized Baxter.

"We've got to do something to help him, John Robert," Ira said, ignoring his mother's sarcastic remarks. "You know how bad things are here on the farm with all this dry weather and all. Most of the cattle are going to have to be sold because there is not going to be enough feed to winter them.

"That means I won't get to work nearly as many hours. If the sheriff don't get re-elected, so I can get that deputies job, things are really going to be tough around here. I think both of us should go into town tomorrow and talk to as many people as we can."

"I want to go too, fellows," Ida Mae interjected. "I have hardly been off this farm all summer, except going to church. I think it's time

I get out once in a while. Maybe I can persuade some of the younger people to support our sheriff."

"Oh, sure," Mary Sue giggled, "and maybe you can go by the service station and persuade Dooley to take you to a movie."

"Oh, shut up, Mary Sue! You're just mad because I'm a full-grown woman now and can do whatever I want to."

"Sounds like a great idea to me," John Robert suggested. "Me and Ida Mae might even get a lead on some of them young fellers that's been hauling that shine."

"Yeah! And if Ida Mae gets to talk to old Dooley, she'll be the one shining," Mary Sue made one more stab.

"We'll be ready to leave as soon as the sheriff comes by with our pay," Ira said. "He'll he pleased to know that we're spending every spare minute drumming up votes. Especially you, Ida Mae. You should really be excited about spending all day in town, helping the sheriff win the election."

Ida Mae was excited about spending the next day in town all right, but she wasn't as concerned as much about the election as Ira would have liked. She was more interested in letting all her friends know that she was no longer Daddy's little girl. And that's exactly what she set out to do.

The next morning, Ida Mae was out of bed shortly after sunrise. She did not even take time to eat breakfast. She was too busy readying herself for the trip into town. She put on her only store-bought dress and matching blue sandals, which she only wore to church on Sunday. She brushed and tied her long blonde hair into a ponytail. Behind each ear, she had dabbed a tiny dot of "Evening in Paris," which she borrowed from her mother. For two hours, she pranced the floor waiting for Baxter to arrive.

"A body might think you were going to Hollywood to see Humphrey Bogart, instead of just down town to see old Dooley," Mary Sue giggled.

"Get lost," Ida Mae said and went into the front yard to wait.

The sheriff made his regular Saturday mid-morning appearance. He gave Ira their pay for the week and complimented Ida Mae on how beautiful she looked.

"The three of us are going to spend all day in town trying to talk everyone we can into voting for you," Ira explained. "John Robert and

Ida Mae think they can swing some votes from the young people who have never cast a ballot before. They are also going to try to get a lead on them young bucks that are hauling illegal whiskey. They will be discreet, of course."

"Is that true, young lady?" Baxter asked, as Ida Mae jumped into the back seat of the family's Chevrolet.

"Sure is, Mr. Baxter," Ida Mae sang out.

"Then, take this," the sheriff smiled as he pulled a new ten-dollar bill from his wallet. "You hang around Sid's Grill and buy as many Cokes and pay for as many pinball games as this will allow. A good-looking gal like you can talk those young folks into doing about anything she has a mind to."

"Thanks, Sheriff," she said, stuffing the money into her bosom. "Let's go, Daddy. We don't want to let any of them good votes get away."

"Anything you need, Mother?" she yelled out the car window to her mother who was standing on the porch.

"Sure enough," Mary Sue answered. "Bring her some more perfume. She didn't have but half a bottle last night and I'm sure she's plum out, now."

"Remind me to kill her as soon as we get back home," Ida Mae mumbled.

"That's the first time I ever heard you call Baxter, 'sheriff,'" Ira said as John Robert started moving down the lane.

"That's the first time he ever told me I was good looking and gave me a ten-dollar bill," Ida Mae giggled.

Chapter Five

A DAY TO REMEMBER

Ida Mae sat in the back seat of the car as it made its way along the winding gravel road that led onto the paved surface heading into town. This was no new journey, but it was the first time she was free to do whatever she wanted, without being under the watchful eyes of her mother or father.

They had traveled a mere mile or so when she became caught up in her plans for the day. They would arrive before noon, and she was sure not much would be happening that time of morning. Dooley did not start work until noon, at which time she would pay him a visit.

She knew John Robert would show her around as best he could. After all, this was the first time she and her older brother had been anywhere together since he'd come home from the army.

Now that she was of age, she expected him to show her some of the wild spots in town; the ones she heard Preacher Kyle refer to so often. That would have to wait, of course, until their daddy got busy, doing whatever he did every Saturday.

Honk! Honk! It was John Robert, blowing his horn at an elderly man nailing an election poster on the same post with the sign that read, Honaker Corporation Limits.

"Looks like we are going to have our work cut out for us," John Robert said as he slowed the car down to within the posted speed limit.

"We can handle it," Ida Mae answered. "Remember the sheriff

said I was pretty enough to talk them young men into doing anything I wanted. Oops, that's not exactly what I meant, Daddy!"

"I hope not," Ira said. "Maybe you better keep an eye on your little sister, John Robert, and you can let me out right here."

Her brother pulled his automobile up in front of the railroad depot where three or four men were gathered. Two or three of them were admiring a large pocketknife. A shotgun was leaning against the wall at the end of a bench, where one of them was setting.

"Looks like the fellows brought some trading material today," Ira grinned as he got out of the car. "Mind you watch your raising, young lady," he said as John Robert backed away.

"What are we going to do first?" Ida Mae wanted to know.

"I don't know," her brother answered. "We can rob the First National Bank or go burn down Hillman's Furniture Store. Seems like you can't wait to start enjoying your freedom."

"Let's go burn the furniture store, smart aleck. I've already got plenty of money," she said whipping the ten dollars from her bosom.

John Robert smiled. "Suits me," he answered, "but let's go by the restaurant and have a cup of coffee first."

Her big brother knew why she must be anxious to start enjoying her newfound freedom. Their parents were really strict on the girls where the young men were concerned. To even ask to go on a date before the age of eighteen was totally out of the question.

"Once you become eighteen, you can do what you want, but until then you need to have my permission," her mother instructed her and her younger sister.

The couple drove around for about half an hour before parking in front of Sid's Grill, one of the only two restaurants in town. They went inside and seated themselves in one of the booths near a window.

A handful of older gentlemen were sitting on stools at the bar, having breakfast. Their main topic of discussion was the torturing hot weather.

The only other customer was Dewey Combs, one of the town police officers, who was seated at the far end of the bar. John Robert and Dewey were about the same age and had gone to high school together.

Dewey recognized her brother immediately. He strolled over to their booth, coffee cup in hand.

"When did you get back into town, soldier?" he asked. "And who is this beautiful young lady you brought with you?"

Ida Mae sat blushing as the young officer seated himself in the booth beside her brother.

"About a month ago, and this is my little sister, Ida Mae."

"My goodness, why haven't I been seeing you around?" Dewey asked.

"Because I just turned ..."

"Because she has been real busy helping out on the farm," her brother interrupted.

"What'll you have?" a waitress asked, smiling at John Robert.

"Just coffee, please?"

"And put that on my tab," Dewey instructed.

Ida Mae spent most of the next hour listening to the officer and her brother catch up on old times. She sipped her coffee and watched the traffic on Main Street. She paid little attention to the two gentlemen seated with her, although she did think the young officer looked rather handsome, especially in his blue uniform.

"Hear your landlord is not doing so well in his bid for re-election," she heard Dewey remark.

"Sure hope he beats old man Fletcher," he spoke softly so no one else could hear. "I think a public office would go straight to Fletcher's head," the officer continued.

"I think the sheriff would do just fine if he could catch those fellers with a load or two of that illegal whiskey," John Robert stated.

"Got my own ideas about who those birds are," Dewey answered. "Nothing I can prove, of course."

"Time to get out there on the streets and start earning my pay," he said as he stood up to leave. "Let's go out for a beer sometime soldier, when I'm off duty. I sure hope I get to see you again real soon, Pretty Lady," he added.

Again, Ida Mae blushed and turned her head as if she were looking onto the street.

"There he is," she said, her voice filled with excitement.

"There's who?" John Robert questioned.

"Dooley," she yelped, he just went by riding with Mr. Hale.

"His dad is probably taking him to work, don't you suppose? Let's play a game of pinball."

His sister stood watching Mr. Hale's car until it was completely out of sight. "A game of what?" she asked. John Robert knew she hadn't been paying attention.

"Pinball, little sister. Isn't that what the sheriff asked you to do? Besides, I thought you told Kevin you didn't have a heartthrob."

"Don't you start on me, too," she warned.

John Robert got a handful of change from the waitress and dropped several coins into the pinball machine. The backboard lit up and he flipped one of the steel balls onto the surface of the game board.

Ida Mae had never seen anything like this before. She had always gone into the only other café in town and the proprietor did not have games in his establishment.

"No wonder all the young people eat here," she determined. She was fascinated by her brother's ability to keep the ball in play.

"Where did you learn to do that?" she asked.

"In Uncle Sam's Army," he replied. "Pinball and poker was about all there was to do during our time off, and I never was much at cards. I did enjoy shooting a game of pool, occasionally," he added.

Ida Mae watched as her brother kept the ball moving across the playing surface. In a little while, other young couples about her age, started gathering around. At last, when the game ended, one of the fellow spectators commented, "You are the best I have ever seen."

"Nothing to it," John Robert smiled. "It just takes practice."

"May I try?" Ida Mae asked.

"Sure thing," he said and he watched while his sister tried her first game. The balls slid past the flippers on the machine so fast, her game ended almost before it began.

"Remember, it just takes practice," he said. He dropped several more coins into the machine. "Why don't you young folks take turns, while I see what else is going on in town? I'll see you back here in an hour or so. Remember what that gentleman told you this morning, Ida Mae," he winked.

"Sure enough," Ida Mae said. "Bring us all a soda pop," she told the waitress as her brother made his exit.

Ida Mae spent the next hour and a half practicing pinball and visiting with the young people who were crowding into the restaurant. Many of them were people she had gone to high school with, so she knew they were of voting age. She did as best she could to convince them William Baxter would make the better sheriff.

"This is not a bad arrangement," she decided, letting the sheriff finance drinks and recreation and all she had to do was try to persuade her friends how to vote.

She had blown almost half of her funds by the time John Robert came back to the restaurant.

"Let's go find something else to do for a while," he told her.

"Suits me," she said. "What are we going to do next?"

"It's up to you, but I really need to get a haircut if I'm going out on the town tonight."

"Then take me to Fuller's Clothing Store, and I'll look at their new dresses," she said.

"Why don't I just take you to the service station and you won't have to wait until I'm out of sight and cross the street," John Robert teased.

"Think you're so smart, then take me to the service station."

Her brother did as she requested. "I'll get a haircut, check on Daddy, and see you in a little while," he said.

When Ida Mae got out of the car, Dooley was nowhere to be seen. The station manager was pumping gas so she made herself busy straightening a rack of road maps.

"May I help you, Miss?" the manager asked.

"Yes, sir. Is Donald working today?"

"I'm sorry. There is no one by that name working here."

"Are you sure, sir? I was certain Donald Hale had been working here for the past few weeks."

"Oh, you must mean Dooley," the manager said. "Sure does, he's back in the pit."

"Where's the pit?" Ida Mae wanted to know.

"Back there," the manager motioned toward another section of the station.

"Mind if I go back and talk to him while he works?" she asked.

"Not if he don't," the manager said. "And if he does, you can stay up here and talk to me."

Ida Mae made her way back to where the manager directed. Someone was backing a car from over a deep hole in the floor.

"Hi! Is that what he was calling a pit?" she asked of Dooley who was standing in the bottom of the hole, looking straight up at her.

"Uh! Uh! Uh! Sure is," Dooley finally managed to mumble.

Ida Mae realized she was standing too close to the edge of the pit, being clad as she was. She quickly took a couple of steps back from the edge of the pit.

"I mean, what are you doing working down in a place like this?" she asked, hoping he could not see the red she knew was glowing on her face.

"Greasing and changing oil in the customers automobiles."

"Why on Earth would you want a dirty job like this?"

"The pay is good and I am going to buy myself a car."

"Your daddy's got plenty of money, why don't he buy you a car?"

"He does alright, I guess, but mother won't hear of it. My father says that if I get a car of my own, I'll have to work it out myself."

Ida Mae knew, as did everyone else, that Mrs. Hale was over-protective of her son, but she had no idea that she did not want him to have an automobile of his own. She had seen Dooley drive his father's car very few times, but she thought that was because the Hales lived in town, and everything was within walking distance.

"What time do you get off work?" she asked.

"Six o'clock sharp, if I'm not in the middle of a service job, I reckon. Why do you ask?"

"Because I thought you might want to take me to a movie or something," she stammered.

"How on Earth did you talk your folks into letting someone take you to a movie?"

"I don't have to talk them into letting me do anything, now that I'm eighteen," she flirted.

"Sorry," he said as he climbed out of the pit. "I think that would be nice but I have already made plans for the evening."

"Who is she?" the words were out of her mouth before she could stop them.

"No, it's not like that at all," Dooley tried to explain.

"Then, what's more important than taking a girl to the movies?"

"I can't tell you," he said, "but if I don't do what I promised I'd be telling a lie."

"Then, I hope you have an enjoyable evening," Ida Mae said, feeling embarrassed that she had mentioned going to the movies in the first place. A lady should never ask a gentleman to take her out, but to be turned down just made matters worse.

"Sorry I bothered you," she said as she turned to leave.

Dooley started to reach for her arm and realized both his hands were completely blackened with grease.

"Oh, what the heck," he thought, "she wouldn't understand anyway."

He let her leave without trying to explain further.

Ida Mae walked to the barbershop, where she knew John Robert would be getting his hair cut. She waited across the street for him to come outside.

"Boy, that was a short visit," he said.

"The place was so busy, Dooley didn't have time to talk," she lied.

"Just as well," John Robert said. " We better go find Daddy. He will barely have time to get the grocery shopping done, get home and eat his supper before Preacher Kyle comes calling."

"What are you doing tonight, Big Brother?" Ida Mae asked as she jumped in the front seat along side John Robert.

"Haven't fully decided, maybe just cruise around town and check out what everyone else is doing. Why do you ask?"

"Because I want to ride along with you. Do you mind?"

"Sure I mind, and I have a feeling Mother wouldn't take too kindly to the idea either."

"She wouldn't mind as long as I'm with you, please?"

"Don't sound like a good plan to me. Don't sound like a good plan to me at all. Besides, I never know what I might get into or what hour I will get home. Anyway, haven't you had enough fun for one day?"

"Tell you what. If Mother doesn't object too strenuously, I guess I could let you tag along, but it's not going to be habit-forming, mind you. You can call it a belated birthday present."

"Thanks, John Robert," she squealed as she leaned over and planted a big kiss on his cheek.

"Remember, only if Mother don't object," he reminded her.

John Robert pulled in front of the grocery store where he knew his father would be shopping. A 12-gauge shotgun was leaning against the wall near the entrance door. Within a few moments, Ira came out of the store carrying a large brown bag. He picked up the gun and placed both items in the trunk of the car.

"What sort of day did you have, Daddy?" Ida Mae asked.

"Wonderful," Ira replied. "Made at least six or eight good trades, ended up with a three-bladed Tree Brand pocket knife and only got a buck and a half in that old shotgun. I got at least a half dozen of them fellers to promise to vote our way, too."

They had just cleared the outskirts of town when Ida Mae yelled, "Stop! Stop!"

Now, what on Earth could be the matter?

John Robert slammed on the brakes and pulled to the side of the road. Ida Mae jumped from the car, ran a few feet back to the post bearing the corporation limit sign. She tore Fletcher's election poster from the post, jumped back into the car, threw it into the floor and yelled again, "Go! Go!"

"Getting to be quite the little politician, 'eh, Sis?"

"I really don't know if we are going to be able to pull this off," Ira said, with a concerned look on his face.

The young couple could tell their daddy was tired, because he had little else to say on the ride home. As soon as the car came to a stop in front of their gate, Ida Mae sprang from her seat. She went bouncing up the steps to where her mother was waiting on the porch.

"John Robert wants me to go out riding with him tonight, Mother. Says we might go to a movie or something. He told me it would be my birthday present. You don't mind do you, Mother?"

Mary Ellen looked toward her son, who was a short distance behind his sister. "Is that right, son?" she asks.

"Only if it is alright with you, Mother," he replied.

Mary Ellen stared at her oldest daughter a moment and then nodded her approval. "I guess you're of the age to have a mind of your own, and I know John Robert will take care of you."

Ida Mae was far more excited than she had been that morning. She had no idea where she and John Robert would go or what they would be doing, nor did she care. This was going to be the first time in her life she was to have a night out. She knew she would have fun, for this surely had already been a day to remember.

Chapter Six

SISTER'S FIRST NIGHT OUT

John Robert could hardly believe he was ready to leave before his little sister. He sat in his car a full five minutes, waiting, after he told her he was ready to go.

"Thought I was going to have to leave without you," he said, when she finally appeared.

"Not on your life. How do I look?"

"If you act as good as you look, I won't be sorry I brought you along."

She did look great, too! She exchanged the blue dress and sandals for a pale green skirt, white blouse, and a pair of white flats she'd borrowed from Mary Sue. Her hair was no longer in a ponytail, but fell loosely down her back.

They had barely reached the end of the lane, when she took a tube of lipstick from her small white clutch purse and began to apply it to her lips.

"Why didn't you do that before we left home?" John Robert questioned.

"Didn't want to push my luck," she smiled.

It was almost dark by the time they had driven to where the narrow gravel country road met the hard surface. John Robert came to a stop when he reached the intersection. Somewhere in the distance, they could hear the sound of a siren. Curiosity caused him to wait. To their left was the road leading from the top of the mountain. A sharp left-hand downhill sweeping curve, was just beyond the intersection. The sounds of the rapidly approaching siren told the couple something was flat out. The next instant told the story. A set of headlights was coming into the curve at a high rate of speed. Another set of headlights was a short distance behind and seemed to be gaining ground. No mistake, the red light on the top of the car in the rear told them it was Sheriff Baxter and he was in hot pursuit.

John Robert knew that only an experienced driver would be able to maneuver the curve at the speed they were traveling. The car in front seemed to slide to the inside of the curve, causing both wheels on the driver's side to leave the pavement. Once the automobile was fully in the turn, the driver gunned the heavy machine, sending gravels from the shoulder flying in every direction. The car swerved and began scooting sideways, coming straight at John Robert and Ida Mae. Before he could react, the big machine clipped the end of the driver's side bumper, knocking his Chevrolet a few feet backward. The impact was just enough to allow the speeding driver to regain control. He down shifted, mashed hard on the accelerator and sped away. The Sheriff was not so lucky. His cruiser spun around and around in the curve, and slid through the grass and stopped several yards down the road against a fence.

"Horse manure!" Sheriff Baxter yelled as he pulled himself from behind the steering wheel."

"No. Hudson Hornet," John Robert corrected.

"Say what?" he shouted again, as he tried to pound the dents from his hat with his fist.

"It was a dark blue Hudson Hornet, 1948 model with fender skirts."

"What else do you know about it?" the sheriff asked, unable to hide his frustration.

"I know it now has a dent in the right rear fender, and will run like a scalded dog," John Robert continued.

The sheriff spent the next few minutes collecting all the information he could from the Duncans. Just as he was about to leave, another automobile pulled behind John Robert's Chevrolet. "Have an accident Sheriff?" the driver yelled.

"No thank you, I just had one, Fletcher," the sheriff yelled back as he jumped into his cruiser and sped off.

"Started out to be quite an evening, Sis. What do you think?"

"Appears that way, John Robert. Let's get into town and see what else happens."

He threw the end of his bumper into the trunk, and they were on their way.

It was well after dark by the time the couple reached their destination. Most of the restaurant crowd had already gone home and the local hotspots were beginning to get busy. For the first hour, John Robert and Ida Mae cruised the streets, stopping now and then; to speak to someone one or the other of them knew. They were driving past Willie's Billiard Parlor, when Ida Mae caught sight of Dooley going inside.

"So, that's what's more important than taking me to the movies," she gasped.

"What on Earth are you talking about?" her brother asked.

"I asked Dooley if he would like to take me to the movies tonight, and he said he already had plans. I just saw him dart into the pool hall. What do you think of that?"

"I think that's what you get for asking a guy to take you to the movies," he laughed.

"It's not funny, John Robert! Let's get out of here."

"Wasn't planning on stopping," he laughed some more. "Ever been skating?"

"No."

"Then, you are about to make your first trip."

A short while later, they were walking into the local skating rink. The jukebox was turned up loud and twenty or thirty young people were going around in circles, moving in rhythm with the music.

"That looks like fun, let's try it."

"If you are sure you want to."

"Sure, I want to," she said looking out over the skaters to see if there was anyone she recognized.

John Robert rented skates for both of then and started walking to the arena. Someone spoke to him and he stopped long enough to exchange a friendly hello. He told Ida Mae to try her skates.

When he turned back to where she had been standing, she was gone. He looked out at the skaters and there she was. Dewey Combs, the policeman, had one arm around her waist and the skating lesson had begun.

"Look, John Robert," she called over the sound of The Tennessee Waltz, "I'm learning to skate." The words were barely out of her mouth when down she went, taking her skating partner with her. John Robert helped Dewey get her back up on her skates.

"Find out who he thinks is hauling that booze out of Buchanan County," he whispered. He skated away and left her to continue her lesson.

John Robert renewed some old acquaintances, leaving his sister to get whatever information she could from the young officer. About an hour later, she'd had enough.

"Let's go do something else," she said. "My legs are so tired, they will hardly move."

"Did I notice you're sort of taking a liking to Mr. Combs?" Her brother asked when they were out of the building.

"He's alright, I guess. He did ask me to go to the movies sometime."

"What did you find out about our moonshine buddies?"

"Two brothers by the name of Johnson, he's pretty sure. One of the automobiles they use is a Hudson Hornet, he thinks."

"Dark blue I'll bet."

"You got it. He says the cars they use are hot rods, geared to outrun anything any law enforcement officer in this country has ever seen."

"I hope you didn't say anything about our little accident."

"Not a word."

"You are a smart girl. What do you want to do now?"

"I would like to go play a game of pool, if you really want to know."

"Hey, wait a minute little sister, playing the pinball machines and skating is one thing, but hanging out in a place like Willie's Billiard Parlor is something else altogether. I don't think that is something a little lady like you should want to do. Besides, I thought you told Kevin you didn't have a heartthrob."

"I don't have a heartthrob, but when you think about it, if Dooley hangs out there, it couldn't be all that bad. He is one of our church deacons, you know."

"Whatever you say. But if Mother ever finds out, she will never let you go anywhere with me again."

The couple walked in the back entrance of Willie's place and John

Robert made his sister sit beside him on a high-rise stool near the doorway. The room was dimly lit and if anyone saw them come in, they didn't acknowledge it.

Ida Mae had no idea what to expect, but this was different than anything she could have imagined. A row of eight pool tables filled the center of the narrow smoked-filled room. A large light bulb hanging from the ceiling encircled by a shield illuminated each of the tables. Some of the customers sipped from beer bottles, while their opponents took their turn at the table. It took a moment or two for her eyes to adjust.

"There he is," she said, pointing to a table near the center of the room.

Dooley and someone she did not know waited, while another gentleman placed a few of the pool balls in a triangular mechanism near one end of the table. Dooley's buddy pitched a dime to the man who had placed the balls and took a seat on one of the stools. Ida Mae watched as Dooley took his turn.

Each time he shot, one of the balls fell into a pocket. The fellow on the stool pitched another dime on the table and the man with the triangle repeated the process.

"Why don't the other fellow get to take a turn?" Ida Mae asked.

"Because Dooley just ran the table," her brother remarked.

"What does that mean?" she wanted to know.

"That means Dooley won the game without the other guy ever getting a turn. The winner gets to shoot first and the loser has to pay for the game."

"Does that mean Dooley is good?"

"The best there is in these parts, so I've heard. We're going to watch a couple more games and then we're out of here."

The couple watched as Dooley ran the table two more times and left without him ever knowing they were there.

"It's almost midnight; time to get you home."

Ida Mae did not object. She was worn out from the events of the day.

"Thank you, John Robert," she said, as her brother turned his car into their lane. "This has been the best birthday a girl ever had, and I've still got money left," she giggled as she pulled a five dollar bill from her bosom. "Maybe I will spend this next weekend if you will take me with you."

"We'll see," John Robert yawned.

Everyone was in bed when they got home. There was not a light in the house. John Robert closed the front door behind them and whispered, "No use waking anyone if we don't have to. Good night, Sis."

Ida Mae tiptoed upstairs and into the room she shared with Mary Sue. She undressed by the light of the moon and slipped into her gown. She stretched out on top of the bed sheet and let the events of the day rush through her mind. She took a deep breath to welcome a restful nights sleep.

"You better not have scuffed my white flats," was the last thing she remembered hearing.

CHAPTER SEVEN

SUMMER SLIPS AWAY

Sunday morning found Ira and John Robert in the back yard in the shade of the maple tree. Mary Ellen was putting the finishing touches on breakfast and the girls were putting the finishing touches on themselves in preparation for church. John Robert was recalling the accident of the night before. The twins were enjoying their favorite hobby, practicing with their slingshots.

"Looks as if someone is in a mighty big hurry," Ira said, drawing attention to the cloud of dust boiling up behind an approaching vehicle.

The car came to a stop near the gate at the far end of the lane.

"Why! That's the sheriff," Ira said. "What could he want this early on a Sunday morning?"

"Appears like the old windbag is in a mighty big hurry to tell you," his mother snapped as she stepped from the back porch and started around the back of the house.

The sheriff pulled his car up along side John Robert's damaged automobile. He hesitated a moment in front of the Chevrolet and then rushed up to where the two men were relaxing. He seated himself on one of the few areas still covered with grass as he asked, "Where is the rest of your car, John Robert?"

"Darn!" A woman's voice rang out before he could answer.

Baxter sprang to his feet and in an instant had his revolver in hand. "What on Earth was that?" he wanted to know.

"Nothing, just Granny in the outhouse," Kevin answered; laughing so hard he could hardly speak. "Let's see that fast draw again, Sheriff."

"Got to find time to replace that loose board," Ira grinned. "Now, what were you saying, Sheriff."

Baxter holstered his pistol and resumed his position beside Ira and his son.

"The rest of the car, the end of your bumper," the sheriff said. "Where is the end of your bumper?"

"I threw it in the trunk. Why do you want the end of the bumper?"

"Paint," the sheriff said. "Let's see how much paint is on that bumper."

John Robert went to his Chevrolet and raised the trunk lid. There on the end of the bumper was embedded a huge amount of dark blue paint.

"I need you to help me find that car, John Robert. I know that Hornet was loaded with moonshine. Fletcher has already told half the voters in town about that load of whiskey getting away from me last night."

"How did he know what happened, and even if he did, how did he know it was a load of whiskey?" Ira asked.

The sheriff shuffled his feet for a moment and began scratching the back of his head. "Now, isn't that a mystery?" he asked. "Did you or Ida Mae say anything to anyone about what happened last night?"

"Not a soul."

"As I was about to say, John Robert, I need you to help me find out who was behind the wheel of that flying machine. I had an idea it was about time for another shipment, so I was backed into the trees near the county line.

"It was almost dark when he came across and it wasn't hard to tell he was heavily loaded. He saw me as I sped onto the highway, and the race was on. If we had not been traveling downgrade, I could never have stayed in sight. The weight was the only thing that kept him from losing it in that curve. Man, could that son-of-a-gun drive."

"My Chevrolet was the only thing that kept him from losing it," John Robert reminded him. "Did you get his license number?"

"License number, my rear end," the sheriff grunted. "As fast as we were moving, I could hardly get my breath."

47

"How am I supposed to find out what you need to know?" John Robert asked.

"Go to Buchanan County next week, drive all over that county if you have to, until you find that blue Hudson. Go every day if necessary. If we can find that car before it's been repaired, we got our man. I'll pay you ten dollars a day and buy all your gasoline. What do you say? The election is getting closer every day, and if I don't stop some of that moonshine traffic, I'll be turning in my badge."

"And that big check he draws every month," Granny hooted as she came back into view, one hand rubbing the cheek of her butt.

"Ten dollars a day to ride around on free gasoline — how can I say no?"

"We can't count on the sheriff over there to do anything to help us. In the first place, the fellows who are making and hauling the booze are the ones keeping him in office. In the second place, he and Fletcher are best friends."

Ira was glad John Robert agreed to help Baxter find the Hudson. He knew how badly the sheriff wanted to stay in office and he wanted the job as deputy just as bad.

"What about working the crops?" John Robert asked, as the sheriff started to get into his car.

"Forget about the crops," he said, as he stood for a moment staring down over the parched fields. "Your daddy will save what he can. The only thing that looks worse than that cornfield is my chances for re-election," he added as he drove away.

"Come and get it, or we'll be late for church," Mary Ellen called from the kitchen as soon as she knew their guest had gone.

"What did old Easy Money want?" Granny asked as Ira and John Robert took their seats at the table.

"Just wanted to know that you weren't going to vote for him more than twice," John Robert teased.

"He just better be glad I don't vote," she snarled. "Let's eat."

The family was not late for church; as a matter of fact they broke tradition and arrived a good bit early.

Reverend Kyle stood on one side of the entrance and Dooley on the other, greeting the congregation as they arrived. Ira, Mary Ellen and Granny were ahead of the others. After a cordial handshake, Ira ushered the ladies to their seats. Ida Mae waited until the reverend was busy talking, and then slipped across to where Dooley was standing.

"Good morning, Ida Mae. You sure look nice today." He leaned forward and whispered, "Sorry we didn't get to go out last night."

"Oh, I just chalked it up to a lost evening."

"I should have cancelled something, so we could have gone to the movies. I guess I'm just not on the ball."

"Don't mention it, Dooley. Some days, none of us are on the ball."

"What are you doing this afternoon?" he asked.

"Don't have a cue, I mean clue," she said tilting her head slightly backwards and stepping inside, leaving him to sort out the meaning of what she had said.

"Good to see you this morning, Dead Eye," the reverend said, as he shook hands with Kervin. "Have you got your weapon with you today?"

"Never leave home without it, Preacher," Kervin said, expecting to be complimented further.

"Better let me hang on to it until after the service, young man. Remember what I told you the Good Book said when I visited your home the other evening."

Kervin slipped his slingshot from his hip pocket and gave it to the reverend. "I thought you were talking about blackbirds, Preacher. You didn't say nothing about them darn rats."

The day was hot and the sermon short. So short, in fact, Granny did not have time to take a nap. When the preacher asked the congregation to stand for the closing hymn, Dooley made his move toward the door. Ida Mae was sitting in back and he was not about to let her get away. He had to have her clarify the remarks she made earlier.

"Do you have any plans for this afternoon?" he asked when they were outside.

"Maybe, maybe not, why do you ask?"

"Let's go for a ride. My parents will let me use the car after church, as long as I'm home before dark."

Ida Mae could not believe her ears. A man at least 25 years old, and his parents want him home before dark. But, she could not believe he had asked her to go for a ride, either.

"I'm really sorry, Dooley. I have already made other plans," she said, recalling his comment from the day before.

"Oh," he said as he turned to walk away.

"But, I'll cancel if you really want me to," she was afraid he might never ask her again.

"Pick you up at two."

Ida Mae was so excited, she could not eat her lunch. At last, she was going to be alone with Dooley. Maybe she was going to find out what made this bashful boy tick.

Dooley must have been excited too. He was at the Duncan's place at two o'clock sharp. What Ida Mae was to learn about the deacon was far different from anything she could have imagined.

They drove the back roads and talked the entire afternoon. Dooley told Ida Mae about many interesting parts of his life. He told her about his mother's little brother, who'd been in a terrible, late-night automobile accident many years before.

The child had been thrown from the vehicle and suffered a severe head injury. He would be in a mental institution for the rest of his life.

"That's why Mother won't travel much in a car, nor does she want me to after dark," Dooley told her. "We once lived in the country as you do," he continued, "but, when I became a teenager, Mother insisted we sell our farm and move into town.

"She wanted me to be near as many activities as possible, without having to drive. She would never allow my father to purchase an automobile for me. I did odd jobs and started saving money to buy my own vehicle, but when she realized what I was doing, she made sure that none of our neighbors had any odd jobs they would allow me to do. I started hanging out at Willie's Pool Hall and learn to play the games for money. Got to be pretty good too, if I do say so myself."

"I know," Ida Mae interrupted. The words were out before she could think.

"How do you know?' Dooley looked surprised.

"I mean I've heard you are pretty good," she stammered. "Did you win much money?"

"For a while," he went on, "and then, I guess I became too good, nobody would play me for money. I just quit hanging out a Willie's very often. That's when Preacher Kyle talked me into joining the Baptist church and before I knew it, I became one of the deacons. And, as you know, I am now also the treasurer."

"Why does your family drive all the way on the mountain to attend our church?"

"It was the closest church to our place before we sold, and my parents never wanted to join anywhere else."

"Do you ever play pool any more?"

"Occasionally, but only at night."

"Why at night?"

"Now that I've taken a job at the service station, I work days. And to be honest, I'm afraid that if I go there in the daytime, some of the church members might see me and I'm sure that would be hard to explain."

The afternoon passed much more quickly than the couple would have liked. They were nearing Ida Mae's home just as darkness was closing in.

"If your father allows you to use his car, why do you want one of your own so badly?"

Dooley pulled in front of the Duncan's gate. "There is a young lady I'm very fond of and I would like to be able to ask her out whenever I choose."

"Oh! If it's not being too personal, do you mind if I ask if it's someone I know?"

"It's you, Ida Mae."

"Thanks for a lovely afternoon," she said. She squeezed his hand and let herself out of the car.

Ida Mae walked around to the drivers' side. "How long will it take you to earn enough to purchase a car of your own?"

"A long time, unless I find another way to earn more money," he said.

"I'm sure you will find another way. Good night, Dooley."

CHAPTER EIGHT

THE SEARCH BEGINS

John Robert could not wait to begin the task of trying to find the Hudson that had damaged his car a few days before. Not only did he want to help the sheriff catch the moonshiners, he had a personal score to settle, too.

He wanted the joker who'd damaged his car to pay for the repairs.

John Robert was crossing the county line on Route 80, as soon as he was sure it was light enough to distinguish one vehicle from another. The only way he could be sure not to overlook every place the subject could be, was to take every off-road and every driveway off every road.

He also planned to talk to as many county residents as was possible. This was going to be a time-consuming ordeal, but he was being paid by the day, so he didn't mind. After all, it was a far cry from working on the farm in the blazing sun.

The first day went by without a hitch. Most of the people he talked to were friendly, but he did not learn anything of value.

He pretended to be looking for one of his old army buddies by the name of Ernie Johnson, who he thought drove a dark blue Hudson.

It was nearing suppertime when he called it a day. It had been a long day. He was far up on one of ridges, eight or ten miles from Route 80, which would take him back out of the county. He drove the dusty road back to the blacktop.

"I'll start again at this point tomorrow," he thought, as he waited for an oncoming vehicle to pass. The car slowed as it went past the intersection, just enough for him to recognize the driver.

It was Fletcher.

What on Earth could he be doing over here, John Robert wondered. One would think he would be spending his time in his own county, trying to land more votes.

Maybe just visiting, he thought. After all, Baxter did say he and the Buchanan County sheriff were very good friends. Anyway, he was too tired and hungry to think about that, now.

The next couple of days went pretty much as the first. John Robert drove every back road he could find. He went up every hollow and across every ridge, one after the other. Several people knew of Johnson families. Seems there were several in the county, but they did not know of one named Ernie, nor did they know of one who drove a blue Hudson.

Late on the fourth day, John Robert stopped at a service station for gas. While he was filling his car, he saw Fletcher again. This time, he was driving a gray pickup truck with cattle racks. The bed of the truck was half filled with loose hay. Fletcher honked his horn as he passed, so John Robert was sure he recognized him.

"That's strange," he thought, "Fletcher is in the lumber business. He doesn't own a farm; he doesn't even own a cow, why would he be hauling hay?"

He did not dwell on the matter, however, again it was getting late and he needed to be getting home.

By the end of the week, he had worn out his welcome in Buchanan County. No one would talk to him. The few who did knew no one by the name of Johnson or had any information about the car he was looking for.

Twice, county deputies stopped him. One gave him a ticket for speeding, although he knew he was well under the limit. The next day was Saturday, and the sheriff would be coming to the farm. He had better report this matter to him, he decided.

The next morning, John Robert was waiting when Baxter arrived. He went over the details of the previous week and asked what he should do.

"I'll figure something out," Baxter told him. "I'll come back tomorrow afternoon. Take the weekend off."

John Robert looked toward the twins, who were playing in the front yard.

"Think I'll take my little brothers down to the Clinch River fishing today," he said, raising his voice so the twins could hear. "If I can persuade them to dig us some fishing worms," he added.

"Did you hear that?" one of the twins yelled and went running into the house to tell his mother.

Within minutes, the boys were headed to the barn lot. One of them was carrying a garden hoe and the other had a large empty tobacco can.

The sheriff lingered a while to gather all the information John Robert had and to pay him for the weeks work and the gasoline he used. He was barely out of sight when the twins came running up to their big brother with enough bait to fish the entire day.

"Good job fellows," he said. "Now let's go eat breakfast and ask Daddy if he would like to go."

Ira was standing near enough to hear his sons talking. "Sure would," he said. "Haven't had a fish dinner since John Robert went to the army. We'll stop in town and get whatever your mother needs on the way home."

All the male members of the Duncan household gobbled down their breakfast threw what was left in a basket for lunch, and they were off.

"Better stop in town for fishing licenses in case the game warden should come check us out," John Robert suggested.

"Sure enough," Ira agreed.

They pulled into the service station where Dooley worked, which was the only place in town that sold fishing licenses. The station manager was pumping air into a tire on the same pickup truck John Robert had seen Fletcher driving in Buchanan County earlier in the week. The hay had still not been unloaded.

Ira and John Robert started inside, leaving the twins to play around on the parking lot.

"Good morning, gentlemen," Fletcher said as he exited the station. "How's my old friend, William Baxter doing these days?"

"Better than some people think," John Robert answered.

They watched as Fletcher started toward the pickup. "Tell your boss to keep those patrol cars shined up. I'll want to make a good impression on my constituents after I'm elected."

A large bumblebee came to rest on the hay as Fletcher got under the wheel. Kervin could not resist. Out came his slingshot and he took aim just as the truck started to move away.

Crack! It was the sound of the pebble as it hit the load of hay.

"You missed," Kevin said to his brother as Fletcher drove off the lot.

"Wouldn't have missed if he hadn't been moving," Kervin explained.

John Robert had watched all that had transpired and he had heard the sound of the pebble, but he assumed Kervin had missed his target and hit the bed of the truck.

A few moments later, Ira and his son came out of the station, licenses in hand. John Robert dropped some of the coins the attendant had given him right where the pickup had been parked. One of the coins rolled into a pool of liquid and he stooped over to retrieve it. When he did, he was shocked.

"I'll be darned," John Robert said as he signaled his father to come to see what he had found. The liquid was, without doubt, moonshine.

Kervin had not hit the bed of the truck, but a glass container of whiskey hidden in the load of hay.

"Don't say a word," Ira said, as they got back in the car. "This could be the break that we've been needing."

Darkness drove the fishing party home. John Robert enjoyed the day's outing with his father and two little brothers, not to mention helping to catch the large string of fish they brought home. He also cherished the thought that he may have stumbled onto something that would insure Baxter winning the election. He could hardly wait to tell the sheriff what he had learned. And tell him he did. The sheriff came to the farm the next afternoon as he had promised.

Although Baxter was elated at the information John Robert relayed to him, he was also troubled.

"We have to be able to prove he is bootlegging, and we have to do it quickly," he said. "Time is running out, the election is only two months away."

"Then, I'll work around the clock if I have to."

"I'm afraid that won't work. Fletcher has used his influence to get the word out all over Buchanan County. It's going to be impossible for you to get any information. We need someone he and his friends don't know. Someone he would never suspect."

John Robert was just about to ask if he had anyone in mind, when Dooley stopped his father's car at the end of the lane. Baxter had not noticed.

"There's our man," John Robert said, pointing in the direction of the gravel road.

"You got to be kidding! He's a deacon of the church."

"All the better. You said we needed someone no one would ever suspect."

"He'll never do it."

"Let's ask him," John Robert said, as Dooley drove up to where they were standing.

"I don't think he'll ever go for it, but give it a whirl."

Ida Mae was also aware of Dooley's arrival. She came onto the porch to wait for him. She was surprised to see her brother and the sheriff approach him as soon as he got out of his car. She had no idea why they would want to talk to Dooley.

John Robert got Dooley's promise of confidentiality before explaining their situation. When he explained what they needed him to do, Dooley seemed interested.

"If I didn't have a job, I would do it," he said.

It was then the sheriff joined the conversation. "How much do you make?"

"A dollar an hour."

"I'll pay you twice that."

Dooley's eyes widened. He looked at Ida Mae sitting on the top step. The thought of making that much money made him realize he could have his own automobile much quicker.

"This will only be temporary. What if I am not able to get my job back at the station, once I find out what you need to know."

"Tell you what," the sheriff said, feeling that Dooley might yet be persuaded. "If you help me get the evidence I need, I'll give you a five hundred dollar bonus."

"How can you do that?" Dooley questioned.

"Campaign money, son. Lots of campaign money."

Again Dooley looked at Ida Mae. Five hundred would be enough to finish paying for a good used car and he would be in a position to ask her out any time he wanted.

"What will I drive?"

'I'll take care of that," Baxter said.

"When do I start?" he asked.

"First thing in the morning, right after you go by the service station and let them know you quit, and don't worry about getting your job back. If we are able to pull this off, being re-elected will be a cinch. I'll promise them enough county business if you're rehired, they will be happy to give your job back. The three of us will meet in front of Willie's place at six o'clock in the morning and develop a game plan. Right now, I'm sure there's someone else you would rather be talking to."

"Six in the morning," he said, and started toward the porch where Ida Mae was still waiting.

"I've heard politics can be a little shady," John Robert said.

"What would make you say a thing like that, boy?" the sheriff smiled as he got into his car and drove away.

Chapter Nine

THE DEACON PLAYS DETECTIVE

John Robert pulled in front of Willie's place next morning at six o'clock sharp. Dooley and the sheriff had both gotten there ahead of him. They were standing along side of an old pickup truck.

"How do you like Dooley's transportation?" Baxter asked.

"Not much to look at. Will it run?"

"Like a Singer sewing machine, and that's just what we need for what I have in mind. I'm sending Dooley into Buchanan County pretending to be looking for work. He's going to tell folks that he's planning to get married soon and he really needs a job. When they take a look at this chariot he's riding, I'm sure they will agree. Since logging and mining is about the only industry there is in that county, excluding running the stills, he will have an excuse to be on every back road there is."

"There are only three roads out of that county without driving miles out of the way. With three deputies, you, and myself, I figure we can watch everything that moves on these roads around the clock.

"The deputies and I will stop every car that looks as if it has more than twenty pounds in the trunk or can run more than forty miles per hour.

"John Robert, you will hang out at Mickey's Tavern and the other beer joints in the county and make note of anyone who is buying shine, either at the bar or out the back door. I'm not out to get any of your buddies in trouble, mind you, I've been known to take a little nip now and again myself.

"We'll meet at your house at nine o'clock tonight, John Robert, and at a different location each night thereafter, so not to arouse anyone's curiosity you understand."

Baxter was pacing back and forth as he talked. It was not difficult to tell he was becoming more nervous with each passing day.

"Mind if I take Ida Mae along with me?" Dooley asked.

The sheriff considered the idea for a moment before he answered.

"I think that would be a great idea Mr. Hale, if Ira and her mother have no objections. That will make it more convincing to folks that you are about to get married and are in need of a job."

"See you gentlemen at nine o'clock tonight," Dooley said, and he was off to see if Ida Mae and her parents were receptive to the idea.

When he explained to Ira and Mary Ellen the importance of having Ida Mae along, they offered no objections. Ida Mae made it sound as if she was more than happy to do whatever she could to help get the sheriff re-elected. She did not want her family to know how happy she was to get to spend the entire day with Dooley. She had never confided in anyone, how many times she dreamed of being Mrs. Donald Hale.

It was less than a fifteen-minute drive from the Baxter farm to the top of the mountain. As soon as the couple crossed the county line, Ida Mae slid as close as she could to Dooley.

"Better act as if we are really fond of each other if we want to convince people we are going to get married," she giggled.

The couple spent all morning riding the back roads, pretending to be looking for work. No one made a job offer, but everyone seemed sympathetic. Most even made suggestions of other places to look for work.

This was working out just as Dooley had hoped. Ida Mae, on the other hand, was hoping he would not take this assignment so serious. They had been on one lonely back road after the other and she thought how nice it would be, if she and Dooley could stop and take a break, if only for a little while.

If this were to happen, it would have to be at her suggestion. It was getting late in the afternoon when she came up with an idea she thought might accomplish her goal.

"Let's get something to drink," she said, when she realized they were nearing a small country store. "Maybe a bite to eat also," Dooley said. "I would have brought a lunch if I had known we were going to spend the day together."

They stopped and Dooley purchased a loaf of bread, a few slices of luncheon meat, and cold drinks for each of them.

"Let's find a secluded spot and have a picnic," Ida Mae suggested, when they were back to the truck.

"Where do you have in mind?" Dooley asked.

"Drive back up to the road we were just on, and I'll tell you where to stop," she said, remembering a wide spot with a path leading off into the woods.

Dooley did as she suggested. He turned onto the road they had just traveled, which looked as if it was seldom used.

"Stop here," she told him, when they reached the place she remembered. She gathered their picnic lunch and told him to follow her, having no idea where she was going. She led him about two hundred yards along the path until she found a small, flat area suitable for what she had in mind.

"Just sit there and relax," she told him, "while I fix you something to eat."

Dooley happily stretched himself on the cool bed of leaves that covered the forest floor. The only sound that could be heard was the singing of a flock of sparrows fluttering in the treetops. He watched a gray squirrel jumping from limb to limb as Ida Mae prepared their lunch.

When they were finished eating, he lay down again on the cool surface, sipping the last of his Coca-Cola. Ida Mae gathered the remainder of their food, placed it into the paper container, and lay down on her back beside him. She pulled her knees slightly toward her chest, causing her dress to slide up a few inches.

She had dreamed many times of having Dooley alone where she could let her emotions run wild and she was not about to let this opportunity get away.

"Wouldn't it be nice if we were not pretending?" she asked.

"Not pretending what?"

"To be getting married, Silly."

"Would you really marry me, Ida Mae?"

"Are you asking me to marry you?" she smiled.

"I guess I am," he said as he rolled onto his side and took her into his arms.

The couple stayed in their secluded grove until they barely had time to meet with the sheriff back on the farm. For the next three days, Ida Mae packed their picnic lunch and she also hid a blanket in the bottom of the picnic basket. Each morning, they worked hard at finding Dooley work, but by noon, they were back at their private spot where they would spend the remainder of the day.

It was paradise. They talked of when they would get married. Ida Mae also broke every dating rule her mother had ever taught her.

They met with the sheriff each evening but by the end of the third day, they still hadn't learned anything at all. Dooley had been offered a job, however, hauling lumber from three of the sawmills in Buchanan County across the mountain to the railroad yard in Honaker.

If he were to begin work, he had to report by 7 a.m. the following morning. At first, Baxter was reluctant to advise him to take the job. Most of the lumber trucked to the railroad yard was what Fletcher purchased at the mills and shipped to furniture factories in the Carolinas.

William Baxter wanted nothing to do with helping put money in Fletcher's pockets. But, because the sawmills were deep in the hollows of Buchanan County and hauling lumber would give Dooley an excuse to be on the roads where he could watch for suspicious traffic, the sheriff told him to take the truck driving job.

Dooley liked this arrangement; all he had to do was to drive. He shuttled loaded trucks to the rail yard and empties back to one or the other of the mills. The loading and unloading was left to others. He was being paid by the owner of the mills to drive the trucks, by the sheriff to keep an eye out for suspicious vehicles, and if he were lucky enough to help catch whomever was hauling the booze, he would earn a handsome bonus. If he could earn the bonus, it would mean that he could buy a good used car of his own. He missed having Ida Mae with him, but he knew that if they were to get married, he would have to earn every dollar he could.

Ten days went by without yielding anything that would prove of value to the sheriff. At the end of the second week, the sheriff informed Dooley that if nothing had been discovered by the end of the upcoming week, he should go back to his old job at the station.

Monday of the next week began like all the other days, except Dooley paid more attention to every vehicle. Still, he was unable to find the blue Hudson or anything about any other automobile that might arouse suspicion. The chances of him owning his own car was rapidly slipping away, as were Baxter's chances of winning the election.

The meeting place for that evening was again at the Baxter farm. Neither Dooley nor John Robert had anything to report. It was almost dark, and clouds were beginning to gather in the west. An occasional streak of lightning and a deep rolling rumble of thunder gave evidence that some much needed rain might at last be on it's way.

"Better call it a night," the sheriff grumbled. It was clear that he had all but given up.

Dooley and Baxter left and John Robert made ready for bed.

Driving in the hot sun had taken its toll. Dooley did not realize that such an easy job could make one so tired.

"If it would only rain, maybe tomorrow would be more bearable. Like John Robert, he was completely exhausted. He fell into his bed and was asleep almost at once. He was awakened often throughout the night by the constant booming thunder and the scary streaks of lightning, but it was almost dawn before the first huge drops of rain began pounding their metal roof. Moments later, a steady downpour began. It would last all day. The weight of his truck cut deep ruts in the muddy roads leading to the mills, which sometimes made him almost lose control. He was glad when quitting time drew near and he knew he was delivering his last load.

He managed to wrestle the heavy vehicle out of the hollow and onto Route 80, leading up the mountain.

He was within a hundred yards of the top when the rain started coming so hard, he had to pull onto the shoulder. After almost an hour, the rain let up. Dooley started to pull back onto the hard surface and realized his load would not move. The heavy rain on the dirt shoulder had caused the weight of his truck to sink into the mud.

He could not move in either direction.

"What do I do now?" he pondered.

Suddenly, he came up with a solution. Take a few pieces of the lumber from the top of the load and place them behind the rear wheels. This would allow the tires traction, and besides, the truck would be moving downhill.

Dooley climbed to the top of his load, loosened the dogs that were holding the chains and climbed back onto the ground. He slid four wide pieces of lumber from the center of the load and placed one on top of the other behind each wheel. The lumber allowed him to back his vehicle onto the hard surface. He carefully drove to the top of the mountain and pulled over in a wide area where he knew he would have no trouble reentering the highway.

No need walking back to retrieve those few pieces of muddy lumber, he decided. He climbed back to the top of his load to retighten the chains. What he saw almost caused him to lose his balance and fall from the truck. The lumber was stacked in such a manner as to leave a huge hollow area in the center of the bed. At least fifty gallon jugs of white lightning were neatly stacked in the hollowed space with sawdust poured around each glass container.

Suddenly, Dooley felt as important as if he were a member of an elite group of law enforcement. He alone had solved the case of illegal whiskey being shipped into and through Russell County.

Fletcher himself was, no doubt, the ringleader. He was buying lumber sawed at the mills in the hollows of Buchanan County. He was also buying moonshine from the same people and shipping both products together.

A clever operation, Dooley had to admit, but what was he to do next? Neither Fletcher nor any of his men must know what Dooley had learned. He was glad that it was his last load for the day, but still, he had no choice but to deliver his load to the rail yard. He carefully rearranged the top layer of lumber and retightened the safety chains.

Dooley hurried back to where he had been stuck and quickly threw the muddy boards over the embankment. There was nothing for him to do but park the truck at the rail yard and get word to Baxter as quickly as he could.

He was glad that their meeting place was again at the Baxter farm. After all, they each had good reason to be there. Each time they were to meet where he would see Ida Mae, he always finished his day's work and went home to bathe and freshen up. Today, he did not bother. He was too anxious to share what he had learned. He and John Robert were standing just inside the barn shed, sheltered from the still slowly falling rain, when the sheriff came into view. Dooley had already shared everything he had learned with both, John Robert and his future father-in-law.

The sheriff got out of his car and began slowly walking to where the three men were waiting.

"Cheer up, Sheriff," Dooley said. "You look as if you just lost your best friend."

"It's not my best friend, but the election I'm going to lose," Baxter growled.

"No, you're not," Dooley smiled. He handed the sheriff a milking stool and told him to sit down.

As he recounted the happening of the day, Baxter's expression changed. It went from disbelief, to pure excitement, and then to a look of deep concern.

"Why such a worried look?" John Robert asked, when Dooley finished talking.

"Knowing is one thing and proving is something else," Baxter said. "We have to catch that rascal with his hands in the cookie jar, or in his case, the moonshine jar," he smiled. "If I can pin this on him, I will not only win the election, I'll be the hero of the county."

But how?

"Let me think," Baxter said, and he started pacing from one end of the shed to the other.

"Fletcher is a smart cookie," he said. "I'm sure that the booze is always on the load that is delivered to the rail yard at the end of the day.

"That way it can be unloaded from the truck onto the flatcars after the depot agent and any other railroad employees have gone home.

"So, this is what we will do. Dooley will take a short detour and come here to the farm with his last load each day. Ira and I will hurriedly examine the load, and he can be on his way. If what we're looking for is being transported, we will stake out the railway station and wait for it to be unloaded. I'm sure Fletcher will be there, and if he is, the race for re-election will be over."

"Will I get my bonus, then?" Dooley asked.

"You bet," Baxter said, "and we might even keep a jug or two of old Fletchers' shine to celebrate. Oh, sorry about that, Deacon," he added.

The following week went exactly as planned. Each day, Dooley brought the last load to the farm, but it was mid-week before they found what they were looking for. The moonshine was neatly placed in the center of the load as Dooley had described.

"Now, all we have to do is lay low near the railway station and hope my most worthy opponent makes an appearance," Baxter grinned.

"I sure would like to be there to see how this bust goes down, Sheriff," Ira said.

"By all means," he agreed.

Things went better than the sheriff had hoped. He, Ira, John Robert and one of the deputies sneaked into a vacant house, two hundred yards away, directly in front of the station. They each wandered in, one at a time, in plain clothes without anyone ever knowing they were there. Another one of the deputies was waiting a short distance away in an unmarked car and in plain clothes.

They watched while Fletcher's men unloaded a truck onto a railroad flatcar. It was one Dooley had parked alongside the tracks earlier in the day. When the truck was completely unloaded, one of the men moved it to another location and pulled the one that contained the moonshine up near the flatcar. Just as they suspected, it was the last one to be unloaded.

Baxter was becoming more nervous with each passing moment; Fletcher had not shown up. He knew that it would help to confiscate the whiskey, but he would have to catch Fletcher red-handed if he wanted to guarantee himself the election.

The workers did not start unloading the truck at once. All four of them sat on the edge of the flatcar as if they were taking a break or waiting for something to happen. One of the men kept looking at his pocket watch. At exactly seven o'clock, they got up and started loosening the safety chains on the truck. Within five minutes, Fletcher came driving up and parked his pickup truck beside the load of lumber. It was the same pickup Ira and his sons had seen at the service station a few weeks earlier and it was partially loaded with hay as it had been then.

"Bingo!" the sheriff said, "Now all we have to do is wait until we know he is connected with the booze and we can make a move."

The wait was not long. The men started unloading the lumber as fast as they could move. They stacked it onto the flatcar exactly as it was stacked on the truck, leaving a vacant space in the center. As soon as the first jug of home-brew came into view, Baxter gave the order to move.

He stepped outside and raised one hand in the air, which was the signal for his deputy to pick them up. In less than a minute, they were beside the tracks and Baxter was out of the car. The workers stopped what they were doing immediately. They each had a horrified look on their faces. Fletcher, on the other hand, remained calm.

"Good evening, gentlemen," Baxter shouted. "Fine-looking load of building material you have there."

"First quality," Fletcher bragged. "Thinking about going into the lumber business after the election?" he asked.

"Might," the sheriff said, as he climbed onto the bed of the truck.

Ira, John Robert and the deputy stood at the back of Fletcher's pickup waiting to see what would happen next.

The sheriff lifted one of the jugs out of the sawdust and set it on top of the stack of lumber.

"This belong to you, Fletcher?" he asked.

"Nope," Fletcher replied.

"Does this load of lumber belong to you?"

"Sure does."

"I guess you don't know what's in these jugs."

"Sure don't."

"Mind if I open a few of them to find out?"

"Sure don't."

The sheriff opened three or four of the containers and sniffed the contents. "Smells exactly like shine to me. What do you think?" he asked, as he handed one of the jugs to Fletcher.

"Whatever you say, Sheriff," he said, but would not take the container in his hand.

"Mind explaining how this stuff came to be on the same truck that is hauling your merchandise."

"Have no idea," Fletcher stated, still as calm as if he were talking about the weather. "I simply buy my goods from the mills and the price includes delivery to the rail yard. I have no control over what else might be delivered on the same trucks."

"Bullcrap," the sheriff bellowed, it was clear to see he was getting much more upset than Fletcher. "Then, what are you doing here?" Baxter asked.

"Making sure I'm getting all that I'm paying for, so I can make a profit, but if you need some lumber I'll cut you a deal, Sheriff," he laughed.

Baxter was turning red. He knew that although he had the evidence, he had no way of proving it belonged to Fletcher or that he had knowledge it was on the truck.

Ira was standing behind Fletcher's pickup with one foot on the rear bumper, taking in all that was going on.

"Got the makings, Charlie?" he asked the deputy.

"Sure thing, but I didn't know you smoked," the deputy answered, as he handed Ira a can of Prince Albert tobacco, a book of cigarette papers and a box of matches.

"Just started," Ira grinned. He tore a paper from the packet and poured in some tobacco. He rolled up something that resembled a cigarette and struck a match. When the cigarette was lit, he slowly dropped the match into the pickup bed of dry hay, acting as if it were an accident. The hay started burning so fast, one might have thought it had been soaked with gasoline.

Fletcher made a dash for the truck, but it was too late. Enough of the hay had burned so that several jugs of clear liquid came into view.

The sheriff was once again all smiles. "Don't need any lumber," he said to Fletcher, "but what sort of a deal will you give me on this load of hay? You are under arrest for possession and transporting illegal whiskey," he added.

Fletcher and the others offered no resistance. They were placed into handcuffs and delivered to the county jail. The following day, Fletcher posted bond for him and the four workers and resigned from the race for sheriff.

The weekly newspaper made no mention of his arrest. It simply stated that he had withdrawn from the election due to bad health.

Chapter Ten

IDA MAE MEETS A STRANGER

The day following the arrests was a Saturday. The news spread faster than a wildfire in dry grass. Dooley was at the Duncans' place bright and early, driving his father's automobile.

He was there to pick up Ida Mae so they could go car shopping. He had the bonus the sheriff promised, plus a few dollars he had managed to save, since he'd been working at the service station. Dooley had no idea where they were going or what kind of car he would buy, but he knew that if he had a vehicle of his own he would have his freedom. He could take Ida Mae out and not have to be back home before dark, to please his mother.

Ida Mae was even more excited. She knew he would take her to places she had never been and they could do things that neither of them had ever done.

The couple's first stop was at the only used car dealership in their hometown. Ida Mae wanted the first car they tried, a black 1941 Mercury. They spent the remainder of the day, going to every lot in the county, but she insisted Dooley buy the Mercury.

Before sundown, the deal was closed. Dooley was the proud owner of his first automobile, although it took almost every penny he had.

Her heart sank when the dealer told Dooley he would not be able to drive the car until he purchased license plates, come Monday morning. She was looking forward to their first night out.

"Guess we'll just have to wait," Dooley told her. "I have to take you home, so I can be home myself, before dark. You know how Mother is."

She knew too well how his mother was, and she didn't like it one little bit. She had dreams of Dooley someday being her husband, but she could tell she and Mrs. Hale was not going to see eye-to-eye where her son was concerned. The only time she had ever visited the Hales' home, Dooley's mother had barely been cordial.

Ida Mae got the feeling she would not have been the one chosen as a daughter-in-law. Little did she know how right she was.

Dooley let her out of the car in front of her gate and hurried off. Ida Mae started toward the house just as John Robert was leaving.

"Going out tonight?" she asked.

"Yes, but you're not going, little sister."

"Got a date?"

"Not yet, and if I take you along I'm not likely to have," he said.

"Please, John Robert," she begged. "I won't get in your way. Drop me off at the skating rink and pick me up on your way home."

He hesitated a moment before he spoke. Looking into her sad eyes, he could not say no. "Go ask Mother," he said.

"Give me ten minutes," she said and she was up the steps and into the house.

John Robert sat in his car and waited for her to return. In a little while Ida Mae bounced onto the porch and down the steps.

"What did she say?" he asked.

"She said no at first, but I convinced her that as long as I was with you I'd be alright."

"You lied," he smiled. "You won't be with me all the time."

"I know, but you won't tell," she said as she jumped into the car beside him.

John Robert dropped her off at the rink shortly after dark. He gave her five dollars and promised he would pick her up before the place closed at midnight. He was confident she would be safe there with her friends.

Ida Mae could not believe this was happening. She had never been allowed to go anywhere without one of her parents or Mary Sue accompanying her.

John Robert waited until she was safely inside before he drove off. He was going to Mickey's place to have a few beers and chat with some of his buddies.

Ida Mae went in and was about to rent her skates when John Robert's friend, the policeman, Dewey Combs came up to where she was standing.

"Size six for the lady," he told the attendant behind the counter.

Ida Mae looked at him surprised. "How did you know what size skates I wear?" she asked.

"Just a lucky guess I suppose, not to mention I heard you order your skates the other day when you were in here with John Robert. Sure was a fine job he and your daddy did in helping the sheriff catch Fletcher," he added.

Ida Mae and Dewey skated together for the next hour. In a while, the policeman had to excuse himself to go on late duty. When he left, Ida Mae decided she would step outside to get some fresh air. She was standing alone, near one end of the building, when a new Oldsmobile pulled in front of where she was standing. The driver blinked his headlights a couple of times and whistled.

"What in the world is a beautiful lady doing out here all by herself?" the driver asked.

"Pretty car," Ida Mae said choosing not to respond to his question.

"Just bought it three days ago. Want to go for a ride?" he asked.

"No, thank you."

"At least take a look at it from the inside," he urged.

"Now, do I strike you as the type of girl who would get into a car with a fellow she just met?" she asked.

"Certainly not," the stranger replied. "Do I look like the type of gentleman who would harm a beautiful lady such as you?"

"But I don't even know you."

"And you never will, if you don't allow me to introduce myself."

Another couple exited the rink toward a parked vehicle near the entrance. They were close enough to hear everything Ida Mae and the handsome stranger were saying.

The gentleman jumped from the driver's seat and ran around to the passenger's side and opened the door.

"My name is Jacob," he said.

"I'm Ida Mae. This is the prettiest car I've ever seen."

"Sure you won't go for a ride?"

"I'm sure," she said.

"Then at least let me pull to the back of the parking lot away from all these lights, and we can get acquainted."

Ida Mae nodded her approval.

Jacob parked the Olds in the darkest area of the lot and reached behind the seat.

"Have a cold one," he said as he opened a Blue Ribbon beer and handed it to Ida Mae.

Not wanting to admit she had never tasted beer before, she accepted the bottle. The stranger opened a beer for himself and tuned the radio to the Grand Old Opry and turned the volume down low.

"Live around here?" he asked.

Ida Mae proceeded to tell him where she lived and to take small swallows of the awful tasting liquid. She did not know this fellow, but he seemed nice enough. He had a nice new automobile, so she thought he must be a decent sort of guy. After all, she did not want to spend the evening alone. Dooley had to have the family car home before dark, but that did not mean that she had to sit home and do nothing.

During the first hour she told Jacob all about herself; about how she had grown up on a farm and how she was not allowed to date until she was 18 and even about Dooley's being homebound.

She also told him that Dooley was a church deacon with an excellent pool shot.

By eleven o'clock she realized she had done most of the talking and had learned next to nothing about this stranger she'd just met. But, she did not care; she was finishing her second bottle of beer and becoming more relaxed.

"This stuff doesn't taste too bad once you get used to it," she said as Jacob handed her a third bottle.

Before she knew it, she was scooted over close to this fellow who no longer seemed like a stranger and he had his arm around her shoulder.

For the next 45 minutes the couple said very little.

She was feeling the pleasant effects of the alcohol and enjoying the soft sounds of the country music. She even began humming along with some of the Grand Old Opry entertainers.

Ida Mae was so relaxed she did not even object when Jacob brushed parts of her body that no one ever had, except Dooley. It was an accident, she was certain, because he was reaching over her to constantly adjust the volume on the radio.

It was not until she heard the announcer say, "The last quarter-hour of the Opry is brought to you by Duck Head Overalls," that she realized what time it was. She quickly raised her head from off Jacob's shoulder and reached for the door handle.

"I have to go," she said. "My brother will be picking me up before midnight."

"When will I see you again?" he asked.

"Before long I hope, but don't let anyone know that you even know me," she said as she slid out of the car.

Jacob watched as she teetered over to a bench in front of the building and plopped down near the entrance. He watched in darkness until John Robert drove up to where she was.

"Glad you are here," he heard her say to her brother as she was getting into the car. "I've been skating so long, I really feel dizzy."

Having consumed a goodly amount of beer himself, John Robert was not even aware that his little sister had been drinking.

When she was home and in bed, her thoughts wandered back to the stranger. She was having feelings she had never known before. Probably the beer, she thought just before sleep overtook her.

When she awoke Sunday morning, her aching head felt as big as a pumpkin. She was so thirsty, she thought she could guzzle a bucketful of water, but she did not dare complain. She could not bear the thought of eating a single bite of her breakfast, but she did manage to get herself ready for church.

Dooley was in his regular place behind Reverend Kyle, but she tried not to look directly at him. Ida Mae felt ashamed.

"Why should I bother to feel this way?" she thought. "I would have been with him were he not such a mama's boy."

She paid little attention to the services. She just wanted to get back home and lie down. She was glad when the preacher announced that the building materials for the new Sunday School rooms would be delivered the following day and Ira had agreed to begin construction at once.

"Deacon Hale has informed me that there is an ample amount in our treasury to make full payment for the materials and Mr. Thompson will have his money just as soon as the job is completed. If there is no further business, the congregation is dismissed."

Dooley asked Ida Mae if he could come to see her that afternoon, but she told him that car shopping the day before made her so tired she needed to rest. "Come by later in the week, or I'll see you next Saturday."

Chapter Eleven

THE BUILDING BEGINS

Brother Ezra Taylor was at the Baptist Church before sunrise the following morning. At last, his dream of seeing the new addition was about to become a reality. He'd helped his father, who was the pastor, and others build this building ten years prior to the Great Depression.

The log church they had been using had burned to the ground, so another one had to be built hurriedly. The plans were to enlarge it the following year, but funds would not permit.

More than three decades had passed, and still it was its original size. Each year thereafter, there was talk of building more rooms but due to helping needy families, or sending money for missionary work, the project was put on the back burner.

Although it had been his father's dream to see the church grow, the elder man had died without seeing it happen.

Brother Ezra promised his father on his deathbed that he would see his dream carried out. Now, far into his sunset years, he was afraid that he, too, would not live to fulfill his promise.

As he sat watching the sun rise, the shadow of the building began to take form. The outline of the bell tower was as clearly visible on the churchyard, as if someone had painted it there. He let his mind wander back to those days more than thirty years ago. His aging father had honored him by letting him nail the last shingle on that very tower, which made the project complete.

His reverie was cut short by the arrival of Ira and John Robert. Within an hour, about twenty other men from the congregation were there, anxious to get started. Shortly thereafter, Thompson's truck pulled in with the first load of materials.

The workers brought every tool they'd possibly need: picks, shovels, hammers, squares, levels, handsaws and more. Several of the men began unloading Thompson's truck while others helped Ira measure and drive stakes, which outlined the size of the building.

Unable to do any physical labor himself, Brother Ezra could only sit and watch. Watching the men reminded him of his childhood days, when everyone in the community gathered to participate in a house-raising for some new family moving into the area. There were so many workers, they sometimes seemed in each other's way, but everyone pitched in.

By mid-day, the group had dug several large holes. Massive stones were lowered in to ensure a solid foundation. Several of the workers were mixing concrete in a large pan. The concrete was to hold the stones into place, so the foundation could not move.

Shortly after noon, Reverend Kyle arrived with a half-dozen women from church. They had large baskets of food for the workers. There were ham biscuits, fried chicken, potato salad, cole slaw, lemonade and two large chocolate cakes for dessert.

None of the laborers had to be asked twice to quit working. The sun was boiling down as lunch was served. The sight of the wonderful offering, set out on blankets beneath the massive shade trees, rejuvenated the overheated workers Within minutes after the pastor asked the blessing, the food began to disappear.

The men seated themselves on the ground under the trees to eat their lunch and listen as Brother Taylor recalled helping to build the existing church. A silence fell over the crowd when a tear appeared in the old gentleman's eye, as he told of his promise to his father.

"My doctor tells me that I have but a short time left," he continued. "And to see this project completed, will make my going out much easier."

The group was touched. They finished their lunch and resumed work with renewed vigor

They worked until it was almost dark, and Brother Taylor was the last one to leave. Ira and John Robert watched him as they drove away.

With a cane in one hand, he was walking the well-trodden path that led from the church to his home.

Brother Taylor's wife died many years earlier and since her passing, he had devoted his life to watching after the Baptist Church. He was not only the oldest member and one of its deacons; he was its jack-of-all-trades, self-appointed janitor and maintenance man until the years had slowed him and he'd handed over the reigns to a younger man.

For the next two weeks, the men worked from early morning until sundown. They stopped only long enough to eat the wonderful lunches the ladies brought each day. Their goal was to complete the project so they could have a dedication service the following Sunday. By mid-day Saturday of the second week, they knew their goal would be reached.

Just about sundown, Ira and John Robert were up on the roof. In one hand, Ira was holding a hammer and in the other he had a shingle. As if by cue, all the other workers gathered at the base of a ladder that was leaning against one side of the building.

"Brother Taylor, I believe this task is yours," Ira said.

Several of the men helped the old gentleman pull his feeble body to the top of the ladder. A moment later, the only sound that could be heard was the gentle tapping of the hammer as Brother Taylor drove the nails into the last shingle.

The church was once again whole, and again Brother Taylor had been honored.

Chapter Twelve

DOOLEY BREAKS OVER

Dooley could not believe so much could happen in so short a time. With Fletcher out of the sheriff's race, William Baxter was sure to be re-elected.

Dooley's future father-in-law would be chief deputy; he was driving his own automobile, had nearly a hundred dollars in his pocket, and had gotten his old job back Monday morning.

Only six weeks earlier, he'd been worrying about how he would ever be able to take Ida Mae out on a date, and now, she was about to become his wife. Now it seemed nothing could go wrong.

Ida Mae stood on the front porch watching as the Mercury, shining like brand new, slowly approached. She knew Dooley must have spent most of the day cleaning and waxing and he was driving as careful as he could so as not to raise any dust.

Before Dooley even had time to climb out, Ida Mae jumped in the car. She gave him a big kiss on the cheek before they slowly drove away.

"What would you like to do first?" Dooley asked.

"Let's get something to eat and then just drive for a while and try out your new car."

Dooley drove into town and pulled the Mercury right up in front of Sid's Grill so everyone would know he now had a ride of his own. They went inside and ordered burgers and Cokes.

They had just about finished eating their meal when a tall stranger walked into the restaurant and took a seat at the end of the bar. He ordered coffee and started a conversation with one of the waitresses.

"Who is the second-best pool shot in the county?" they overheard the stranger ask.

"The best shot in town is right over there," the waitress told him, pointing to the booth where Dooley and Ida Mae were sitting.

The stranger turned and gave a quick glance in their direction. "Not while I'm in town," the stranger grinned.

"Sounds to me like you've just been challenged," someone at the other end of the bar called out.

"Not me," Dooley said as he approached the bar to pay for their food.

"It's on me," the stranger said, as he slipped a fifty to the lady at the cash register. "You and the lady have a fine evening."

He winked at Ida Mae when he was sure her friend wasn't looking.

"Mighty kind of you, mister. I don't believe we've met. Name's Donald Hale and this is my fiancée, Miss Ida Mae Duncan."

"Jacob Hurd," the stranger said, extending his hand, "but most people just call me Jake. 'Jake the Stick,' that is."

Dooley stood.

"Well, 'Jake the Stick,' you didn't have to do that, but thanks again, and see you around," Dooley said as he ushered Ida Mae toward the door.

When they were outside, they could not help but notice the brand-new light green Oldsmobile Ninety-eight and its Illinois plates, parked right beside Dooley's Mercury.

"What a beautiful set of wheels," Ida Mae commented, never letting on that she had ever seen the Olds before.

"And what beautiful cue sticks," Dooley said, pointing to the back seat.

"Maybe that's why everyone calls him 'Jake the Stick.'"

"Most likely. Let's go for a ride, then we'll go see a movie."

The couple spent some time riding and trying to decide on a date for their wedding. They both agreed they would not get married until they could afford a place of their own. The Duncan household was already crowded enough, and Dooley was sure Ida Mae would not tolerate his nagging mother.

"I know of a beautiful apartment in town," Dooley told her. "But I need a fifty dollar deposit plus another fifty for the first month's rent.

There's food, electricity, gasoline, insurance, and we have to buy furniture, of course."

"How much will we need?" she wanted to know.

"At least five hundred, best I am able to figure. I don't know how I'll ever come up with that much cash."

She scooted a little closer to him and whispered in his ear as if they were in a crowded room, "I bet you'll find a way."

They were back to the theater 45 minutes before showtime, so Dooley drove around town for a while.

They returned to find Jake's big Olds sitting in front of Willie's Billiard Parlor.

"Guess he's inside teaching some of our local boys how to shoot," Dooley said.

"Let's go see if he's as good as he claims," Ida Mae coaxed.

"Are you kidding? If any of our church members were to see me go into Willie's place, they would withdraw my membership, and if your daddy found out I took you in a place like that, we'll have to elope."

"Let's wait until dark and we will slip in the back door," she said.

"How did you know Willie's place has a back door?" he asked.

"Every place has a back door, Dooley."

"Thought you wanted to go to the movies."

"Please, Honey, just for a little while."

Dooley relented.

"Alright," he said, "but just for a few minutes."

They cruised until dark. Dooley parked his car a good distance away and they strolled around back of Willie's place.

At the doorway, he grabbed Ida Mae's hand and they hurried inside. The place was much like it was when she and John Robert were there a few weeks before.

"Watch your language, fellows, there's a lady in the house," Willie announced when the couple made their entrance.

"Thanks, Willie," Dooley said as he and Ida Mae took a seat near the table where Jake and a couple of other fellows were playing.

"Grab a stick, Dooley," Willie said. "This fellow Jake is pretty good. He's been winning quite a bit in the last two hours."

"No thanks, I'm just a spectator."

Dooley and Ida Mae watched as Jake and his opponents played several games. Jake made some mighty fine shots, but he also missed some shots that Ida Mae knew Dooley could have easily made.

They were playing for a dollar a game. After a while, the two fellows he was playing decided to leave.

"Better try your luck, Mr. Hale," Jake said. "Show the lady how well you can shoot."

Dooley shook his head.

"Go on, Dooley. You are a lot better shot than he is," Ida Mae whispered. "You can win a few dollars."

"How do you know?" he whispered with a puzzled look on his face.

"I've watched you shoot," she said.

"When?"

"Well, I—I was with my brother some time back and he came in here looking for someone," she fibbed. "We sat back there in that dark corner and watched you and some fellow shoot nine ball. You beat him every game. I bet you can beat this guy, too, Dooley, then maybe he won't brag so much," she added.

"What do you say, Mr. Hale?" Jake extended another invitation.

"Maybe one game, and the name is Dooley, if you don't mind."

"Buck a game, Dooley?"

Dooley looked at Ida Mae. She nodded her approval.

"Buck a game, name your poison."

Willie racked the balls and took a coin from his pocket.

"You call it, Dooley," Jake said.

"Heads," he said, just before the coin landed on the table, tails up. Jake broke the rack and ran the table.

Dooley lost without getting a shot.

"Rack 'em," he said to Willie as he handed Jake a dollar bill. Two more times, Jake ran the table; each time Dooley lost another dollar.

"He's got to miss sometime," Ida Mae whispered.

She was right; on the fourth rack, no balls fell when Jake made the break.

At last, it was Dooley's turn to show his expertise and that is exactly what he did.

He ran the table four times in a row while Jake watched, slack-jawed.

Halfway through the fifth rack, Dooley scratched. Jake dropped the remaining balls. After eight games, the pair were even; neither won nor lost any money.

"You're good," Jake interrupted, "and maybe the only man I've played against who is as good or better than I am."

Dooley laid his cue stick on the table and turned to Ida Mae.

"Time to go," he said.

"You can't quit now," she insisted. "We're right back where we started."

"See," Ida Mae whispered, "even he admits you are better than he is. Get over there and win us some money."

"Are you sure? We're already late for the movie."

"I'm sure. Watching you make some of those near impossible shots is much more fun than watching a movie."

"Then rack 'em up, Willie," Dooley smiled.

"Since we are so evenly matched, why don't we make it a little more interesting?" Jake suggested.

"How much more interesting do you have in mind?"

"Say five bucks a game."

Ida Mae's eyes widened.

Dooley won three or four games and Jake would even the score, Jake would get a few games ahead and then Dooley would catch up. And so it went for the next couple of hours. Then, luck made a sudden change in Dooley's favor. The longer they played, the better Dooley became. It was nearing midnight, when Jake had had enough.

"I'm getting tired," he said, "but I hope you will give me another chance to get my money back."

"Anytime," Dooley said, "and bring plenty of cash. This pretty lady and I are getting married soon and we can sure use the money."

"Tell you what," Jake said. "I'm on my way to North Carolina to visit my brother, but I'll be coming back through in a couple of weeks. What you say we go at it again?"

"Two weeks from tonight," Ida Mae said.

"That'll work," Jake smiled.

The couple could hardly wait to get back to the car. Ida Mae got more and more excited as Dooley counted his winnings.

"Fifty dollars exactly," he said, "what do you think of that, Lady?" he asked.

"I think, if old Jake comes back in town in two weeks, you can win enough so we can get married much sooner than we thought."

Dooley was secretly thrilled. He was compiling net worth faster than he could ever dream possible. As he drove Ida Mae home, they could talk of nothing but their future together.

He came to see Ida Mae almost every day after work. They went to look at the apartment they would soon be able to share. Their future landlord was a friend of Dooley's father, so he agreed to hold the place until they were married.

The couple spent the following Saturday selecting the furniture they were sure they could soon be able to afford.

Their future looked bright. All they needed was for Jake to get back into town.

But it was still vital for none of the church members to find out how Dooley was getting ahead so fast. He was afraid the news of his winnings would leak out.

He took his seat behind Reverend Kyle on Sunday morning, but was overwhelmed by his feelings of guilt. He felt that every member of the congregation was staring directly at him. He could not look at Ida Mae, because each time he did, he could feel his face flush.

How rapidly his life had changed. How could he ever make amends?

"I'll give ten percent of Jake's money to the church," he decided. After all, once the building materials were paid for, there would be almost nothing left.

He pulled a five-dollar bill from his wallet and rolled it up tightly as he waited for the collection plate to pass in front of him. As the offering plate drew near, his feeling grew worse.

He quickly took another five from his wallet and dropped both bills into the plate. He took a deep breath and exhaled. His guilt subsided, but he could hardly wait to be dismissed.

When the last word of the final hymn had been sung, Dooley scooped the offering from the collection plate, which he would deposit in the cigar box at home, and he was out the door.

The following week passed slowly. When the couple was together, they talked of little other than the upcoming Saturday night. They hoped that above all else, nothing would keep Jake from getting back into town, because Dooley had asked for Saturday off from work at the station.

He had drawn another check for the previous two-week's work, which made his cash in hand almost $250. He was halfway to the amount they agreed they would need to be able to say their vows.

At last, the big day arrived. Dooley was to go by Thompson's lumberyard before it closed at noon and pay for the church building supplies, and the remainder of the day was his own. The cigar box containing the cash, now totaling almost nine hundred dollars, was safely tucked away in the trunk of his car. It was barely past mid-morning, so he decided to pick up Ida Mae first and he would still have time to take care of the church business later.

When he arrived at the Duncan's place, Ida Mae was waiting. She was decked out in her prettiest blue dress and she was bubbling over with excitement. "Let's go back and look at our furniture," she said as she jumped into the Mercury and scooted as close to Dooley as was possible.

"Whatever you say, dear," Dooley replied, "but let's stop and get something to eat first. I'm starved."

"That makes two of us," she replied, and they were on their way.

When they arrived at the restaurant, the place was crowded. Dooley gave the waitress their order and they watched some teenagers play the pinball machines while their food was being prepared. It was not until they had finished eating and he started to pay their bill, that he realized he had forgotten to take care of the church business at Thompson's. "No big deal," Ida Mae declared. "You can take care of it first thing Monday morning."

The remainder of the day, the couple spent looking at furniture and riding around. Ida Mae had it all figured out. If Dooley could just win a hundred and fifty dollars, his next payday would make almost exactly what they needed for them to set their wedding day.

"At five bucks a game, I'd have to win thirty games more than Jake does, and he's good. Remember?"

"Then, play for more money," Ida Mae said. "He's good, but you're much better."

They continued to drive and make plans for their future until it was almost dark. Finally, curiosity overtook them. Dooley just had to drive back into town to see if Jake's Oldsmobile was anywhere around.

Sure enough, there it was — parked in exactly the same spot it had been two weeks earlier.

"Let's go on in now," Ida Mae coaxed.

"Not a chance," Dooley replied. He drove back out of town, so he would not be tempted to go into Willie's too early.

Finally, the time had arrived. Ida Mae was so anxious she was squirming in her seat. As usual, Dooley parked a short distance away and they strolled up the street as if they were window-shopping. This time, when they arrived at the back door of the pool hall, it was Ida Mae who grabbed Dooley by the hand and rushed him inside. They were surely grateful there were no windows in Willie's establishment.

Once inside, the couple strolled in and took seats on two of the stools that lined the walls. Jake recognized them at once.

"Glad you could make it, Dooley," he said. "How are you this evening, Miss Duncan?" he added.

Before Ida Mae could answer, the fellow who was playing at the same table with Jake spoke.

"Grab a stick, Dooley. I've just been helping this gentleman pass the time while he was waiting for you to arrive."

Dooley selected the best stick he could find. Jake replaced the stick he had been using with one he removed from an expensive-looking cylinder case. Both men chalked their cues and Jake asked Dooley to name the game.

"Nine-ball is fine with me," Dooley smiled. "Lag for the break?" he asked.

Jake nodded his approval.

Each of the players shot one ball to the far end of the table simultaneously. Dooley's ball came back and stopped closest to the rail, entitling him to be the first to shoot.

Willie racked the balls and the two men were ready to begin.

"Same as before, five dollars a game?" Jake asked.

"Make it ten," Ida Mae spoke before Dooley could answer.

"Okay with you?" he questioned.

"Make it easy on yourself," Jake replied.

At the mention of ten dollars a game, almost everyone in the house laid down their cues. Few had ever seen anyone shoot for this amount of money. Most of the other players became spectators as Dooley prepared to make his first break. Jake took a stool and waited his turn.

Dooley made the break and three of the nine balls disappeared; he was off to a great start. He ran the table five times before missing a shot.

The room got so quiet, one would have thought they were attending a wake. The only sound, other than that of the billiard balls clicking, was a loud belch made by some fellow who had just guzzled down half a bottle of beer.

Ida Mae sat quietly calculating their winnings. They were already fifty dollars ahead and Jake had not yet gotten a turn. The tide turned rapidly, however. Jake was also starting quite well, and within twenty minutes, he had won forty dollars of his money back. The lead swung back and forth like the pendulum on Willie's wall clock. Dooley was three games ahead at about half hour before midnight. The two had been going at each other nonstop for well over two hours.

"How about a fifteen-minute break?" Jake asked. "I'm beginning to get a little tired."

Dooley quickly agreed.

"Just what we wanted to hear," Ida Mae whispered. "Remember the other time the two of you played? When Jake began to get tired, you really started winning."

"He did miss a few shots I thought he could have surely made," Dooley replied.

They did not realize they had spoken loud enough for Jake to overhear.

"What time do you close?" Jake asked when they were ready to resume play.

"Two a.m. sharp," Willie answered. "It's a city ordinance and one of our officers is usually here by 2:15 to make sure I'm in compliance."

"Then, since we are so evenly matched and I don't know when I'll be back in town, why don't we raise the ante?" Jake suggested.

"Fifteen a game?" Dooley asked.

Jake reached for the case that had held his cue. He unscrewed a secret compartment in one end and extracted a large roll of green backs.

"I was thinking more like 25," he answered.

"Too rich for my blood," Dooley complained.

Ida Mae cleared her throat two or three times in rapid succession. Dooley looked at her and then back at Jake several times before answering.

"Twenty-five it is," he said. "I believe it's my break."

The next two games were Dooley's and Ida Mae was all smiles. Halfway through the third, he missed a shot. Jake sank only two of the remaining balls before he scratched, which caused him to lose his turn.

"Guess I should have been happy with just fifteen a game," he said.

"Wish I'd suggested fifty," Ida Mae giggled.

"Guess I could afford to lose a few games for that amount," Jake said. "After all, it's only money."

"Go for it, Dooley," one of Willie's regulars encouraged, and suddenly the spectators, who until now, had been almost silent, became a cheering section.

"You guys are crazy," Dooley shouted.

"No, they're not. Go for it, Dooley," Ida Mae said in an almost pleading voice. She had not yet told him that the afternoons they spent on the mountain road, watching for moonshiners, had created an urgent need to get married as soon as possible.

"Do it for us," she whispered.

Dooley could not say no. He stood, staring at Ida Mae for a moment, and then toward his opponent. He nodded his approval.

"With the stakes so high, what you say we make a couple rules," Jake suggested.

"What do you have in mind?" Dooley asked.

"Neither of us may call it quits until it becomes his turn to break, unless he is out of cash. We are allowed one five-minute break and the games end promptly at two o'clock, regardless who's winning."

"Sounds fair enough," Dooley agreed.

"A beer for everyone in the house," Jake told Willie, "and bring me two Blue Ribbons," he added.

"What will you have, Miss?" he asked Ida Mae.

"Never tasted the stuff," she answered, looking at Jake who just smiled.

Willie did as he was asked and Jake emptied one of the bottles without ever taking it from his lips.

It was Dooley's turn to go first. Jake set on the stool beside Ida Mae, calmly sipping his second bottle of beer while Dooley made his shots. Jake watched as he ran the table three times before he missed.

Each time, he peeled a crisp fifty from the roll he had taken from the case and handed it to Ida Mae. Counting what she knew Dooley had in his pocket, they now had just over four hundred dollars. One hundred short of what they would need to start their life together.

At last, it was Jake's turn at the table. He guzzled down the remainder of the Blue Ribbon, chalked his expensive cue and broke the rack.

At least half the balls disappeared. Three more shots later, he had fifty dollars of his money back.

A hush fell over the onlookers. No one in the place had ever witnessed such skill. The hooks, combinations, and bank shots he made were simply unbelievable. Within minutes, he had eight games under his belt.

Dooley was broke.

"Time to call it quits," Dooley started to say, but Ida Mae interrupted.

"Time to take our five-minute break," she said. She pulled Dooley aside and whispered," Give me the car keys."

"Not in a million years," he said. He knew exactly what she was thinking.

"It will only be a loan and only for a few minutes," she urged. "You know he is getting tired. Give me the keys."

Dooley reluctantly did as she asked. She rushed out the back door and quickly returned with the cigar box from the trunk of his car. She opened the box and the large number of bills came into view. Jake's eyes widened. When the game resumed, it was still his turn. He broke the rack more gently than the previous times and not a single ball fell into the pockets.

Ida Mae smiled; at last Dooley could recoup their losses. He took his turn, but was so nervous that he sank only three of the balls before he scratched. It was Jake's turn again and it was near one in the morning.

Ida Mae watched the clock as Jake won game after game. Dooley was watching the cigar box as the stack of bills dwindled. With a quarter hour left to play, Dooley had to call the game; both his funds and that of the church treasury were depleted.

He laid his cue on the table, took Ida Mae by the hand and made his exit without uttering a word.

Preacher Kyle's warning was ringing in his ears. "He who gambles for the wages of another will commit greater sins."

"You got any more bright ideas?" he snapped when they were out on the street. It was the first time he had ever spoken in such a manner to Ida Mae.

"No, but I'll come up with one before Monday morning," she said. During the ride back to Ida Mae's home, neither she nor Dooley spoke a word. Such a short time before, he felt as if everything had been going his way, now his whole world was crashing in around him. He was unable to help on the building project because of his job, he had gambled away all the church funds and his dream of marrying Ida Mae had gone with them. If anyone ever found out what he had done, he would bring disgrace on himself and his family.

Dooley was numb; Ida Mae felt just as guilty. It was her fault they had gone into Willie's place and she was to blame for him loosing money that did not belong to him. They also had another crisis that Dooley was not yet aware of; she was sure she was carrying his child. She had planned to tell him on their way home, after he won enough money for them to get married, but now she felt it better to keep silent.

When Dooley brought his Mercury to a stop in front of the Duncan's gate, Ida Mae scooted as close to him as she could.

"Don't worry," she whispered, "we're both in this together. I'll see you at church tomorrow." She kissed his cheek and got out of the car.

CHAPTER THIRTEEN

IDA MAE BREAKS THE NEWS

The next day, everyone was anxious to get to the church early — everyone except Dooley, who was so ashamed, he'd been unable to sleep. Although he was certain no one knew what he had done, his conscience was tearing him to pieces. He wondered if Ida Mae felt as bad.

The Duncan family, like everyone else in the congregation, was excited to see the finished building project. Even Granny was up early, and for the first time since anyone could remember, she was not grouchy. After all, it was her son who did the supervising on the project, so she wanted to get there early enough to brag a little before the services started.

They were on their way at least a quarter hour earlier than what they were accustomed. They were not the first to arrive, however. Several of the members were already gathered near the front entrance when they drove onto the parking lot.

Brother Ezra Taylor was sitting on the top step, but something clearly wasn't right. His head was bowed, but his body was slumped forward. An open Bible lay across his lap.

Ira and John Robert knew something was wrong as soon as they got out of the car. A hush had fallen over the crowd. It was not until they moved closer, that they realized Brother Taylor was dead.

Four of the male members picked up the cold frail form, carried it inside and placed it on one of the back pews. They stepped to the outside of the church and closed the doors behind them. By then, it was time for services to start and the congregation was gathered in front of the building.

Reverend Kyle asked that everyone bow his head in silent prayer.

"In view of the passing of Brother Ezra, I am canceling today's worship service. I'd like to ask you menfolk who're able to please meet me at the cemetery at two in the afternoon.

"Our dedication service will be in conjunction with Brother Taylor's funeral," he continued. "I think that would be appropriate. Consider us dismissed."

The passing of Brother Taylor saddened Dooley, along with everyone else, but he was glad he did not have to sit for an hour, looking at the people from whom he had stolen.

"I must go to the grave site," he told Ida Mae, "but I will come by later today."

By two, a large crowd had gathered to start digging the grave. The men took turns working as they talked. They discussed the life of Brother Taylor and the great job the sheriff had done in catching Fletcher with all that moonshine, but most of the conversation centered on the new church addition.

Although the church was at least a half-mile from the cemetery it could be seen clearly. Each time Dooley looked in that direction, he was reminded of the terrible wrong he had done and knew Brother Taylor would have been ashamed of him. He took a turn at working in the grave at the earliest opportunity. He did not want to leave without helping, but he could hardly wait to see Ida Mae.

He felt that if he did not have someone to talk to, he would surely explode from the guilt he was feeling. When someone asked to relieve him, he excused himself and took off. He went straight to the Baxter farm to visit with Ida Mae. He was grateful Mr. Thompson had not come to the graveyard and that no one had mentioned the money owed for the materials.

"What are we going to do?" he asked Ida Mae when she met him at her front gate.

She could tell he was so nervous he could hardly speak.

"I don't know what we'll do later," she said "but right now, let's go for a walk."

They strolled past the barnyard and through the pasture field leading toward the woods. The couple sat down in the shade of the same oak tree that had caused the damage to John Robert's car a few months earlier. They discussed how they would get the money to replace what they had lost. They also talked about how they could postpone paying Mr. Thompson without having to tell him what they had done.

"We will have to forget about getting married for a while," Dooley said.

"Oh no, Dooley," Ida Mae raised her voice, "that's one thing we can't do."

"Why not," he asked.

"I'm going to have your baby," she blurted out.

Dooley's face turned the color of a fresh fallen snow. Several moments passed before he was able to speak.

"Within the last month I have become a liar, a thief, and on top of all that, I'm going to be a daddy. What else can happen?" he asked.

"You tell me," she said.

"Alright, I will," he went on. "I'll lose my position as deacon, not to mention being thrown out of the church. I will be put in jail for stealing, and if I'm lucky, your daddy will kill me with the first shot."

"Oh, shut up, Dooley," she said as she burst into tears.

Dooley sat down beside her and took her into his arms. They held each other a long while without saying a word.

At last Ida Mae composed herself.

"Something good will happen, Dooley. You just wait and see."

"Tell you what," he said, "we will give it one week. I'll make up something to tell Mr. Thompson tomorrow morning and if we don't have a plan by next Saturday morning, we will run away and get married."

"Where would we go?" she asked.

"Wherever you say."

"Well, I've always wanted to see New York. Or Boston. And, we could go to Illinois."

"Yeah, that's it," Dooley said. "Why don't we go to Illinois? Maybe I can find Jake and win all our money back and then we can get married on the way home."

Again Ida Mae burst into tears. "Let's go," she said.

He helped her up from where she was sitting and they began walking the path back toward the barn. When they reached the open-ended shed, Ida Mae stopped. "Let's sit here on the hay for a while," she said. "I don't want you to leave feeling as you do."

She pulled Dooley toward her as she fell back on the pile of loose hay. As she fell backwards, she bumped her head on something solid. Wondering what it could be, she began to uncover the object she had struck. A full gallon of moonshine came into view. She moved more hay and more and more jugs became visible.

"Where did this come from?" she asked.

"That's the whiskey we took from Fletcher," Dooley answered. "The sheriff needed some place to hide it until trial day. It's evidence."

"How much is here?"

"About sixty jugs would be my guess."

"How much is it worth?"

"About twelve dollars a gallon, I reckon."

Ida Mae grabbed a twig and began making numbers in the dust on the barn floor. "Sixty times twelve. That's seven hundred and twenty dollars. When is trial day?"

"Don't know yet."

"This is it," she said smiling. "This is how we're going to get the money back. This is how we're going to get you out of trouble, and this how we're going to get married," she said, as she grabbed him and pulled him down beside her again.

"What are you talking about?" he asked.

"We're going to sell this whiskey," she giggled.

"Are you out of your mind?" he whispered, not knowing if anyone was within hearing distance. "We can't steal this stuff."

"Why not?" she giggled again. "Is that worse than stealing cash from the church?"

"We could never pull it off."

"You just leave it to me," she said. "You come by here tomorrow as soon as you get off work. I'll bet you I'll have it all figured out."

In a little while, Dooley had to leave. Ida Mae sat down on one of the porch steps and watched as he drove down the long lane to the gravel road. She knew what to do to get them out of this awful situation; she just had to figure out how they were going about getting it done. It was almost dark and Ira and John Robert were just getting home from the cemetery.

"I'm starved. I'll see if your mother has our supper ready," Ira said, as he entered into the house.

John Robert sat down beside his sister, but she did not even acknowledge his presence. He scooted closer to her and placed his strong arm around her shoulder. "Something bothering you?" he asked.

"It's nothing," she answered.

"Come to think of it, Dooley wasn't exactly himself today, either. You two haven't been arguing, have you?"

"He was probably upset about Brother Ezra," she said.

"Come and get it," Ira called from inside.

John Robert got up and started inside. He hesitated, aware that his little sister was deeply troubled. "If there is anything I can do, you only have to ask," he told her.

She followed her brother into the kitchen and they joined the others at the supper table. John Robert could not help but notice she hardly touched her food. For the first time in many days, their conversation did not center on Baxter and the election. Everyone talked about Brother Taylor and his untimely death.

"The grave is all finished and the wake will be tomorrow night at the church," Ira commented. "Everyone for miles around will be there."

John Robert watched as his sister sat staring into her plate, as if she were in some kind of a trance.

At once, her demeanor changed. A smile came on her lips and she looked as if she had just been invited to a square dance, instead of being informed of a wake.

She'd told Dooley she would figure out how they were going to get out of their predicament and already a plan was beginning to take shape. They would take the whiskey out of the barn while everyone was at the church.

"Sure they will," Ida Mae said. "Everyone in the community will be there. Pass me the cornbread, Granny."

No one else in the family seemed to notice, but John Robert could tell his sister was up to something. He had no idea what it was, but he was determined to find out.

After supper, the family gathered on the front porch, as usual. They talked about the new addition to the church, Brother Ezra's death, and the upcoming election. Ida Mae did not take part in the conversation. Again, she sat in silence, as if she was in a world of her own. When the subject of the whiskey finally came up, she suddenly developed an interest.

"Who did Fletcher sell that moonshine to?" she asked.

"Only he knows that and I'm sure he won't ever tell," Ira said. "He's in enough trouble himself and he's not about to involve anyone else."

"What will happen to him?" Ida Mae went on.

"Hard to say," Ira answered. "If he'd only had a gallon or two, he would probably have gotten off with a small fine, but with the quantity he had in his possession, he may have to stay a good long time in the county jail."

"I bet he would pay a lot, not to have to do that, wouldn't you say?"

"I bet you got that right," Ira grinned.

Already, another phase of Ida Mae's plan was coming together. She had figured out how to get the whiskey out of the sheriff's hiding place and now she was about to come up with a way to turn it into cash. For the remainder of the evening, she did not take part in any of the other conversation. She was trying to formulate the details of her plan. By bedtime, she was sure she had everything figured out, but she would need to solicit John Robert's help.

Chapter Fourteen

DOOLEY GETS IN DEEPER

Just before sundown the following day, the Duncan family was getting dressed for Brother Taylor's wake. Everyone, except Ida Mae, was anxious to get to the church. She was stalling in hopes Dooley would make an appearance before her family was ready to leave. She had plans for Dooley and herself, but she was careful not to do anything to arouse suspicion. She was really becoming nervous by the time Dooley's car came into view.

"The rest of you go ahead and I'll ride with Dooley," she said when she saw his car pull to a stop at the end of the lane.

She was relieved when the family was loaded into John Robert's Chevrolet, and he drove away.

"We'll wait until we're sure they're out of sight," Ida Mae said, as soon as Dooley's car came to a stop.

"Why do we want them to get out of sight?" he wanted to know.

"So we can load that moonshine, Silly, unless you wanted to ask them to help us."

"I do believe you have taken total leave of your senses," he said.

"You got any better ideas?" she asked.

"I reckon not," he had to admit.

"Then, back the car out here to the barn shed and let me do the thinking," she demanded.

Dooley reluctantly did what she told him. They hurriedly loaded all but two jugs of the whiskey into the back of his car. They carefully placed portions of the loose hay around the jugs so they would not get broken.

When the last jug was in the trunk, Ida Mae jumped into the passengers seat and said, "Hurry up, we're going to a wake, remember."

"It'll be my wake if we get caught," he snapped. "What are we going to do with this stuff?"

"Sell it. You didn't think we were going to drink it, did you?" she laughed. "We're going to put the money back in the church treasury."

"Sure we are. I guess we're going to take it to Brother Taylor's wake and auction it off. I'm sure Baxter will be there, so maybe he will be the highest bidder."

"You worry too much, Dooley," she said as she scooted up real close to him. "You wouldn't want our baby to grow up while you were in jail for stealing money from the church would you?"

"Oh no, I'd much rather he think I was in there for selling bootlegged liquor," he snapped.

"So, I take it you think we're going to have a little boy," she said as she snuggled even closer.

When they arrived at the wake, a large crowed had already gathered. The building would not hold all the people who had come to pay their last respects. Most of the women were seated in the sanctuary and the men were gathered in small groups outside.

Ida Mae and Dooley made their way to where Ira and John Robert were standing. They were talking to some of the church members about the new addition. Ida Mae waited until Dooley joined in the conversation and she took her brother by the hand and led him away from the gathering.

"What time is the funeral tomorrow?' she asked.

"Two o'clock."

"Will you take me to town in the morning, so I can buy a new dress to wear to the service?" she asked.

"If it doesn't take too long," he said. "I have some things I need to do."

"Dooley will bring me back home. He's not working tomorrow because of Mr. Taylor's funeral."

Ida Mae breathed a sigh of relief. Another part of her plan was beginning to unfold, but she needed to proceed as quickly as she could.

She wanted desperately to tell John Robert that she was expecting, but she wanted to do it when she had him all to herself. She knew he would be upset, but she also knew he would keep her secret. Tomorrow, on the way to town, would be the perfect time to tell him, she decided.

What Ida Mae had in mind was known only to her. Although Dooley had gone along with her, so far, she did not even want him to know what she planned to do next.

They had only been at the church for a short while, but Granny was too tired to stay any longer. Ida Mae and Dooley volunteered to take her and the two younger children home. She was glad to have an excuse to leave. She wanted to be by herself where would be better able to think.

She told Dooley of her plans to be in town the next day and that she needed him to meet her at Sid's Grill around noon and bring her back home. As soon as he was gone, she went upstairs and fell into bed. If the next day went as she hoped it would, Dooley would be able to repay the money. They would not have the money they needed to get married, but she would worry about that after she solved the problem more closely at hand.

The next morning, John Robert took her to town around mid-morning and dropped her off at a clothing store. She waited until he was gone and walked quickly to Sid's Grill, where she knew she could find someone to help her carry out the next step of her plan.

Her luck was running better than she hoped. As soon as she stepped inside the restaurant, she saw her new policeman friend, Dewey Combs, sitting at the bar in civilian clothes.

"Good morning," she said as she took the stool beside him. "Wouldn't want to buy a girl a cup of coffee, would you?" she asked.

"Certainly would, Pretty Lady," he said. "Would you like something else?"

"As a matter of fact, I would," she said.

"Just name it," he told her.

"I'd like you to take me somewhere."

"Not a problem. Where would you like for me to take you?"

"To Mike Fletcher's place," she said.

"If you don't mind me asking, why would you want to go to Fletcher's place?"

"I have a friend whose car was involved in an accident sometime back, a hit and run, and I thought he could give me some information about the driver of the other vehicle."

"Does Fletcher know that you are Ira Duncan's daughter and you live on Sheriff Baxter's farm?"

"I'm sure he does."

"Then, you're wasting your time, he wouldn't give you the time of day."

"I already know what time it is, it's other information I'm after. How far is it to his place?"

"About five miles is all, I reckon."

"Are you going to take me or not?" she asked.

"He don't like me very much, but come to think of it, I guess he don't like you very much either. Let's go."

As Dewey pulled into the driveway, Fletcher was about to get into his truck. "No need to wait for me," she said, "Mr. Fletcher will bring me back into town."

"You've got to be kidding," Dewey said.

"You underestimate my power of persuasion," Ida Mae grinned. "Tell you what, if I'm not back at the restaurant in one hour, you come back for me. And please don't tell anyone you brought me here," she added.

"Whatever you say."

Ida Mae strolled up to the passenger's side of Fletcher's truck as if she was one of his best friends. "Where are we going?" she asked, as she got in the truck and closed the door.

"I'm going into town. I have no idea where you're going or how you're going to get there," he snapped.

"I'm going back into town with you," she said, "but you have to listen to me first."

"I don't have to do anything I don't want to do," he said, as he reached across her and opened the door. "Get out."

"You don't have to go to jail, either, but that's what's going to happen if you don't hear me out. Now, do you still want me to get out?"

Ida Mae knew she was being extremely bold, but she had to make Fletcher understand that she wasn't bluffing. She was afraid that if she appeared to be humble, he would think she was weak and offer less than what she demanded.

"What are you talking about?"

"I'm sure I can help you stay out of jail, Mr. Fletcher," she said.

"Why would you want to help me Miss, Ida Mae, isn't it?"

"I have to help you to help myself," she told him.

She told Fletcher that she and Dooley were planning to get married as soon as they could save enough money to get a place of their own. "It's going to take a long time to get the amount we need on Dooley's pay."

"What does that have to do with me?" he asked.

"Just hear me out," she went on. "The sheriff has about sixty gallon of moonshine, enough evidence to send you away for a long time. Do you agree?"

Fletcher shook his head.

"If there was no evidence, he wouldn't have much of a case, right."

Again, Fletcher shook his head.

"I know where that moonshine is hidden and I want to sell it back to you. I know it is worth about twelve dollars a gallon to most people, but I figured you would be willing to pay more."

"How much more?" he asked.

"Twenty bucks a gallon."

"This has got to be some kind of a trick," Fletcher snapped. "I know that was the town cop that brought you here. If they catch me with another batch of illegal whiskey, I never will get out of jail," he said.

Ida Mae went on to explain that officer Combs had no idea about the real reason she was there. She also told him that her daddy and the sheriff must never know what she was doing. "If they were to find out, we would be in more trouble than you."

"Who's 'we'?" Fletcher asked.

"Dooley and myself."

Ida Mae could tell things were not going as smoothly as she had thought. It was clear Fletcher did not trust her. She was not about to tell him the real trouble they were in, but she knew she had to do something.

"I'm carrying Dooley's child," she blurted, "and we want to get married before anyone finds out."

"You don't say," Fletcher smiled. "Then, I understand why you also need a little help."

He sat for a little while before he said anything more. After a while a look of relief came upon his face. "I'll do it," he said, "but you have to take the whiskey out of the county. If you take it across the county line where Baxter has no jurisdiction, we got a deal."

"Where do we have to take it to?"

"Into Washington County. Can you do it tonight?" he asked.

"Sure can, but not for twenty bucks a gallon," she said. "That's a long drive."

"How much do you have in mind?"

"Five dollars more on the gallon."

"Two-fifty and not a penny more. I might just as well die in jail as on the poor farm," he said.

"You got a deal, but I need half the money now, and the balance when we make the delivery."

"Wait here," he said.

Fletcher got out of his truck and went inside his house. In a short while he was back and handed Ida Mae six hundred and seventy-five dollars cash.

"Thank you sir. Now, take me back to town."

Fletcher frowned, but he offered no objections.

On the way back, Fletcher told her the details of the delivery. They were to cross the county line at nine o'clock. He would be waiting and tell them where two of his men would be waiting to take the delivery. Once they had the evidence in their hands, they were to drive back to the county line and he would give her the balance of the money.

"Sounds fair enough to me," she said as she got out of his truck a short distance from the restaurant. "See you at nine o'clock tonight."

Ida Mae walked inside to find that both Dewey and Dooley had just ordered something to eat. Dooley was already dressed for the funeral. She took a seat at their table and gave the waitress her order.

"How long have you been in town?" Dooley asked.

"Just a few minutes. Had to do some shopping for a new dress," she said, as she gently kicked Dewey's leg.

It was just past noon by the time they finished eating. "Time to go," Dooley said. "We don't want to be late for the funeral."

Ida Mae waited for Dooley to go pay for their food and she turned to Dewey. "Thank you," she whispered.

They were approaching Fuller's Clothing Store when she remembered why she told John Robert she had to come into town. "Stop here," she told Dooley. "I have to pay for that new dress."

He parked his car in front of Fuller's as Ida Mae pulled several greenbacks from her bosom. She selected a twenty and handed the remainder of the money to Dooley.

"Hold onto this," she said as she got out of the car. She rushed into the clothing store, grabbed the first garment she knew was her size and was back in less than five minutes.

When she got back to the car, Dooley was as nervous as a long-tailed cat in a room full of rocking chairs. "Better get out of town as fast as we can," he said. "I know you've robbed the bank."

"Better drive as careful as you can," Ida Mae replied. "That's expensive cargo we're hauling."

One the way back home, she told Dooley about the deal she made with Mike Fletcher. She could not tell if he was happy about what she had done, or scared they would get caught with the moonshine, but he could hardly keep the car on his side of the road.

"By this time tomorrow, you will be able to pay Mr. Thompson and then it won't be long until I will be Mrs. Donald Hale. Now what do you think of that, Dooley?"

"I think if we pull this off, I need to quit working and let you go into the boot legging business," he smiled.

Before the couple arrived at Ida Mae's, she had convinced Dooley the outcome of their adventure would be well worth the small amount of risk that was involved. She had plenty of time to convince him, for he drove so slowly one would have thought he was hauling a load of eggs.

When they finally arrived at the Duncan's place, Dooley sat on the porch talking to John Robert, while Ida Mae and her family got dressed for the service. At last, everyone was ready and the family loaded into both automobiles. Granny and the twins chose to ride with Ida Mae and Dooley. When they pulled close to the front of the church, some gentleman opened the door and helped Granny from the car. "Only feller I ever knew that drives slower than Taylor," Ida Mae heard Granny mumble as she got out of Dooley's car and closed the door behind her.

The church was filled to capacity and as many were standing outside by the time the Reverend Kyle stepped to the podium.

He spoke of the life of Brother Taylor and the many good things he had done. He told about how he and his father were instrumental in building their church and his dream of seeing it grow larger.

Reverend Kyle told of many more happenings in Brother's Ezra's life, but Ida Mae did not hear. She was dwelling on the task that lay before herself and Dooley later that day. After about an hour, she began to get nervous. She could also tell that Dooley, who was seated behind the reverend, was also becoming restless. The afternoon was slipping away and they still had to go to the burying. She was afraid that if Reverend Kyle went on much longer, it would be difficult for them to make their nine o'clock appointment. She breathed a sigh of relief when she heard him say, "and in conclusion, from this day forward, the new Sunday school rooms will be referred to as the Taylor addition."

The men from the funeral home rolled the coffin out of the church and placed it on the front lawn. They opened the coffin, so everyone in attendance could file by and view the remains. By the time the last person filed by, the sun was beginning to go down. Both Ida Mae and Dooley were getting really nervous. They were glad it did not take long to place Brother Taylor in his final resting place.

"Let's hurry and take Granny and the twins home. I'll change, and we'll be on our way," she told Dooley as they left the cemetery. She was glad the rest of her family had not yet arrived by the time they were ready to leave.

"Tell Mother, Dooley and I are going for a drive and I might be late," she told Granny as she hurried out of the house.

CHAPTER FIFTEEN

WHAT A SURPRISE

Ida Mae and Dooley arrived at the pre-arranged meeting place a full half-hour early. Dooley parked his car on a wide spot a few feet from the county line. It was well after dark and there was very little traffic. The couple was glad because all they could do now was to sit and wait. Ida Mae tried to talk about their wedding and what they would do once they were married, but Dooley kept interrupting with his fears of all the things that might go wrong.

At exactly nine o'clock, a vehicle pulled behind Dooley's car. Ida Mae almost panicked. She did not know what kind of vehicle it was, but she was certain it was not Fletcher's pickup truck. After a moment the driver walked up beside Dooley's car and shined a flashlight inside.

"Having trouble folks?" he asked.

Ida Mae recognized Fletcher's voice at once. "Not if you brought cash," she answered.

"Mind if I see what I'm buying?" Fletcher asked.

Dooley did not move, but Ida Mae took the keys from the ignition and unlocked the trunk.

Fletcher uncapped a couple of the containers and sniffed their contents. He then turned the jugs upside down and looked at the bottoms. Only then did Ida Mae notice that each of the jugs had a small white mark painted on them. She was sure that was how he marked all the whiskey he bought and sold.

Fletcher replaced the containers and closed the trunk lid.

"Go one-half mile west and turn left onto the gravel road," he said. "Two cars will be waiting a short distance from where you turn and both will have only their park lights on. Unload this stuff as quickly as you can and come back here. I will have the rest of your money."

"Why two cars?" she asked.

Fletcher smiled. "Because if one of those boys gets caught, I'll still have half of my investment," he said. "Now get going before we all get caught."

The couple did exactly as Fletcher instructed. They turned onto the gravel road and within minutes two cars came into view. Both were sitting beside the road and each had their park lights on. Dooley pulled in front of the two vehicles and both he and Ida Mae got the surprise of their life. One of the cars was the dark blue Hudson Hornet that had ran into John Robert's Chevrolet and the other was a brand new light green Olds.

"Well I'll be — ," Ida Mae started to say. Before the words were out of her mouth Jake was standing beside their car.

"Do you folks need us to help you take some weight off your tires?" he said, before he realized to whom he was speaking.

"That would be nice," Ida Mae answered as she got out of the car.

Jake looked as if someone had thrown ice water in his face. "Oh! I'm sorry," he stammered, "I thought you were someone else."

"Now, who else would be delivering moonshine to you this time of night?" she asked.

"No one I guess. It's just that we have never taken a delivery from a lady before. Back your car up to the back of ours," he said to Dooley who was still sitting behind the wheel.

Dooley, Jake, and the other fellow, who Ida Mae recognized as the one who had been playing pool with Jake, hurriedly transferred the cargo. Dooley got back in his car, anxious to get away before anyone came by.

"Meet me at the skating rink Friday night just after dark, Pretty Lady," Jake whispered, when he was sure Dooley could not hear.

Ida Mae was taken by surprise, but she did not let on. She was as relieved as Dooley to get the illegal whisky out of their hands.

"What if Fletcher doesn't show up with the rest of our money?" Dooley asked, when Ida Mae was back in the car.

"You worry too much, Dooley, and what do you mean our money?" she giggled.

She wrote down the license numbers of both the other cars as they drove away.

When they got back to the county line, Fletcher was waiting just as he promised. "Did everything go alright, and were those strangers nice to you?" he asked.

"Couldn't have gone better, and those strangers treated us like we were old friends," she smiled.

"Mind if I look in your trunk once more?" he asked.

"Not at all," Dooley answered, and this time it was he who got out and unlocked the back of the car.

After Fletcher was certain the merchandise had been delivered, he gave Ida Mae the balance he owed.

She carefully counted the cash and handed him back twenty-five dollars. "We were a couple of jugs short," she smiled.

Fletcher looked somewhat bewildered but he put the money in his pocket and drove away.

When Fletcher was well out of sight the couple put all their money together and started counting. There was enough to pay Mr. Thompson, the five hundred they needed to get married, and almost fifty dollars left over.

"What are we going to do with this extra cash?" Dooley asked.

"Just hold on to it for a while," Ida Mae giggled. "I think I know where we can get a good deal on another load of liquor."

"We can't get involved with any more of this stuff," Dooley said. "We could get into a lot of serious trouble."

"Then we will use it to hire someone to give you pool-shooting lessons," she laughed.

Dooley did not find the any humor in Ida Mae's comments. In fact, he felt rather embarrassed. He and this fellow, Jake, were not far from the same age, yet in comparison Dooley felt he did not measure up. He was less than fifty dollars from being flat broke, was driving a car that was almost ten years old, and was working in a grease pit to make a living. Jake, on the other hand, always had a large roll of cash, was driving a shiny new Oldsmobile, wore nice cloths, and as far as he knew did not even have a job. Not to mention he had proven he was a master at the game of pool. Unlike Ida Mae, who seemed to be enjoying the thrill of doing things outside the law, he was so nervous he could hardly control his trembling.

During the ride back to the Baxter farm Dooley had little to say. He should have been happy with their accomplishment of the last few days, but such was not the case. He was grateful to have gotten out of the dilemma he had incurred, but for the first time he was beginning to resent having had such a sheltered life. The thought of Jake's success kept pounding in his head.

It did not matter that Dooley was not in the mood for a lot of conversation, for Ida Mae chattered all the way home. She would ask him a question and before he could answer she would follow with another. She talked about their apartment, the new furniture, his job, their upcoming wedding, and their unborn child. He did not mind because he could tell she was bubbling over with excitement. What did concern him were her repeated comments about how easily they had made their money. By the time he had Ida Mae home most of his trembling had ceased but he still felt consumed by guilt.

"Go home and calm down," she said, as she handed him the cash and kissed him good night. "If delivering a small load of white lightning makes you this jittery, next time I'll drive."

Dooley did not even get out of his car. He watched as Ida Mae ascended the steps onto the porch and went inside. He loved her dearly. She was the only girl he had ever been out with, but he was glad to at last be by himself.

He was also glad that when he got home his parents had already retired for the night. He went to his room, placed the exact amount of money he had taken back into the cigar box, kicked off his shoes and stretched himself on top of his bed. He did not even bother to undress; he was mentally exhausted.

The thought of Ida Mae being so thrilled at what they had done troubled him, the thought of Jake's success made him envious, and beginning a life as a husband and father scared him to death.

"I'll just find a job with a better income," he thought just before he was overtaken by sleep.

The next morning Dooley was awake at the crack of dawn. It seemed like hours before he heard his mother moving in the kitchen. She would not hear of him starting the day before eating breakfast. He deposited two spoons of sugar into the steaming hot bowl of oatmeal his mother set before him. He blew on the cereal until it was cool enough to put into his mouth. He rushed through half the oatmeal and one of the half-dozen hot buttered biscuits he would normally consume and he was gone. Nothing was going to prevent him from paying Mr. Thompson this time. Only then would his life return to some form of normalcy.

Dooley was sitting in front of the office at the lumberyard when Mr. Thompson arrived. He followed him inside and paid the church bill in full. Once back in his car he felt that the weight of the world had been lifted from his shoulders, not to mention the weight that had been removed from the trunk of his old Chevrolet.

Chapter Sixteen

FLETCHER MAKES A DEAL

The next few days were filled with excitement. Dooley returned to work and Ida Mae, Mary Sue, and her mother were making plans for her wedding. Both she and Dooley thought everything was moving along without a hitch. Little did they know what was about to take place? Two days after Dooley returned to work, Fletcher came to the station. He pulled up to the gas pumps where Dooley was standing and handed him a folded piece of paper and drove away without uttering a word.

Dooley unfolded the message and what he read almost threw him into shock.

"I would like to see you and Miss Duncan at my place at eight o'clock tonight. I would also appreciate your votes in the upcoming election," it read.

Dooley folded the paper and put it in his pocket as another vehicle pulled to the pumps. "Fill 'er up with oil and check your grease," he said.

"Are you alright?" John Robert asked.

Dooley was so awestricken he had not noticed who was driving.

"Uh, Uh, I'm fine, John Robert. Would you tell Ida Mae I will pick her up right after work?"

"Sure will."

"Thanks," Dooley said as he started walking toward the service bay where he had been working.

"Would you also like for me to tell her that you didn't want to sell me any gasoline?"

"I'm sorry," Dooley said as he returned to the pumps and put the nozzle into the tank of John Robert's Chevrolet. "Must have had something else on my mind."

Indeed he had something else on his mind. Fletcher was up to something and he was sure it was not going to be to his liking. The very thought of Mike Fletcher getting back into the race for sheriff sent cold chills up his spine. He had reservations about taking Ida Mae to his place, but not knowing what he might have up his sleeve frightened him even worse.

"I'll just leave this matter up to her," he decided. "She always has a way of working things out."

Somehow, Dooley got through the day. When quitting time came, he rushed home, did only that which was necessary and hurried off to pick up Ida Mae. As he drove to the Duncan home, he pondered the happenings of the last few weeks.

"How did I get myself in so much trouble in such a short time," he wondered?

Just a short time before, Dooley's only concern had been to get enough money to buy a used car so he might date the prettiest lady at church. But since winning her affection, Dooley had endured enough wrongdoing for an entire lifetime.

"Maybe living a sheltered life wasn't so bad after all," he thought as he pulled in front of Ida Mae's home.

John Robert had given her Dooley's message and she was waiting when he arrived. As soon as she was in the car Dooley handed her the folded piece of paper.

"Fletcher stopped by and delivered this message," he said, his voice almost quivering. "What do you think of that?"

Ida Mae read the message and handed it back to Dooley.

"What do you think?" Dooley repeated.

"I think we should go see what the gentleman has on his mind. Maybe he has another business deal. Wouldn't it be nice to make some more of that easy money?"

Dooley could not believe what he was hearing. He had let Ida Mae talk him into gambling away money that belonged to the church, steal evidence that belonged to the sheriff, and sell illegal liquor. For days he had worried himself sick about how he was going to get out of all the trouble she had gotten him into. He was not about to let her get involved in anything else outside the law.

"We're not going to have any part of any more of Fletcher's illegal business deals," Dooley insisted. "If that's what he has in mind, you tell him we're not interested. There is more in life than making money."

"Yeah, and there has got to be more in life than greasing cars and having babies," Ida Mae snapped.

When the couple arrived at Fletcher's home he met them at the door. "Come in," he said, greeting them as he would a member of his own family.

They stepped inside and hesitated for a moment. This was, without doubt, the most beautiful home either of them had ever seen. Expensive furniture sat along three walls of the huge living room. Drapes, which matched the fabric on the living room furniture, adorned the large picture window behind the sofa. An oil painting of a beautiful lady, whom Ida Mae assumed was the late Mrs. Fletcher, hanging over a baby grand piano, made up the decor of the remaining wall.

Fletcher ushered them into a large dining room, which was as elaborately furnished. A gigantic oak table surrounded by eight chairs sat in the middle of the room. A matching hutch with leaded glass doors, displaying fine imported china, sat in one corner and a solid brass chandelier overhanging the table illuminated the room. Burning candles in the center of the table filled the air with the aroma of fresh lilacs.

"Make your self at home," Fletcher said, as he slid one of the dining room chairs from the table and waited for Ida Mae to be seated.

She scooted her chair closer to the table and watched as Dooley seated himself at the opposite end of the table, as if to distance himself from the conversation.

"Have some refreshments," Fletcher said, as he placed a glass containing miniature ice cubes and a bottle of Coca-Cola in front of each of them and sat down directly across from his female guest.

Ida Mae had no idea what Mike Fletcher had in mind but she knew whatever it was she was not going to be intimidated. As curious as she was to know why he invited them to his home, she was not about to ask.

"You are a shrewd business lady," he began. "I am intrigued by your ability to negotiate when it comes to business matters, so I'll get right to the point."

"Fire away," Ida Mae said.

"How did you get your hands on that whiskey the sheriff took from me?"

"He had it hidden on the farm and I found it."

"So you stole it," he went on.

"You might say that," she smiled.

"Why didn't you get all of it?"

"Because that would have been greedy, and besides I didn't want to take all the evidence the sheriff had on you."

"Does Baxter know his evidence is missing?"

"Not yet, but I am sure he will real soon."

"Which brings me to the reason I invited you here," Fletcher went on. "My attorney has talked to the judge and my case will come before the grand jury later this week. The election is two weeks from tomorrow and he is giving me a chance to get this matter behind me as quickly as possible. When Baxter cannot produce the whiskey he claims to have taken from me, he is going to look like a fool."

"As you know, I have every intention of getting back into the election. Now that Baxter does not have the evidence to get a felony conviction for transporting illegal whiskey there's only one small obstacle I need to overcome."

"What might that be?" Ida Mae asked.

"The sheriff took sixty gallon of whiskey at the time of my arrest. When you made the delivery the other night you were two gallon short. I assume he still has the two-gallon in his possession, which is enough for a misdemeanor charge against me."

"What does that have to do with me?" Ida Mae asked.

"I have a feeling you might be able to sell me that other two-gallon if the price was right. Then he would have nothing he could prove in court. I am prepared to offer you an amount that I believe will be appealing to you."

"Not interested," Dooley said.

"What amount might that be?" Ida Mae asked, ignoring Dooley's comment.

"One hundred dollars," he said.

"Not interested," Dooley repeated.

"Not enough." Ida Mae insisted, again paying no attention to Dooley.

"One hundred dollars per gallon," Fletcher upped his offer.

He did not wait for her to answer. "I know this is not an easy decision, but I also know that you and the deacon are planning to get married. With a new baby coming on, I'm sure you can use the money."

"How did he know about the baby?" Dooley stammered.

Ida Mae did not acknowledge he had spoken.

"I also have another proposition," Fletcher continued. "I want the two of you to help me get elected."

"How are we supposed to do that?" Ida Mae wanted to know.

"There are a lot of men in this county who are known to enjoy the taste of a toddy on occasion. Many of them are friends to both Baxter and myself and could care less which of us is elected. It is my opinion that they could be easily persuaded which way to cast their ballot. Many of them do not own a vehicle and have no way to get to the polling places. That's where the two of you fit into my plan. I would like for you to pick them up on Election Day, give them a few shots of homebrew on the way to the polls, and help them make up their minds how they should vote."

"What's in it for us?" she asked.

"I'll pay you a hundred dollars the day before the election and another hundred if I win the race for sheriff."

"Not a chance," Dooley interrupted.

Again Ida Mae ignored him. "Where are we supposed to get the homebrew you mentioned?" she asked.

"I'll tell you where and when," Fletcher told her.

Ida Mae sat for a moment without saying a word. She was considering every aspect of the proposition. She surveyed her surroundings and wondered if she and Dooley would ever be able to afford such luxuries. Not on Dooley's salary she was certain, yet she had Dooley's reputation and the baby to think about.

If it were not for the baby, I would do it with or without Dooley's help she thought. As much as she wanted the money, she felt she had to decline the offer.

"Sorry, but we can't do it, sir," she said. "If the members of the church ever found out, Dooley would lose his position as deacon. Think of what that would do to his reputation not to mention the devastating effect it would have on his mother."

"That's my girl," Dooley smiled as he gulped another large drink of coke.

Fletcher was shocked that she had refused his offer. His face turned red, his breathing became labored and the veins in his neck pushed against his tight fitting shirt collar.

The anger, which Fletcher was unable to conceal, told Ida Mae it was time for them to leave. She stood up as if to make her exit.

"Just another moment please," Fletcher said, and he motioned for her to keep her seat and left the room.

Ida Mae toyed with her small purse that lay on the table in front of her.

"Now what do you suppose he has in mind?" Dooley asked when Fletcher was out of the room.

Before she could answer Fletcher reappeared. He placed a quart fruit jar filled with clear liquid on the table in front of them. He uncapped the container and poured a portion of the contents into his glass of Coca-Cola.

"Help yourself," he said just before he placed his glass to his lips and emptied the entire contents with one swallow.

After what seemed a good fifteen seconds Fletcher exhaled, an act that erased any doubt of what the white liquid might be.

"Sure you won't join me?" he asked.

"Was there something else you wanted to discuss?" Ida Mae asked, ignoring his offer.

"As a matter of fact, there is," Fletcher continued, talking to Ida Mae as if she were the only one present. "How is it going to affect the good deacon's mother and the members of the church when they find out he has fathered a child out of wedlock. Not to mention the large amount of cash he lost down at Willie's Pool Hall a few nights ago."

Upon hearing Fletcher's comments, Dooley emitted such a mouthful of Coca-Cola that he put out the candle that was burning in the center of the table.

Both Ida Mae and Fletcher waited until Dooley regained his composure and was certain he was not going to die as a result of strangulation.

"How do you know about the money Dooley lost at the pool hall?" Ida Mae demanded.

"There is very little that goes on in this town that I don't know about young lady."

"You wouldn't dare tell anyone," she insisted.

"Not if the two of you accept my offer," he smiled.

"That's blackmail, sir."

"I prefer to call it good business. Do we have a deal, or not?"

Ida Mae looked to her companion for assistance, but none was forthcoming. Dooley's face was the color of half-skimmed milk, his hands were trembling, and his eyes looked like that of a whipped puppy. Ida Mae felt that his next motion was probably going to be throwing up.

"Go outside and get some fresh air before you render yourself unconscious," she snapped. "I'll handle this."

Fletcher waited until Dooley made his exit. "Well, what have you decided?" he asked.

Ida Mae turned to make sure the deacon was well out of the house. She picked up the quart jar and poured a healthy portion into her own glass. She gulped it down in the same manner Fletcher had done. She placed the glass back onto the table and replied.

"I have decided it will be two hundred the day before the election, two hundred the day after, and I want a piece of your whiskey business, or I'll tell the sheriff what happened to the moonshine he confiscated. I'm sure the law would go easy on an expectant mother who turned states evidence."

Fletcher stood up, reached into his pocket and pulled out a large roll of cash. He counted out two hundred dollars and handed it to Ida Mae.

"Have the deacon bring the other two gallons to the station tomorrow. I'll pick it up when no one is there but him. After I have the remainder of the evidence, I'll give you the details of the rest of my plan. I can see you are on your way to becoming a wealthy young lady, if you just learn that the best way to succeed in business is to eliminate your competition."

Ida Mae took the money and made her way back to the car, where Dooley was waiting.

Neither of them spoke for a good while, but Ida Mae could tell Dooley was so angry he was about to explode.

"Guess I better resign as deacon before next Sunday's service,"

Dooley said, when they were some distance from Fletcher's home.

"No need for that," Ida Mae answered as she slipped the cash into Dooley's shirt pocket. "A lot of money for such a small task, don't you think?"

"I think you're crazy," Dooley said. "I can't believe you would let Fletcher blackmail you into doing such a thing. The very thought of you trying to get people to vote for Fletcher makes me furious. You saw what kind of a home he lives in. You don't think he makes that kind of money in the lumber business, do you? He's using the lumber business as a front to bootleg whiskey, and who knows what else he's doing. We don't need someone like that in the office of sheriff. In fact, we shouldn't even be associating with people like him."

"You're right, Dooley. We shouldn't have anything to do with anyone who sells bootlegged liquor," she laughed. "And, what makes you think I'm going to try to get someone to vote for Fletcher? He just said for me to help them make up their minds how to vote, he didn't specify I had to convince them to vote for him."

"What are you talking about, Ida Mae?"

"Here's what we're going to do," she began. "Tonight after it gets dark, you and I will walk to the barn and get the other two gallons of whiskey. Tomorrow you will give it to Fletcher when he comes to the station Then we will have earned this two hundred dollars. Election day, we will haul voters to the polls and earn another two hundred dollars. We will persuade them to vote for Sheriff Baxter instead of Fletcher, but if by chance Fletcher should win, we will get another two hundred dollars."

"Now I know you're crazy," Dooley said.

Ida Mae did not answer. She acted as if she were in a deep state of meditation.

"I bet if I tell Baxter we are trying to get him re-elected, he will pay us well to haul those voters too. I think Fletcher was right," she added, "I might be on my way to becoming a wealthy lady."

"I think you're on your way to becoming a lady convict," Dooley snorted. "If you don't mend your ways, our baby will be born wearing a black-and-white striped nightshirt. Now what do you think of that?"

Ida Mae considered what he'd said for a moment and then scooted up real close and whispered in his ear.

"I think we should try to find out if night shirts come in polka dot," she laughed.

Dooley angrily jerked the car to the side of the road.

"You have got to promise me you will give up this wild way of living," he began. "How would it look if the people of our church found out one of their deacons' and his bride were enticing voters with corn liquor? Sooner or later, we are going to get caught. You have got to promise me you won't do it, Ida Mae."

"Okay," Ida Mae giggled, "I promise we won't get caught."

Dooley became so angry he was out of control. He jumped from the car, walked to the rear, and started pounding the trunk lid with both fists.

Ida Mae had never witnessed this side of Dooley before. She sat calmly in her seat until his tantrum passed. When it seemed he had somewhat regained his composure, she stuck her head out the window and said, "If the drumming lessons are over, we had better be on our way. We still have to go for a walk out to the barn, remember?"

Dooley got back into the car, slammed the door, and threw the Chevrolet into gear.

"I refuse to have anything to do with any more of your illegal activities," he stammered.

"Whatever you say, sweetheart," Ida Mae whispered trying as best she could to get him to calm down. "Help me get Baxter re-elected and I will never again ask you to do anything illegal. How is that for a deal?"

"I don't like it but I'll do it," Dooley answered, "but after we're married, you are going to start doing as I say."

"That's what you think Brother Dooley," she started to say as the anger boiled up inside her but she decided it was better to say nothing at all.

It was late when the couple reached the gate at the end of the lane that led up to the Duncan's home. A full moon hung in the western sky like a giant lantern.

"Turn your headlights off," Ida Mae told Dooley as she got out of the car to open the gate. "We'll park the car halfway between the house and the barn and wait until we're sure everyone is in bed before we get the booze," she told him.

Dooley did exactly as he was instructed. He needed no headlights. The moonlight illuminated the farm so well one could have gone rabbit hunting. He drove up the long driveway and parked about a hundred feet from the barn. They sat in the car, speaking barely above a whisper until they were sure no one had seen them arrive. Ida Mae talked about what they could do with the money they were going to make but Dooley was so scared he paid little attention. He was getting more nervous with each passing moment. Each time she would start to say something he would interrupt:

"What if someone finds out you are going to have a baby? What if Fletcher tells the people at church?"

At last, Ida Mae had had enough of his complaining.

"Ah, be quiet Dooley," she said. "Why don't you sit here and dream up something else to worry about while I go into the barn and get what we come here after."

Dooley made no comment.

Ida Mae slipped out of the car and made her way to the hay shed where the moonshine was hidden. She needed nothing more than the light of the moon to find the whiskey for she knew exactly where it was. With a container in each hand, she rushed back to where Dooley was waiting.

Once the hooch was in Dooley's possession, he was so anxious to leave he did not even take time to kiss her goodnight before he drove away.

Ida Mae sat down on the porch step, and watched as the taillights of Dooley's car faded into the distance. She gazed down over the fields that lay on either side of the lane between their home and the gravel road.

Sparsely placed shocks of corn dotted the field to her left, and two medium-sized stacks of hay reflected the meager harvest in the field on the other side of the lane. One-fourth the amount the fertile land would have produced had there been ample rainfall.

"Not much to show for a year of hard work," Ida Mae thought as she watched the slow moving clouds cast ghostly shadows on the fields that lay before her. The smell of wood smoke drifting from a neighbors chimney somewhere in the distance and the chill of the late October evening reminded her that winter was coming.

Winter was a fun time for the Duncan family — a time of togetherness and a time of sharing. This winter was to be much different for Ida Mae.

Farm life was a hard life — but a good life, she reasoned as she tried to imagine what lay ahead. For her, there would be no sleigh riding, no building snowmen, or friendly snowball fights with Mary Sue and the twins.

No games of checkers or fox and goose while eating popcorn before bedtime on those cold winter nights. She would miss watching her father sitting in front of the large fireplace cracking walnuts while Granny and her mother busied themselves at the quilting frame that sat in one corner of the large living room. Instead of the fun times with her family, she would spend her days sitting alone in a small apartment waiting for a child of her own.

She felt the warmth of an escaping tear as she thought of what she must leave behind.

Why had she let herself grow up so fast?

Why had she gotten herself in the family way with the first boy she dated? There were lots of boys she could have gone out with she thought, remembering Jake had asked her to meet him at the skating rink Friday night.

"Maybe I will meet Jake," she decided as she picked herself up and made her way inside and up to her bedroom. Mother, Mrs. Hale, Mary Sue, and some of the other ladies would be meeting at the church to make plans for the wedding, which was little more than a week away, and Dooley was going to be out of town on some errand with his father.

Maybe Jake will tell me how he got involved with Mike Fletcher and how he always has large amounts of cash without having a job.

"That's exactly what I'll do, I'll get John Robert to take me into town and I'll meet Jake," she thought, as she slipped quietly into bed beside Mary Sue.

The trying events of the evening and Fletcher's moonshine were taking effect.

"If Dooley thinks I'm going to settle down to his dull way of living, he's in for the surprise of his life," she decided just before she fell asleep.

CHAPTER SEVENTEEN

A WILDER SIDE OF LIFE

Ida Mae had no trouble at all talking John Robert into taking her into town the following Friday evening. She told her family she wanted to rearrange some things in their apartment before the wedding. She also told them she wanted to spend the night and have John Robert bring her home the next day.

"What will Dooley have to say about that?" her mother wanted to know.

"I don't really care," Ida Mae told her, "but he's out of town, anyway."

To Ida Mae's surprise, her mother offered no objections.

Everything had gone more smoothly than she had anticipated. John Robert dropped her off at the apartment a good two hours before dark. He told her he had a date with one of his old sweethearts in the next town and asked what time she wanted him to pick her up the next day.

"About noon," she told him, "I may want to sleep late."

"Noon it is," her brother told her and hurried off.

Ida Mae was glad she would not have to worry about John Robert's whereabouts. Now, all she had to do was to wait until time to go to the skating rink.

She seated herself in one of the kitchen chairs that made up part of the furnishings in the three-room second floor apartment, and began staring at the four walls.

119

She knew she should be excited about beginning her married life in such nice surroundings, but somehow that feeling escaped her. The apartment was nice enough, the furniture was new, and the location was not bad, but she felt as if she were being forced to live in a place she did not choose to be. There was no radio that she could listen to; no magazines to read and the walls were as bare as a newborn baby's butt.

"A picture or two is what this place needs," she thought, as she gazed at the bare walls. "Even a large almanac calendar, like the one that hangs on the wall in the kitchen of our farmhouse, wouldn't hurt."

She sat for a while, trying to become accustomed to being alone, and then began pacing from room to room.

She had only been in her own place for little more than half-hour and already she was bored.

How would she ever survive living there all the time, she wondered? She strolled to one of the three small windows and looked down onto the deserted alley below.

Suddenly she realized it was not the bare walls that frustrated her, nor was it the absence of a radio or magazines. It was being away from her family, and life on the farm, that she really missed. She remembered Dooley's statement about her doing as he said after they were married.

"If he thinks I'm going to sit here every day and do nothing, somebody's been beating on his head with a stupid stick," she heard herself say aloud.

She somehow got through the next hour waiting for time to meet Jake. Just after dark he had said, and she planned to be there when he arrived. She made her way down the steps leading from the apartment and began the fifteen-minute walk toward the skating rink.

It was a perfect rendezvous. Just as she reached the entrance to the parking lot Jake's shiny new Oldsmobile pulled up beside her.

"May I give a pretty lady a lift?"

Ida Mae looked around to make sure no one was outside the rink that might recognize her.

"Only if we get out of town," she heard herself say as she jumped into the front seat beside him.

"Not a problem," Jake smiled, "where would you like to go?"

"Let's just drive around, if that's okay with you. Wouldn't want the good people of this town spreading gossip that might get back to the deacon."

Jake took the shortest route out of the city, Route 80 toward Buchanan County.

"I hope you don't get the wrong impression of me Jake, but I really do need to talk to you."

Jake could tell she was nervous. She sat as close to the passenger door as possible. She looked straight ahead with her hands tightly folded in her lap.

"Now, what makes you think I could ever get the wrong impression of you? Just tell me in which direction to go, and when you want to return, your wish will be my command."

"In that case, just keep driving," she said.

"Like a cold beer?" he asked, when they were a few miles out of town.

"Thought you would never ask," she smiled.

Jake pulled the car to the side of the road and took the keys from the ignition. "Excuse me for a moment while I place our order," he said. He got a cooler out of the trunk of the car and placed it on the floor behind her seat. He withdrew two cold bottles of Pabst Blue Ribbon and handed one to Ida Mae.

"Just this one and no more," she said.

"You're the boss, Pretty Lady," Jake said as he pulled his olds back onto the pavement. "Now what was it you wanted to talk to me about?"

"Later," she said as she began sipping from the ice-cold bottle. "First I would like you to tell me more about yourself."

"Not much to tell," he answered. "What would you like to know?"

"First of all, where do you live?"

"Illinois, North Carolina, Virginia, I guess you might say I'm a drifter."

"Then how do you make a living?"

"I'm a hustler, among other things," he stated.

"What in the world is a hustler?" Ida Mae asked as she continued drinking from the frosty bottle Jake had given her.

"A pool hustler. I'm known as the best shot there is in most towns, but there's always someone who is anxious to prove he's better."

"Are you the best?"

"Maybe not the best, but I am two steps ahead of whoever is in second place," he smiled.

"Do you really have a brother who lives in North Carolina?"

"Sure do, North Carolina, Illinois, and two or three other states I reckon. There were seven children in my family and each of us have six brothers."

"Seven boys."

"No less."

"Where do your parents live?"

"Here in Buchanan County. This is where I grew up."

"Why have I never met you before?"

"Beats me, guess you don't get around much."

"You got that right," she said, "I have never been out of the state of Virginia."

"You are about to be unless you would like for me to turn around," Jake said as a sign which read, "Welcome to Kentucky" came into view.

"No way, keep driving! Then I can say I have been in at least one other state. Got another beer?"

Jake leaned behind the seat and retrieved another bottle.

"What time do I need to have you home?" He asked.

"Twelve o'clock."

"Then we had better not go much further, wouldn't want to get you into trouble."

"Twelve o'clock tomorrow, but I guess it wouldn't be ladylike to stay out all night."

Jake smiled as he uncapped the Blue Ribbon and handed it to his companion.

As the miles rolled past, Ida Mae learned more and more about this young man she had no business being with. But the more she learned, the more infatuated she became.

He was so unlike the man she was committed to spending the rest of her life with.

As they drove further into Kentucky, the distance between Ida Mae and the passenger door grew. The alcohol dispelled any thoughts she may have had about whether or not Jake could be trusted.

She felt comfortable in his presence, but she still had not gotten the nerve to inquire about his relationship with Mike Fletcher.

"We're out of refreshments and I bet you could use the ladies room," Jake said as he pulled onto the parking lot of a building bearing a large neon sign that read, West Lexington Bar and Grill.

"That would be nice, you must be a mind reader," she smiled.

Jake escorted her inside the building, which was unlike any place she had ever seen. A long bar ran along one side of the smoke-filled room. A live band, playing one of Hank Williams' latest hits, filled the stage on the opposite side. Ladies with low cut dresses or tight fitting jeans and well-dressed gentlemen were seated in booths that ran along the wall and up to either end of the stage. Three or four pool tables were located near the front entrance and couples dancing to the slow rhythm of the music occupied the remainder of the space.

"All the way back and to your right," Jake told her as they made their way inside.

"Chalk up your cue sticks boys, Jake's back in town," Ida Mae heard someone say as the door to the ladies room closed behind her.

As she exited the ladies' room she saw Jake and a waitress standing near one of the booths near the stage. He motioned for her to join him and asked what she would like to eat.

"Whatever you're having," she smiled.

"The usual," he said to the waitress, "and the lady will have the same."

Several of the patrons either waved or came to their booth to say hello while they were waiting for the food.

"It's not hard to tell this is not your first visit," Ida Mae said as the waitress placed a salad, large steak, and baked potato in front of each of them.

"I eat here as often as I can. This establishment serves the best food in town, and not to mention one of my brothers owns the place."

"Can't imagine Dooley ever taking me to a place like this," she thought as she listened to the band and watched the couples moving gracefully across the dance floor.

"Care to dance?" Jake asked, when they had finished eating.

"Maybe next time," she said, not wanting to admit she had never been on a dance floor in her life.

"Then you'll come back again," he was asking more than making a statement.

"We'll see," she said as the waitress came up to their table.

"Would you and the lady like anything else?" She asked.

"Yes, I would like a dozen cold ones to go, please."

In a short while the waitress returned with a large bag containing twelve cold Blue Ribbons.

"Strange she did not even ask what brand," Ida Mae thought. She was sure she already knew the answer.

Jake placed a twenty-dollar bill on their table and ushered Ida Mae back to his car.

He carefully placed all but two of the beverages into the cooler and pulled the Olds to the edge of the highway.

"Better take you back to Russell County, Pretty Lady," he said reaching her one of the opened containers. "It's almost midnight and I wouldn't want to keep you out too late. It might harm your reputation."

"You are truly a gentleman, Jake," she said, as she begins sipping from the frosted bottle.

Jake smiled and pulled the big green Olds onto the highway for the three-hour journey back to Russell County.

As the miles passed, Ida Mae became more relaxed. She finished her beer, threw both her and Jake's empty container into the tall grass that grew along the highway and scooted closer to him.

"How did you get to know Mike Fletcher?" she asked.

"That's a long story, one that makes me angry even to think about," he answered.

"Please tell me," she begged.

Jake placed an arm around Ida Mae's shoulder and slowed the Olds to half speed.

"It's like this," he began. "My daddy has made his living in the lumber business most of his life. As us boys became old enough we were taught ever phase of the operation. We did the timbering, logging and operated the sawmills. His business did quite well up until a couple of years ago.

"At that time, the local market dwindled to almost nothing. There was little more than enough income to provide a livelihood for him and my mother. My older brothers had no choice but to leave home and find employment elsewhere, leaving Daddy to do most of the work himself with whatever part-time help he could muster."

"One day, while pulling logs from the mountain, he was involved in a serious accident. Something spooked the team of horses he was using, causing them to bolt. Daddy was knocked to the ground, trapping him between two logs the team was pulling. He was dragged several hundred feet and one of his legs was torn off at the knee. After weeks of recuperating he insisted on returning to work but there was little to do. Most of his buyers were no longer in existence or had taken their business to other suppliers. To supplement his income, Daddy began making moonshine. He would make the whiskey at night and one of my brother's and I would haul it into North Carolina where it sold for top price."

"Then, out of nowhere, Mike Fletcher approached Daddy to purchase lumber to resale to the booming furniture companies, which were also in the Carolinas.

"Of course he was thrilled at having the business, although it meant hiring workers to do the logging and run the mills. He and my brother continued making whiskey because the demand was high and the profit was good. He figured people would still want their whiskey, even if the furniture factories went out of business."

Ida Mae rested her head on Jake's shoulder and listened without interrupting. She could feel his body grow tense as his story about Fletcher unfolded.

"Time for some more refreshments," he said, as he pulled onto a wide spot by the side of the highway.

Ida Mae waited while Jake retrieved another beverage for each of them and was once again on their way.

"You still haven't told me what Fletcher has to do with the moonshine," she said.

"That's the part that infuriates me," Jake began.

Ida Mae sat more to the passenger's side toying with the bottle of Blue Ribbon and listened as Jake continued his story.

"One Saturday evening when the mills were not running, Daddy and I were loading containers of shine into the back of my brother's Hudson. Mike Fletcher and his best friend, the upstanding sheriff of Buchanan County, came sneaking up to where we were. They caught us red-handed."

"What happened then?" Ida Mae questioned.

"Daddy and I were both arrested, taken to the county jail and locked in a cell. Early the next morning Mike Fletcher came to visit. He had a proposition for us. He said he could persuade the sheriff to drop all charges if my daddy would give him half of his whiskey business.

Not wanting my mother to find out we had been arrested or having to spend a long time in jail, Daddy agreed."

"That's blackmail," Ida Mae said.

"That's not where the story ends," Jake continued.

Ida Mae sat sideways in the seat staring at Jake's profile. The headlight from oncoming traffic made it easy for her to observe the changes in his expression. His jawbone became rigid, his speech more harsh, and the grip on the steering wheel tightened. He found it difficult to hide the resentment he felt toward Fletcher.

"Part of the deal was that Daddy was to sell whiskey to no one else. Fletcher's theory is the best way to have a successful business is to eliminate the competition."

The more Jake talked the more sympathetic Ida Mae became, and the more her dislike for Fletcher grew. She knew of Fletcher's theory first hand.

"He insists the furniture factories are becoming overstocked and is paying less and less for the materials from daddy's sawmills," Jake continued.

"Is Fletcher really the only person your daddy sells his whiskey to?"

"No, but nobody knows that."

"If Fletcher ever found out he would have his friend, the sheriff, arrest you and your daddy again, isn't that right?" Ida Mae asked.

"You got it," Jake answered, "and then there would be no income from the stills or the sawmills."

"How do you sell the shine without him knowing?"

"About half of it is sold in Lexington and the rest my brother hauls into North Carolina. That was where he was headed the evening he hit your brother's car. If he had gotten caught, Fletcher would have surely found out."

"Was your brother the gentleman who was with you the night Dooley and I made our delivery into Washington County?"

"That it was, and I hope you didn't tell Fletcher you knew me. You don't realize how devious he can be."

"No I didn't, and yes, I know, all too well what kind of person he can be."

Jake had told her enough about himself so she knew he could be trusted, so she began telling him the story about her dealing with

Fletcher. About how the money he won from Dooley belonged to the church, and that she had stolen the whiskey that was to be used as evidence and sold it back to Fletcher. About the upcoming election, and about how Fletcher was also blackmailing her and Dooley. The only thing she did not tell him was about the child she was carrying.

"Someday, he will get what's coming to him," Jake said, when Ida Mae finished speaking.

"I hope I'm there when it happens," she said, as she snuggled close to Jake once again and rested her head on his shoulder. Jake turned on the radio and tuned in a country station. She remained in this position for the next several miles, listening to the soft music and letting her mind absorb what she had learned. She watched as the broken lines in the center of the highway were being gobbled up by the front of Jake's car.

Why had she trusted him enough to stay out with him so late, when she had planned to be with him only long enough to learn about his relationship with Fletcher? What would her parents think of her?

What would Dooley do if he ever found out, and why couldn't he be more like Jake?

She did not know the answer to any of these questions but it did not matter. She was growing much too fond of Jake, and she knew she must not go out with him again.

"Well, what did you think of the state of Kentucky, Pretty Lady," Jake asked, as the Virginia state line came into view.

"I loved it," she admitted, "and I'm sure I would not have enjoyed it as much had I been there with someone else."

"What time is it?" she asked.

Jake turned the inside light on enabling him to see his wrist watch. "A quarter past three in the morning, are you getting sleepy?"

A little, she started to say just as they passed a car parked beside the highway. It was partially hidden by some low-hanging tree branches, but the Buchanan County Sheriff emblem on the door was clearly visible.

Jake quickly turned off the inside light and began looking into his rearview mirror. Within seconds, headlights were approaching from behind at a high rate of speed.

"Better get ready to hang on," Jake said, as the automobile came closer and red lights started flashing.

"Why, you weren't doing anything wrong?"

"It's not me I'm thinking of," Jake replied, "I'm sure the sheriff could tell there is a lady with me and I'm certain curiosity is getting the best of him."

Jake maintained his speed for the next half-mile or so and the officer stayed within a few feet of his rear bumper.

"What are we going to do?" she asked.

"We're going to give the old boy some driving lessons," Jake smiled, as a section of straight road appeared in front of them. He began to slow down as if he were going to pull to the side of the highway. The car following also became slower and fell somewhat further behind.

Jake threw the Oldsmobile into second gear, the rear tires screeched and the race was on. It was evident that he was no stranger to the highway that lay ahead. Ida Mae sat silent as she watched her companion maneuver the heavy machine through one curve after the other at unbelievable speeds.

Within the next couple miles, she had little doubt as to who would prevail. The vehicle that had given chase began to fall further and further behind. Soon the flashing red light was no longer in view. Jake began to slow his automobile and made a sharp right turn onto a gravel road leading away from the highway.

"Better lie low for a while," he said. "If there is one of his deputies near the county line the sheriff will have radioed ahead and have him set up a roadblock."

Jake drove a short distance on the gravel road and brought the Oldsmobile to a stop. He turned the headlights off and waited a few seconds before he spoke.

"Lost him," he said, "but we had better stay here for a while to make certain."

Ida Mae slid closer to Jake and gave him a kiss on the cheek. "You're unreal," she whispered, as she snuggled beside him and laid her head on his shoulder.

Jake placed his arm around her and they sat in silence waiting to see if the sheriff had determined how they had evaded him.

Neither of them was aware of any of the happenings around them until there came a knocking on the driver's side door. They had fallen asleep and been undisturbed while the early morning slipped into dawn. When Ida Mae opened her eyes the first thing she saw was the uniformed police officer standing beside the car. The words "County Sheriff" inscribed on his badge erased any doubt as to his identity.

"Good morning folks, have a restful night's sleep?" he said, smiling like a cat that had just eaten a canary.

Before either of them had time to answer, the officer opened the driver's side door and asked Jake to step back to his car.

Ida Mae sat in Jake's car for what seemed like an eternity. She listened to the chirping sound of the sparrows as they welcomed the arrival of a new dawn. Hundreds of sunrays creeping through the treetops were like tiny swords cutting a path for the approaching day.

A gray squirrel was taking the outer shell from a hickory nut that would be added to the pantry that would insure his survival through the oncoming winter.

She watched as a chipmunk scurried along a path leading further back into the woods. Suddenly she realized that was the same path she and Dooley had taken just a few weeks earlier. Just a short distance beyond where she could see was where she had conceived her unborn child.

"Why did it have to be Dooley's," she questioned, as the officer came up to the passengers side of the Olds.

"What is your name, young lady?" he asked.

Before she had time to consider what repercussions might occur, she gave the officer her real name.

"How old are you, Miss Duncan," was his next question.

"Eighteen, sir."

"You and Mr. Hurd have a nice day," he smiled, as he returned back to his patrol car.

A moment later Jake came back to where she was waiting.

"Did he give you a ticket for speeding?"

"No, he knows all about me hauling booze for his old friend Mike Fletcher. He's not going to do anything that might cause me to have my license suspended. It's like I told you this morning, he saw you in my car and he could not stand not knowing who you were."

"Why did he question you so long?" she asked.

"He wanted to know where I had been, if I had made a whiskey run last night, and why a young lady like yourself was out with me so late. Of course, I didn't give him the correct answers to any of his questions.

"Did you give him your right name, I'm sure that's what he asked?"

"I did Jake, I'm sorry."

"Just as well I suppose, he was sure to find out sooner or later. You can bet your last cow Fletcher will know before sundown."

It was still early when they got back into town. None of the businesses were open and the streets were deserted so Jake drove Ida Mae right up to the steps of her apartment.

"I guess we won't be going out again since you and the deacon will be getting married next Saturday," he said. "Sure you won't change your mind about the wedding."

"If only I could," she answered, as the tears begin to well up in her eyes. She threw both arms around Jake's neck and gave him a slow passionate kiss. "Thanks for the most wonderful time I have ever had."

Jake watched as she ascended the steps leading up to her apartment.

"What I wouldn't give to trade places with Deacon Dooley," he thought, as he slowly drove out of the alley and onto the road leading out of town.

Ida Mae watched until the Olds could no longer be seen before she unlocked the door and stepped inside. She slumped down on one end of the sofa and began to sob. Her head ached, her hands were trembling, and the deafening silence in the lonely apartment seemed more than she could bear. It was a full half-hour before she was able to control her emotions.

"A hot bath and a strong cup of coffee is what I need," she thought. She went into the bathroom and filled the tub to near overflowing. She slipped out of her clothing and let her body sink into the soothing warm water.

"If only I could soak away the thing I wish I had never done, my life could be so different," she thought.

Ida Mae was crestfallen. How could she have allowed herself to believe she was in love with Dooley simply because he was the first man she'd ever dated? And if she must have a child, why could it not have been with someone as exciting as Jake?

These were just a few of the many unanswered questions that were racing through Ida Mae's mind as she pulled herself from the tub and got dressed.

It was still early morning, a good four hours before time for John Robert to pick her up. She was not about to spend so long in a small apartment with no one to talk to. She missed the hustle and bustle of her family in the large spacious home back on the farm.

She missed the twins running in and out, the tricks they played on her, and their occasional teasing. She missed seeing her mother and Mary Sue busy in the kitchen preparing breakfast while her daddy sat at the head of the table waiting for the food to be ready.

Ida Mae also missed John Robert, who was probably outside with the twins, or tinkering with his old Chevrolet, and Granny who she knew would be complaining about not being able to sleep to anyone who would listen.

I'll go down to Sid's Grill on the corner for a cup of coffee, she decided.

As she left her apartment the streets were not as deserted as they had been earlier.

The Saturday morning crowd was already beginning to move about. Even the honking of a car horn, signifying a friendly hello from one acquaintance to another was a welcome sound.

When she entered the restaurant she was pleased to see her friend, Officer Dewey Combs, sitting alone in one of the booths reading the local newspaper.

"Mind if I join you?" she asked.

"Please, be my guest," he smiled.

Ida Mae took the seat across from the officer just as the waitress placed a large plate of ham, eggs and two homemade biscuits in front of him.

"Would you like breakfast, Miss Duncan?" The waitress asked.

"Just coffee."

"Why are you in town so early? Are you all alone?" Dewey wanted to know.

"I guess you might say I live in town now. Dooley and I are getting married a week from today and we have rented an apartment. I stayed there last night, sort of getting used to living away from the farm."

"How do you like city living?"

"I hate it," Ida Mae admitted.

"Did you get the information you wanted from Mr. Fletcher the other day," Dewey asked, wishing to change the subject.

"No, he said he had no idea who it was that ran into John Robert's car."

"Did you believe him?"

"Not for a second."

"I read in the paper that he is reentering the race for sheriff. Something to the effect that his health is not nearly as bad as was first diagnosed. Do you think he has any chance of winning?"

"Not if I can do anything to prevent it," Ida Mae stated emphatically. "But, to answer your question, I don't think he has a ch..."

"Speak of the devil, he just walked in," Dewey interrupted.

"Did you get any more leads about who it is hauling that moonshine through the county," he whispered.

"Not a one."

"Sorry I have to leave, but it's time to go to work," Dewey said.

She sipped her coffee as she watched Fletcher make his way from one customer to the next. He was shaking hands, giving each of them a campaign badge bearing his name, and asking for their support.

When he was finished making his political pitch to everyone in the restaurant, he dropped some coins in the jukebox, and took a seat across from Ida Mae. He handed her one of his badges and told her he would appreciate her vote on Election Day.

"A friend of mine called me early this morning with a bit of interesting news," he continued, in a much lower tone of voice. "He said you were keeping late hours with one of my associates. As a matter of fact, he indicated it might have been the entire night. Not very lady-like for someone who is getting married in a few days, I would say."

Ida Mae made a quick survey to ascertain that no one had overheard what had been said. That was why he was playing records on the jukebox, she determined. She found it difficult to control the anger that was building inside her. She wanted to lash out at him, to tell everyone what a low-life excuse for a human being he really was, but she knew she had as much to lose, as did he.

"How is that any concern of yours?" she snapped, almost forgetting to keep her voice below the sound of the music.

"I just wanted to make you aware of how upsetting it would be if the good deacon were to discover he may not be your only interest. I would also like to assure you that I could guarantee he never found out."

"At what price?" she asked.

"Not much, just a small favor."

"I'm sure I will be sorry I asked, but spit it out."

"My other associates will be elsewhere and I desperately need to get a load of merchandise to North Carolina by midnight next Saturday. I want you and Mr. Hale to make sure it is delivered on schedule."

"Are you out of your mind? Dooley and I are getting married next Saturday."

"That shouldn't be a problem. I understand North Carolina is a great state in which to spend a honeymoon, and since you will be going anyway, I see no reason why you can't run a small errand for a friend."

"Not on your life," she said, "Dooley would kill me."

"Sounds like a personal problem, but if he does, make sure it is after you make the delivery. Have the deacon leave his car at the railroad depot just after dark next Friday night. Tell him to leave the trunk key in the ashtray. My boys will have the cargo loaded and ready for delivery the day of your wedding," he whispered.

"He can pick his car up any time after ten o'clock. If you should get caught, tell the cops everyone you know gave you whiskey as a wedding gift."

He was smiling as he got out of his seat and waved to everyone while making his exit.

Chapter Eighteen

IDA MAE REVEALS HER SECRET

Then Ida Mae left the restaurant, she was so upset she was trembling. When she made the deal with Fletcher to sell him the whiskey Sheriff Baxter confiscated, she had no idea about where it might lead. To even mention to Dooley the thought of hauling another load of illegal whiskey was totally out of the question. To ask him to deliver the load to North Carolina would throw him into a state of panic. But, to have him find out she had been out all night with Jake would be much worse.

She made her way back to her apartment, where there was nothing to do but dwell upon the dilemma she had gotten herself into, and wait for John Robert's arrival. She did not even unlock the door; instead she sat on the landing at the top of the steps and listened to the traffic on the street at the end of the alley. The small apartment made her feel as if she was in a cage. That was the last thing she needed, she already felt trapped.

She hoped John Robert would not wait until noon to pick her up. She needed to get back to the farm, back to her family, where she felt safe.

The warmth of the morning sun felt good to her body but did nothing to ease the uneasy feeling that was gnawing away in the pit of her stomach. The only cure for this ailment was to find a way to free herself from Fletcher's clutches. The effects of the alcohol and Fletcher's demands made her head feel as if it had a jackhammer inside. She buried her face in her lap and began to sob. She was not even aware John Robert was standing at the foot of the steps leading to her apartment.

"Whatever the problem is can't be that bad," he said.

Startled, Ida Mae lifted her head and stared at her older brother through tear-filled eyes.

"I just want to go home," she said, as her sobbing became more intense.

John Robert put his arms around his little sister and held her until she was able to regain some manner of composure. Her trembling body made him aware that there was something more seriously wrong than being homesick.

"Let's go inside and you can tell me what's really bothering you," he coaxed.

"I'm sorry, John Robert, I didn't mean to act so childish," she told him when they were both seated at her small kitchen table.

"I have known for some time that something was troubling you, but I had no idea it was something of this magnitude. I will assure you of one thing," he continued, "we are not leaving this apartment until I find out what's causing you so much grief."

"You would hate me if you knew the kind of person I really am," she said, as the tears once again began to flow.

"Let me make that decision," he said. "Things are seldom as bad as they seem."

Ida Mae was almost too embarrassed to tell him about all her illegal activities. But, she also knew that if there were anyone who would look at her situation objectively, it would surely be her big brother.

"Regardless of what you may think of me, you must promise you will never tell anyone what I am going to share with you."

"Cross my heart," he promised. "Now what little mischief have you been into?"

"It all started the night you dropped me off at the skating rink" she began.

She told John Robert about meeting Jake outside the rink and that the two of them sat in his new Oldsmobile drinking beer until almost time for him to pick her up. She told him about Dooley loosing the church funds gambling in Willie's Pool Hall. About getting pregnant while she and Dooley were spending time together in Buchanan County. About how she and Dooley stole the moonshine Sheriff Baxter had hidden in the barn. She told him about having to tell Fletcher about the baby before he would trust her enough to purchase what they had stolen. About Fletcher blackmailing her and Dooley and that she felt trapped. She confessed she had spent the night with Jake and the two of them had gone to Kentucky.

"But nothing happened between Jake and I," she quickly added. "Jake was a perfect gentleman, and he treated me like a lady."

She told him that Fletcher had already found out about her and Jake and how he was again trying to blackmail her.

John Robert sat quietly, soaking up all that his sister told him.

Ida Mae waited for some comment but her brother did not say a word. She tried to determine if the expression on his face reflected anger or disbelief.

"What do you think of your little sister now?" she asked.

"I think we need to walk down to the grill and get something to eat," he said. "I'll tell you what else I think after I've had time to digest all you have told me."

Ida Mae envied her brother's ability to handle any situation without getting upset. When he came home from service and discovered she had all but demolished his Chevrolet, he did not appear to be disturbed. Even when the Hudson ripped almost half of the bumper off he did not lose his cool.

"How do you always remain so calm?" she asked, surprised that he had not become angry about what she just told him.

"Remember little sister, out of every adverse situation comes an equal or better opportunity. Although sometimes you may have to create the opportunity," he added.

"You won't tell anyone what I have done, will you John Robert?" she begged.

"Not if you pick up the tab after we have eaten," he smiled.

"That's blackmail."

"How did you ever figure that out, Baby Sister?" he asked.

John Robert took her by the hand and led her down the steps and through the alley that led to the restaurant. He ordered a delicious meal for each of them and talked of everything he could think of to make her smile. She knew he was trying to keep her mind off her problems, but she also knew he would help her find a way to deal with Fletcher.

By the time she and her brother finished lunch, she felt as if the weight of the world had been lifted from her shoulders, as if her guardian angel had come to rescue her. Why had she not confided in him earlier instead of waiting until the situation had gotten so far out of hand?

John Robert escorted his sister back to where his Chevrolet was parked. He unlocked the passenger side door, handed the keys to Ida Mae, and got inside.

Ida Mae stood for a moment in total disbelief. "Does this mean you are going to let me drive?" she asked.

"Unless you would rather walk home."

She ran around the car and jumped into the drivers seat. "Tell me what I'm supposed to do," she coaxed.

"Do what you've seen me do when I'm driving," he said.

Ida Mae started the car, slipped it into gear, and began to move down the alley.

Surprised at his sister's ability to handle the machine, John Robert relaxed and leaned back into the seat. She did exceptionally well until she reached the end of the alley, at which time she slammed on the brakes so hard her brothers head bounced off the windshield. Realizing what she had done and wishing to correct her mistake, she pushed hard on the accelerator. The smell of burning rubber filled the air as she raced onto the only main street in town.

John Robert slipped the toe of his shoe under the gas pedal causing the Chevrolet to slow to somewhere near a reasonable speed.

"Now when have you ever seen me drive in this manner?" he asked.

He was relieved that it took less than a minute to be outside the city limits. Once they were on the open highway she did well following his instructions.

"What am I going to do?" she asked, when she felt John Robert was calm enough to carry on a conversation.

"Find me some smelling salts as soon as we get home, if I live that long," he gasped.

"About Fletcher, silly."

"Haven't figured that out yet, Sis. Tell me more about this fellow with the new Oldsmobile."

Ida Mae relayed Jake's story to her brother just as it had been told to her. She knew she could trust John Robert so she was careful not to leave anything out, especially the part about how Jake and his family became involved with Fletcher. She emphasized the fact that Fletcher threatened to cease buying lumber or whiskey if Jake's daddy tried to sell to anyone else.

"Eliminate the competition is his motto," she added.

John Robert listened intently until Ida Mae finished speaking.

"Sounds like it's time someone takes Mr. Fletcher down a notch or two. I want to meet your friend Jake as soon as possible, and stay on your side of the road," he said, as he grabbed the steering wheel, causing his Chevrolet to swerve out of the path of an oncoming pickup.

"You can find him at Willie's Place tonight," Ida Mae said, completely ignoring the fact she had almost caused a head-on collision. "I'd really like to go with you but I promised Mother and Mary Sue we would meet Mrs. Hale at the church this evening to make last minute plans for the wedding."

"Not a problem," John Robert insisted. "If this Jake fellow is the kind of guy you say he is, I'm sure he is as anxious as you to free himself from Fletcher's clutches."

"Do you have any ideas?" she asked.

Before her brother could answer she attempted to stop the car near the wooden gate at the end of the lane that led to their home. Not remembering to engage the clutch, she jerked the Chevrolet forward, causing a portion of the gate to go flying forward.

"I have an idea I had better teach you to drive before you get both of us killed," he said, raising both arms in front of his face for protection. "I'll tell you about any other idea I have after I talk to Jake. Not a word of any of this to anyone, not even Dooley," he added.

"You're the best brother any gal ever had, John Robert," she said, as she slid the car to a stop in front of their gate.

Ida Mae spent the evening at the church, trying as best she could to keep her mind on the plans Mrs. Hale laid out for her wedding. She was not really interested in how many people might attend, what food would be served at the reception, or whether or not the dress Mrs. Hale wore when she got married would fit her. She just wanted to get the event behind her to protect her and Dooley's reputation. Were it not for the baby, she wondered if she would be getting married at all.

The foremost thing in her thoughts was John Robert's meeting with her friend Jake.

A meeting, which would prove very helpful, she was to learn the following day. John Robert told her that her friend was at Willie's Pool Hall just as she had suspected.

"I invited myself to join him and one of the local boys in a few friendly games. After an hour or so I suggested Jake walk outside with me for a breath of fresh air; it was then I formally introduced myself."

"How did he react?" she asked.

"Surprised, and a little apprehensive, I suppose."

"You didn't embarrass him, about us being out all night I mean, did you John Robert?"

"Told him if it ever happened again I would skin him alive."

Ida Mae dropped her head not wanting to reveal her own embarrassment.

"Just kidding," John Robert quickly recanted.

"I made him aware, early in our conversation, that I was not there to pry into your private life, but that I would do whatever it took to free you from the hold Fletcher had on you. I also told him I knew of his families involvement with Fletcher and that I was willing to help them if my assistance was needed."

"What did he say?"

"He invited me to Mickey's Place for a few beers."

"And then what happened?"

"We both got drunk, so I don't remember a word of our conversation," her brother teased.

"Oh, cut it out," Ida Mae scolded, "tell me what the two of you decided."

"We have decided we're going to beat Fletcher at his own game. Jake tells me that he has nothing to do next Saturday night and there is no reason he could not make the run to North Carolina. He is confident Fletcher is simply exercising the power he has over you and the deacon."

"What are we going to do about it?" she questioned. "I haven't yet told Dooley what Fletcher has demanded of us."

"You don't have to do anything except persuade Dooley to take you out of town to spend the night after the two of you are married. Leave everything in the capable hands of your friend Jake and your loving brother."

"But, we are spending our wedding night in our apartment."

"You can't do that," John Robert insisted. "You have to leave town so Fletcher will think you really are going to make the trip to North Carolina."

"Where can we go?" she asked.

John Robert pulled a crisp new fifty-dollar bill from his wallet. "Drive into the next county and get a motel room. Tell Dooley it's my wedding gift to the two of you."

"That will be fun, I've never stayed in a motel before."

"I'm sure it will be," her brother smiled.

Chapter Nineteen

THE BIG DAY DRAWS NEAR

The morning of the day before the wedding was a hectic time at the Duncan household. Several of the church ladies began arriving before the hour of nine o'clock and each was busying herself for the festivities.

Ida Mae's mother was at the ironing board pressing Ira's only suit. She laid a dampened cloth on each leg of the badly worn gabardine trousers and slowly moved the iron back and forth until creases as sharp as a knife blade appeared. Once she was sure she could do no more to better their appearance she carefully hung them on a clothes rack and repeated the process on the sleeves of the matching jacket.

Mary Sue took three pair of different size pans from the oven and gently carried each of them to a small table that had been placed on the back porch. Each pan contained a portion of Ida Mae's wedding cake, and would be closely guarded until they were cool enough to be stacked one on top of the other, at which time the decoration process would begin.

At least three of the church ladies were adding ingredients for potato salad into a huge bowl that set on one end of their large kitchen table. Others were chopping cabbage that would soon be the makings of cole slaw and still others were placing portions of ham on the tiny biscuits that had been baked earlier that day.

Ida Mae watched the buzz of activity from an adjacent room while standing in a straight-back chair. She was modeling the thirty-year old wedding dress Mrs. Hale wore when she married Dooley's daddy. Mrs. Hale was making last minute adjustments to the delicate garment. She talked, more to herself than anyone else, while pinning, tucking, stitching and reminiscing about her own wedding day.

Ida Mae, like everyone else, paid little attention to what she was saying. She would have been perfectly content to get married in one of her own dresses but she did not want to offend Dooley or her future mother-in-law.

She was relieved when Mrs. Hale was satisfied that no further alterations were needed and that she had to make haste to the cleaners.

"I will have Donald bring the dress back by later today," she told her and she made her exit. None too soon for Ida Mae, for the smell of mothballs lingered in her nostrils long after both Mrs. Hale and the dress was out of the house.

By mid-afternoon all the food for the reception was ready for delivery to the church. The only thing left to be done was the decoration for the cake, which Mary Sue insisted she wanted to do all by herself.

The last of the group were ready to leave earlier than anticipated, much to Ida Mae's delight. Not that she was ungrateful for their help, but she needed desperately to talk to John Robert.

He had not yet told her of his plans for the following day and time was running out. Dooley was to have his car at the railroad station shortly after dark, an appointment he was not even aware of, and she had no idea of his whereabouts. In fact, she didn't know where John Robert was, either. He and her daddy had gone into town sometime earlier, to be out of the way of all the ladies, and she could not guess what time they would return. She did know that he was to have another meeting with Jake and she could hardly wait to find out what transpired.

She paced back and forth between the kitchen and the front porch, watching every moving vehicle in hopes that the next one would be John Robert. The afternoon was slipping away and her anxiety was building with each passing moment. She had little doubt that Jake and her brother would devise a plan to offset that of Fletcher's, but not knowing for certain was driving her crazy. Even Granny, who was half dozing in a chair near the cook stove, was aware of the tension that was building inside her.

"If getting hitched is bothering you, you better let go of the deacon while you can," she grunted. "A few years down the road when the babies start coming you might wish you had."

"If only she knew," Ida Mae thought.

Granny's comments were doing nothing to ease her anxiety and neither did the little rhymes coming from Kevin and Kervin who were playing Chinese checkers in the next room. Most of their rhymes went something like:

Ida Mae goes walking down the aisle
With her daddy by her side.
Mother goes looking for old Dooley Hale
But he's done found a good place to hide.

"Stop kidding your sister," their mother scolded as she watched Mary Sue put the finishing touches on her sister's wedding cake.

Ida Mae was nearing wit's end when she finally decided to go onto the porch and wait until her daddy and John Robert got home. She sat in her favorite place on the top step and soaked in the last bit of warmth from the setting sun. The chill of the November air reminded her of the rapidly approaching season. A solid black woolly-worm inching its way along the step just below was a sure indication that they were in for a long hard winter; at least that's what she remembered Granny and many of the other older folks saying.

The autumn air chilled her skin but the thought of sitting alone in her tiny apartment through those long winter months created a frigid feeling that penetrated to the innermost part of her being. She buried her head in her lap and let self-pity overtake her.

Tomorrow was her wedding day. She should have felt warm and elated, but the only warmth she could feel was the tears she could no longer hold back.

"I don't want to get married," she kept telling herself, as the misery worsened. I don't love Dooley enough to spend the rest of my life with him, and I'll never grow accustomed to him being such a mama's boy. I should hate him for the irreversible situation he has gotten us into."

Reality began creeping in. How easy it would be to blame someone else for her own misfortune.

"Dooley's not to blame," she thought. "I did this to myself. I asked him out, I encouraged him to gamble away the church money and it was me who seduced him and got him in the mess with Fletcher."

She had become so lost in her self-examination that she was not aware of John Robert's Chevrolet until it was coming to a stop in front of their gate. She hurriedly used her dress tail to wipe the tearstains.

"Hi fellows, glad you're home," she said, as John Robert and her daddy made their way to where she was sitting.

"Why all the enthusiasm?" Ira asked, as he ascended the steps. "I don't recall you being this excited about us getting home before."

Ida Mae hesitated a moment before answering. "Couldn't wait for you to see my beautiful wedding cake," she stammered.

She could hardly wait until her daddy was inside to ask her brother about his meeting with Jake.

"Well, how did it go?" she asked.

"Wonderful. Dooley helped us work out an ingenious plan."

"Dooley," Ida Mae said, raising her voice louder than she had intended, he wasn't even suppose to know."

"Relax, little sister. I'll tell you all about it in a few minutes."

She followed her brother inside and patiently waited while he indulged in some small talk with Granny and their mother and told Mary Sue what a wonderful job she did decorating the cake. He took a cup from atop the warming closet, filled it with the remaining portion of their breakfast coffee, and invited himself to join the twins in a game of checkers.

Ida Mae was certain he was intentionally letting her anxiety build. She sat watching until one game of checkers was finished before insisting John Robert take her to the church to make sure everything was as it needed to be for the next day. It was the only excuse she could think of to get her brother alone.

"Ready if you are," he smiled, realizing he had kept her in suspense long enough.

As soon as they were in the car, John Robert told her of their plans.

"Jake and I were in the restaurant having lunch, trying to figure out how we were going to outsmart Fletcher, when Dooley walked in. During our conversation we learned that he is to deliver your wedding dress later today. It was then I came up with a plan I knew would work."

"Tell me," she begged.

"I told Dooley that you would be busy with some of the church ladies until about six o'clock, so he agreed to come by near that time. I knew it would be almost dark by then and I could make our plan come together. When he arrives, I am going to pretend to have car trouble and ask to use his Mercury to make a trip back into town. All you need do it to keep him entertained until I return."

"I'm sure I can do that, but what is the real reason you need Dooley's car?"

"I am going to make sure it's parked at the railroad station just as Fletcher requested. I'll hide someplace where I can observe the whiskey being loaded. As soon as whoever puts the whiskey in the car is gone, I will drive it away. Fletcher will never know it was not Dooley."

"How is that going to help anything?"

"That's when our friend Jake gets involved."

"Our friend?" she questioned.

"Well, yes," he grinned, "I've come to the conclusion that Jake is a pretty good Joe. Anyway, as I was about to say before I was so rudely interrupted, we have already decided on a meeting place and we will transfer the cargo to his Oldsmobile. I will drive Dooley's car back to the farm and he will never know what happened. Jake and I will make the delivery to North Carolina tomorrow night after the wedding."

"You and Jake are two of the nicest guys in the whole world," she said, as John Robert pulled onto the church parking lot.

"Better not let the deacon hear you say that. Now what did you need to check on inside?"

"Not a thing," she smiled. "Let's go home. Dooley will be coming by before long."

"Just as I thought."

He pulled back onto the gravel road and in minutes they were home. They had scarcely gotten inside when Dooley came driving up the lower end of the lane. He took a huge dry-cleaning bag from the back seat and presented it to Ida Mae.

"Mother says I'm not supposed to see you wearing this until to-morrow."

"She's right. Come in for a while. John Robert needs to borrow your, I mean our, car to make a quick run into town."

It was a quick run, much quicker than either of them anticipated. About an hour after dark her brother returned. He gave the car keys to Dooley, and winked at Ida Mae, indicating all had gone as planned.

CHAPTER TWENTY

THE WEDDING

Ida Mae's wedding day did not begin as most of her days did. She was awakened by the crack of a pebble striking the side of the house.

Usually, she was normally up hours before the twins so when she realized they were already outside practicing with their slingshots she knew she had slept much later than she had intended. The stress brought on by Fletcher's demands had caused her to lose a great deal of sleep in previous nights. Once she knew of Jake and John Robert's plan she allowed her body to catch up on much needed rest.

She jumped from her bed and quickly raised the tattered shade on her bedroom window. Brilliant sunlight poured in like rushing water from a broken dam. She hurriedly dressed and ran downstairs and into the kitchen.

"Good morning, Miss Duncan," John Robert said, as he finished the remaining portion of his third cup of coffee. "Thought you were going to sleep right through your wedding."

"Wish I had," she said but quickly added, "gotten up earlier, that is."

Mary Ellen removed a container of fluffy biscuits from the warming closet, placed two of them beside a huge slice of ham on a large dinner plate.

"Fried or scrambled," she asked as she broke eggs into a skillet.

"Fried, please." Ida Mae answered.

"Your bathwater is almost hot," Kevin said, pointing to the three filled pails sitting on top and near the back of their large wood-burning cook stove.

"I helped Kevin carry your bathwater and we both helped John Robert wash his car, so it would look good for you to ride to your wedding," Kervin interjected.

"And I've got my white flat slippers polished real pretty for you," Mary Sue told her. "It doesn't matter if they get scuffed a little either."

"The flowers you will see decorating the church are compliments of Granny," her mother told her.

Ida Mae did not try to hide her tears. She knew that her family was going to miss having her around as much as she was going to miss being there.

"Don't you fret now, child," Granny said as she came to where Ida Mae was sitting and placed her frail arm around her shoulders. "You'll be back to visit three or four times a week, we'll make sure the deacon understands that is part of his wedding vows."

Ida Mae could see her daddy sitting beneath the maple tree in their back yard. He was whittling on a piece of cedar and seemed to watch each shaving fall among the brown, gold, and amber leaves that lay at his feet. He had never been one to express a lot of sentiment but she knew he was also finding it hard to see his oldest daughter leave home.

She finished her breakfast and strolled outside to join him.

"Remember the first time I insisted you teach me to whittle, Daddy?" she said as she sat down close beside him.

"Sure do," he said, pointing to the small scar near the end of her left forefinger. "You will always have this to remind us."

They spent the next half-hour reminiscing. Ira was never one to express his feelings openly but the tear he tried so frantically to blink away told her that he too was going to miss her.

"You know I will never be able to stay away for long at a time," she told him, while leaning over to give him a gentle kiss on his forehead.

"Time to start getting ready," her mother called from the back porch.

The family spent the remaining time dressing in their Sunday best. Ira in his freshly pressed suit and Mary Ellen in the dress she only wore on special occasions. The dress, like Ira's suit bore telltale signs that it had not been purchased recently. Granny's attire was her favorite blue and gray-stripped dress that made her appear taller than she really was. The twins resembled a set of bookends. Each wore a pair of starched bibbed overalls and identically colored new shirts their mother made from empty feed sacks. It was not hard to tell which one was Kervin, however. He was the one with the slingshot protruding from his hip pocket.

"I don't think you will be needing that weapon," Ida Mae heard her mother say as she made her way upstairs to where Mary Sue was waiting to help her get dressed.

John Robert, who was wearing his military uniform, at Ida Mae's request, winked at his mother. "Better let him take it along just in case."

"As long as he keeps it out of sight," she agreed.

About half-hour before the ceremony, Ida Mae made her way to the foot of the stairs. Even in Mrs. Hales' thirty-year-old wedding dress, she looked more beautiful than any of the family had ever seen her. She held a yellow corsage that accented the golden blonde hair partially hidden by her snow-white veil. The pleasant fragrance of perfume replaced the smell of mothballs that was so evident the previous day.

"You are the most beautiful bride I have ever seen," Ira commented. "Your mother excluded of course."

"You don't stink like you did yesterday either," Kevin added.

"Everyone except Ida Mae and Daddy load up," John Robert stated when they all quit laughing at Kevin's last statement. "I'll take Mother and the rest of the family to the church and I'll be right back after the two of you. We wouldn't want to get that pretty dress all wrinkled and I'm sure the father of the bride will want to ride with his daughter."

Ira and Ida Mae waited on the porch, for they knew John Robert would return in a very short time, but to their surprise it was not John Robert's Chevrolet that turned into the lane a few moments later. It was the shiny new Oldsmobile belonging to their friend Jake. When the car came to a stop near the gate both Jake and her brother got out and opened the rear doors allowing Ida Mae and her daddy to enter the back seat.

"Good afternoon Pretty Lady. I am honored to be your chauffeur," Jake greeted her.

"I'm the one who's honored," Ida Mae smiled, all the while admiring the expensive suit and the highly shined patent leather shoes he was wearing.

John Robert had little more than enough time to formally introduce Jake and his father before they got to the church parking lot, which was filled to capacity. The only time any of them could remember such a crowd was at Brother Taylor's funeral.

Jake pulled his Oldsmobile to the steps and assisted Ida Mae in getting out of the car. She, Ira, and John Robert waited just outside the church doors while Jake parked his Olds in a reserved space beside Dooley's Mercury.

When he joined them, both he and John Robert opened the two large entrance doors simultaneously. As if on cue the sound of "Here-Comes-The-Bride" filled the sanctuary. Ida Mae's knees almost buckled as the entire crowd came to their feet as her daddy ushered her to the front of the church where Dooley and Reverend Kyle were waiting.

She felt as if she might faint, and probably would have, had she not caught sight of Mike Fletcher standing on the aisle near the center of the building.

The feeling of being overwhelmed was quickly replaced with anger. He was the last person she expected to see at her wedding and why had he come anyway she wondered?

She was so bewildered at his presence the next thing she realized Brother Kyle was beginning to speak.

"Dearly beloved, we are gathered here today to unite two of our young members in the Holy Bonds of Matrimony. Who gives this woman to be wed?"

"Her father, Ira Edward Duncan," her daddy replied.

"Is there anyone present who can find fault with this couple being united?" Brother Kyle continued.

Someone near the back of the church cleared his throat as if to speak. Ida Mae strained to conceal her smile for she was sure it was Jake. The reverend must have thought someone was going to make a comment because he waited for a brief moment before he continued.

Ida Mae was barely aware of what was being said. She just wanted to get this day behind her and get on with her life. She wondered how jubilant this crowd would be if they knew she was a little short of seven months away from giving birth.

She was grateful no one knew of her condition but she was sure that if she were not with child she would not be here now.

She daydreamed through most of the ceremony but somehow managed to say her vows without embarrassing herself. Again her legs weakened when the reverend said, "Let me be the first to present to you, Mr. And Mrs. Donald Hale."

She was just glad the moment had ended and all that remained was meeting the guests in the new addition for the reception.

She and Dooley led the crowd into the adjacent Taylor addition that was decorated in such a manner that would have made the late deacon proud. Beautiful floral arrangements sat at each end of a long table containing an abundance of food. The three-tired wedding cake that Mary Sue had so painstakingly decorated made up the center-piece. Numerous gifts filled a smaller table near one corner of the room.

Ida Mae greeted all their guests and performed all the rituals that were expected of her. She and Dooley opened the gifts and expressed appreciation to each individual. She was truly grateful for everything they received, especially the envelopes containing cash.

Although she was the guest of honor, she felt that she and the other members of her family were outclassed. As she surveyed the crowd, it was not difficult to determine her family wasn't well dressed.

She was not at all embarrassed, for she loved each of them dearly, but she vowed someday she would make enough money to give her family the best, even if her new husband chose not to be part of her endeavors.

To Ida Mae, the best part of the entire day was when their guests began to leave. The afternoon had given way to early evening and she was anxious to get away from all the excitement. She needed to go home and get out of her most uncomfortable wedding dress so she and Dooley could be on their way. Everyone including her own family had just pulled off the church lot and she and Dooley were about to do likewise when Mike Fletcher pulled up along side of their car. He handed her an envelope and instructed her to open it right away. "Drive carefully Deacon, you are hauling some fragile cargo," he added.

Disturbed by his arrogance, she stuffed the envelope into her bosom. She had no idea what was inside but she could not wait to be alone to learn of its contents. Little does he know that we will be nowhere near North Carolina, she thought.

When she and Dooley got to her home, she rushed upstairs to change. As soon as she was alone she opened the envelope Fletcher had given her. Inside was a twenty-dollar bill along with a note giving directions to a motel in North Carolina. A room number was printed at the bottom.

"Someone will be there around midnight to welcome you. I'll come to your apartment Monday to let you know about the election Tuesday."

She heard someone coming up the stairway so she stuffed the envelope into one of her shoes. She quickly removed the wedding dress and tossed it onto the foot of the bed as Mary Sue entered the room.

"Aren't you going to hang Mrs. Hales' dress up nice and neat?" she asked.

"No, I think I'll put it in a feed sack full of mothballs so she can let Dooley's next wife wear it," she giggled.

"You're not serious, are you, Sis?"

"Never know," Ida Mae smiled as she made her way downstairs to where Dooley was waiting.

"We'll be back tomorrow night," she told everyone and waved as she and the deacon drove away.

Chapter Twenty-One

A DARK DAY FOR THE DUNCANS

Dooley and his new bride were well out of the county before dark. The fifty dollars John Robert gave her along with the money they received as wedding gifts, allowed them to be able to do whatever they wanted, even though it was to be only for the weekend.

They stopped at the best restaurant in Washington County and ordered the most expensive item on the menu. After they finished eating, they checked into a motel just across the Tennessee state line.

"Now I can say I have been in three states," Ida Mae thought, but this was a bit of knowledge she was unable to share with Dooley.

Their wedding night was much like she expected it would be. She had intended to sleep until noon and then spend the remainder of the day shopping, but this was not to be the case.

For the first time since she realized she was expecting, she woke up with morning sickness. Much to Dooley's disappointment she was unable to join him for breakfast. She stayed in their room while Dooley, at her insistence, had breakfast in a restaurant just across the street.

When he returned she was almost fully recovered, already dressed, and ready to check out. They spent the next several hours browsing through almost every business place in town. The only purchase either of them made was a few framed pictures to hang on the bare walls of their tiny apartment.

It was late afternoon when the smell of food escaping from a restaurant nearby reminded Ida Mae that she had not eaten all day.

"I'm starved," she told Dooley. A moment later they were standing in front of a large plate-glass window which bore bold letters reading, "Bob's Steak And Ale."

They had barely made their entrance when a well-dressed waiter greeted them. "A table for two?" he asked.

"That's correct, sir," Dooley answered. They followed the waiter past a bar, where several customers were having drinks, to a small table near a stage.

"This reminds me of Kentucky."

The words were barely out of her mouth before Ida Mae realized what she was saying.

"When were you in Kentucky?" Dooley asked.

"Oh, not me, one of John Robert's hangouts I've heard him speak of so often."

"Good answer girl," she told herself, as the waiter came back to their table with a menu for each of them.

"We'll have the largest steak in the house, with all the trimmings," Dooley told him.

"What would you like to drink?" he asked.

A tall frosted mug of beer sitting on an adjacent table almost made Ida Mae's mouth water, but she knew that was not to be one of her choices.

"Iced tea," Dooley answered, and she nodded in agreement.

They finished their meal and were back on the street just before the last rays of sunlight were beginning to fade.

"What now?" Dooley asked, as the sound of church bells echoing through the crisp autumn air reminded him that this was the first Sunday he had missed church since he was appointed deacon.

"Lets go home," she replied. "If we leave right away we can go by the farm before it gets dark."

As they started the long walk back to where they parked their Mercury, Ida Mae was sure home was where she wanted to be. She was no longer hungry, if fact, she had consumed so much food she could hardly breathe and her feet were beginning to ache.

Her brief honeymoon was not at all like she had always imagined. She always dreamed of at least a weeklong stay in some far-a-way place where there was dining, dancing, lovemaking, and all the other things newlywed couples were supposed to do. In fact, it was not until they were walking past a jewelry store that she was reminded neither of them had ever mentioned buying a ring. She almost suggested they do so, but decided getting back home was further up on the list of her priorities.

When they were at last back to the car, Dooley unlocked the trunk and placed the pictures they purchased inside. She remembered what they would have had in the trunk and where they would be, had it not been for the generosity of Jake and John Robert.

As soon as they were in the car, she kicked off her shoes and placed her head on Dooley's shoulder. She was fast asleep before they had traveled five miles.

The next thing she was aware of was Dooley bringing the car to a stop. When she sat up, she realized they were already back home. Dooley had stopped to open the gate at the end of the lane leading onto the farm. It was almost dark but she could see well enough to tell something was out of the ordinary.

Three or four automobiles were parked near the gate, one of which was that of Sheriff Baxter. As soon as they stopped in front of the house, Ida Mae could tell there was something terribly wrong. Her daddy, the sheriff, and some neighbor men were huddled beneath the maple tree near the side of the house. Her mother was sitting on the top porch step with her face in her hands. Granny and Mary Sue were doing their best to console her but Ida Mae could hear her sobs as soon as she got out of the car.

Ida Mae rushed up the steps and inquired as to what had happened. Her mother started to answer but her sobs became more intense. Granny took her by the hand and led her inside. Dooley made his way to where the other men were gathered.

"There has been a terrible accident," Granny told her once they were far enough away so Mary Ellen could not hear. "John Robert and some fellow named Jake were in an awful automobile crash. It happened sometime late last night. They are both somewhere in a hospital down in North Carolina and the doctors aren't sure if either of them will live. The Sheriff just got word a short time ago and came straight here to tell us."

Ida Mae's knees buckled and everything went black. The last thing she remembered was seeing Granny reach for her.

Four days passed before she regained consciousness. When she did,

Dooley and a lady in a white uniform was standing by her bed. It took a few moments for her to collect her thoughts.

"Where am I?" she asked.

A woman in white was the first to answer.

"You are in the hospital and you have gone through a rough ordeal. You must not move until the doctor examines you again."

"What happened?"

"You suffered quite a shock," the nurse explained.

The events of the past few days came rushing back. She sat upright in spite of everything Dooley and the nurse did to encourage her to not move.

"How is John Robert?" And Jake?' she asked.

"We'll talk about them later," Dooley tried to tell her but she would not be put off.

"No Dooley, please tell me now," she begged.

"Both are still in pretty bad shape but they will recover."

Ida Mae breathed a sigh of relief and lay back on her pillow.

"Would you mind to leave us alone for a while?" Dooley asked the nurse.

She did not answer, but slipped out of the room and closed the door behind her.

"There's something else I have to tell you," Dooley said, as he gently stroked strands of hair from her forehead.

Ida Mae lay perfectly still and waited for him to continue.

"You are no longer carrying our child," he whispered.

Dooley watched as his new bride's rosy complexion turned milky white. It was as if the blood was slowly draining from her body.

"Does my family know?" she asked.

"Not yet, but I'm sure they will find out eventually. Your mother and Mary Sue are in the downstairs waiting room as we speak."

"Where's Daddy?"

"He and Reverend Kyle left for North Carolina first thing Monday morning."

"What day is this?"

"Thursday."

Ida Mae remained calm for some time, letting the news of the accident and the thought of loosing their child penetrate her brain. Suddenly her eyes widened and a look of fear came over her.

"Please tell me Fletcher didn't win the election."

"Lost by two votes," Dooley smiled, as the nurse reentered the room.

"Serves him right, the dirty — ."

"Your mother would like to see you now," the nurse interrupted.

"I'll tell you all about the election later," he whispered. "I'll go talk to Mary Sue while you visit with your mother."

Mary Ellen leaned forward and kissed her daughter gently on the cheek.

"I love you," were the first words she spoke.

Ida Mae could tell from the look on her face that she knew.

"I'm sorry I have been such a disappointment," she began to sob uncontrollably.

Nothing Mary Ellen did, or said, helped to relieve the guilt that was eating away at the trembling body that lay before her. The sobbing did not subside but only grew worse.

When, at last, she could no longer bear to see her daughter in such agony, she took her by the hand and began to speak in a tone of voice that demanded attention. " I hope you are not so naïve as to think you and I are the only two ladies who put motherhood ahead of the sound of wedding bells."

Ida Mae's weeping ceased almost as rapidly as it had began.

Mary Ellen did not wait for her daughter to ask questions or make comments.

"You are old enough to know, and most surely mature enough to understand what I am about to tell you," she continued. "Many years ago, William Baxter and I were sweethearts. He was the first man I was allowed to go out with and I thought his only purpose for being on this earth was to love and take care of me. That's how it is when you're young and dumb. I'm sure you understand.

"Anyway, there was another young lady in the other end of the county who was willing to give more than I to gain his affections. Although I pretended not to know, I was well aware of what was going on. It was during that time I met your father.

"By the time he and I were on our second date, I would have paid the other girl to take William Baxter off my hands. Shortly after Ira and I began dating the other girl became Mrs. Baxter and I discovered I was expecting your brother, John Robert.

"As soon as we were certain I was expecting, we got married. Granny always insinuated he could have belonged to William but I promise you that was impossible. Your daddy knows that only he could be his father, but neither of us has ever dignified her suspicions with an explanation."

Ida Mae did not feel any less guilty, but she did feel greater admiration for her mother. Not only for not condemning her but for having shared her deepest secret.

After a long embrace, Ida Mae asked. "How did you find out about the baby?"

"I overheard Doctor Davis talking to one of the nurses the night we brought you to the hospital."

"Does Daddy know?"

"No, but I think he should. He loves you too, you know. I'm sure he will be hurt but he will understand."

Ida Mae hesitated for a moment. "You're right, Mother, and I should be the one to tell him."

Mary Ellen started to respond just as Dooley and Mary Sue entered the room. A middle-aged lady carrying a large covered tray followed close behind. She placed the tray on a small table beside the bed and removed the cover.

The large portions of chicken and dumplings, mashed potatoes, green beans, two homemade rolls, and a bowl of banana pudding made Ida Mae's mouth water. The smell of food reminded her that it had been more than three days since she had eaten. Her family remained in her room and visited while Ida Mae devoured everything on her tray. She had barely swallowed the last mouthful when the doctor came into her room.

"When can I go home?" she asked, before he even had time to say hello.

"Not until you are able to eat something," he smiled, as he surveyed the empty tray setting by her bed.

"Tomorrow?" she questioned.

"In a few days," he replied, as he began reading from a chart the nurse handed him. "You seem to be recovering very rapidly and your appetite speaks for itself. If you continue to improve you will be home real soon."

Chapter Twenty-Two

ANOTHER HURDLE

Ida Mae did improve more quickly than anyone expected. The burden of having kept her pregnancy secret no longer present, and the desire to go visit Jake and John Robert helped to speed her recovery.

She was released from the hospital late in the afternoon the following Saturday. She had no trouble convincing her mother that they should leave for North Carolina the next day.

Dooley agreed to take them immediately following the Sunday morning service but he insisted he would have to be back for work Monday morning. Reverend Kyle had already secured accommodations for Ira and any other family member through one of the local churches so they did not have to worry about where they would stay.

She and Dooley had barely gotten to their apartment after her release from the hospital when she insisted he tell her about the election. She knew something was troubling him, because he had hardly spoken on their way home. But what she was about to learn was far beyond anything she could have imagined.

Dooley waited until she was seated in one of the chairs at their kitchen table then sat directly across from her.

"Please don't interrupt until I'm finished," he said, as his story began to unfold.

"The night we took you to the hospital I sat in waiting room until dawn. No one would tell me anything about your condition except that you had lost the baby. Shortly after daybreak the most honorable

Mike Fletcher paid me a visit.

"As you know, it was the day before the election and he reminded me about our promise to help him get elected. He insisted you were in good hands and he expected me to haul voters. I did not want to leave the hospital but he left me no choice.

"Late Monday, he had me drive him into Buchanan County where he purchased three gallon of white liquor. It was in pint bottles, neatly packed into a cardboard box so it could be easily transported. Oddly enough, the name Hurd was on the mailbox where he made the purchase.

"Anyway, when we were almost back home he asked me to hide the whiskey until the next morning; someplace where he knew it would not be found. When I told him I knew of no such place he became angry."

"Stop right here," he said.

"Unaware of what he intended to do, I pulled off the road onto the parking lot of our church. I couldn't believe it when he took the box of whiskey from the trunk of my car and slid it into the crawl space underneath our new Sunday school rooms. When he got back into the car, he handed me a long list of names."

"These men will be expecting you to pick them up tomorrow and haul them to the polls to vote. Come by here and get a pint or two, pick up as many of these gentlemen as you can haul and take them to the polling place. When they place their ballot in the box, take them back home and repeat the process until the polls close tomorrow night. Just make sure they have consumed enough of that liquid persuasion so they won't mind that someone has already marked their ballot."

"I got so mad about where he hid the moonshine, I told him I wouldn't do it. I told him I didn't care if he told everybody in the county you were pregnant when we got married."

Dooley hesitated for a moment as if trying to figure out if he should go on.

"That's when he asked me if I cared if he also told everyone in the county about you and Jake staying out all night together."

He hesitated again and watched as Ida Mae's face turned blood red. She opened her mouth as if to speak but Dooley raised his hand as a gesture for her to keep silent.

"As you might imagine, he spared no details about how one of the

Buchanan County Deputies discovered you and Jake parked on a lonely back road in the mountains. He made a point to emphasis it was barely past daybreak and that the two of you were fast asleep."

Ida Mae felt her body go limp. She wanted to offer some defense but words would not come. Having lost the baby and the enormous hatred building inside her was taking its tole on her frail body. She buried her head in her hands and wept silently as Dooley continued.

"Believing I had no other choice," he said, "I did exactly as Fletcher ordered. Well before time to start voting I had already picked up four of the gentlemen whose names were on the top of the list. I had no trouble enticing these men to start drinking so early in the morning, but I'm sure Fletcher knew that would be the case. Anyway, by the time the polls opened they were well on their way to being intoxicated. I drove to a prearranged location a short distance from the polling place to where Fletcher and another man were waiting.

"He greeted each of my passengers with a hearty handshake and presented two of them with an election ballot that had already been marked. He instructed each to place the ballot he had given them in the ballot box and bring their unmarked ballot back to him.

"I was surprised they were both sober enough to do as he had asked. When they returned to my vehicle, Fletcher marked the ballots they brought back to him and the other two gentlemen repeated what the first two had done."

Dooley went on.

"As soon as the ballots were cast I would return the voters to where I picked them up and go for another load, after I went back to the church for more whiskey, mind you.

"This went on from early dawn until time for the polls to close. Each time I returned to the polling place there was a larger crowd gathered.

Ida Mae said nothing.

"Those hoping to see Fletcher win were huddled in one group and those rooting for Baxter in another. As time for the voting to end grew nearer Fletcher's supporters seemed to outnumber those of Baxter and Fletcher was becoming more and more excited. He even complimented me several times on the job I was doing. It was not until all the votes were counted that he showed his true colors.

"I was on my way to the polling place with my last two passengers when I blew a rear tire. By the time I made the necessary repairs and got to the polls it was too late for them to vote. That seemed of little concern to Fletcher at the time but the next morning when he learned he had lost the election by only two votes, he was furious. He accused me of intentionally being late with the last two voters, which caused him to lose the election, as if I knew how close it was. But you do realize that if I had gotten there ten minutes earlier he and Baxter would have finished in a dead tie."

Ida Mae waited until she was sure Dooley was finished talking before she raised her head. She took his hands in hers and looked at him with tear filled eyes.

"You have to believe me when I tell you that nothing happened between me and Jake," she sobbed.

Dooley got up from the table and started toward the entrance door to their apartment. "I never will be able to figure that out," he commented.

"What?" Ida Mae asked.

"How Fletcher got his hands on those first two ballots," he answered as if he had not heard anything she had said about her incident with Jake.

"I think I will go for a drive," he added. "Don't wait up I may be late."

Ida Mae's sobbing became more intense as Dooley closed the door behind him. She wanted to beg him to stay and let her explain how she happened to be out all night with Jake but she felt it better to let him have some time to himself.

She made her way to their bedroom and stretched her tired body on top of the covers. She decided to lie and rest until Dooley returned and then the two of them would have a long talk.

Tomorrow he would take her and her mother to North Carolina to visit with John Robert. She had not intended to fall asleep, but the smell of the new bedspread, someone gave her as a wedding gift, reminding her of the interior of Jake's new Oldsmobile was the last thing she remembered until the sound of a car horn awakened her the next morning.

At first, she was unable to comprehend where she was. Early morning sunrays fell across her bed and the smell of fresh-brewed coffee filled the room. She lay still for a moment trying to get a bearing as to where she was. The events of the past few days came rushing back. She jumped to her feet and made her way into the kitchen. Dooley was sitting at the table, a half-filled cup of coffee in front of him. She paused for a moment hoping for some kind of greeting. None came. He took another cup from a cabinet, filled it with coffee and placed it on the table directly across from where he had been seated, but still he said nothing.

"What time did you get home?" Ida Mae asked.

"Just before dawn."

"Why didn't you wake me?"

"Didn't see the need."

"Dooley, we have to talk," she stammered.

"Later," he said. "Its already nearing ten o'clock and we've missed Sunday School class. You'll barely have time to get ready for church and pack whatever you'll need for the trip.

"Remember, I'm taking you to visit John Robert, and your friend Jake," he added sarcastically.

Ida Mae, considering it fruitless to make any further attempt at conversation, spent the next hour getting ready for church and placing most of her clothing in a large paper bag. They were ready to leave before she realized Dooley had bathed and dressed sometime earlier. It was not until later she learned he had spent the night at the home of his parents. She hoped they knew nothing about her episode with Jake but she had too many other matters on her mind to worry about that now.

Morning Worship Service had already begun when they got to the church. Ida Mae made her way to the first empty seat near the center of the Sanctuary. She was surprised when Dooley sat beside her instead of taking his usual place behind the pastor's podium. She was too busy contemplating what she might find in North Carolina to pay attention to anything Reverend Kyle was saying. The only comment she fully comprehended was as the Pastor ended the service.

"Let's all continue to pray for the two young men who were injured in an automobile accident," he said, as the congregation stood to be dismissed.

CHAPTER TWENTY-THREE

NOTHING SHORT OF A MIRACLE

Immediately following the service, Dooley and Ida Mae went to the Baxter Farm to pick up her mother. None of the Duncan family attended church this Sunday morning. They were preoccupied with helping Mary Ellen prepare for the trip to visit John Robert.

When Dooley pulled his car in front of the gate, Mary Ellen, Mary Sue, Granny and the twins were gathered on the front porch. But the faces Ida Mae looked into were not the same ones she was accustomed to seeing. The radiant smiles had been replaced with that of worry and deep somber concern.

Granny sat in a rocking chair carefully stitching the torn hem of her apron. The twins, who would have normally been romping in the front yard or practicing with their slingshots, were sitting beside Mary Sue on the top step.

And her mother, whom Ida Mae admired more than any other living being, was seated in a straight-backed chair near the front door. A tattered brown suitcase lay at her feet.

The tired look in her Mother's eyes told Ida Mae that she had encountered many restless nights. Only once before could she remember her mother looking so dejected; the day John Robert left to become a member of Uncle Sam's Army.

"Its time to get started Mother," Ida Mae said as she gently took Mary Ellen by her trembling hand. Tears began to appear in the corner of her mother's eyes and her grip tightened.

"I want to be with John Robert but I'm afraid of what I will find when I get there," she stammered.

"Everything will be alright, Mother," Ida Mae answered, but she found it hard to control the quivering in her own voice.

"Take care of Mary Sue and my boys," she told Granny, just before giving her a gentle kiss on the forehead.

This made Ida Mae even more concerned about her mother's well being. In all her years, she had never seen her mother show Granny this much affection.

The guilt of having brought so much hardship on her family was gnawing at every fiber of her soul. The anvil in the pit of her stomach and the pounding inside her chest was causing it to be hard for her to breathe. She knew she must do something at once before she took leave of her sanity. She grabbed her mother's suitcase and half staggered down the steps and to where Dooley was waiting.

"Let's get started," she almost commanded. "The day is slipping away, and we have a long way to travel."

Dooley eased his Mercury into gear and they moved slowly down the long drive. When Ida Mae got out of the car to open the gate, which would allow them access to the gravel road, she looked back toward the house she had, until now, called home. Everyone, including Granny, was waving goodbye.

They had barely driven the short distance to the paved highway when Mary Ellen slid to one end of the back seat. "You two enjoy the drive," she said, "I believe I'll try to get some rest." Within moments the gentle snoring from the back seat and the hum of the car engine was the only sound that could be heard.

Ida Mae was glad for two reasons. First, she knew her mother was totally exhausted and needed the rest. Second, the tension between her and Dooley had reached a point where she felt it was best if they did not try to converse. Keeping quiet so her mother could sleep gave her the excuse she needed to remain silent.

She tuned the radio to a gospel music station and turned the volume down low. She pretended to listen as the miles rolled by. Neither she nor Dooley spoke for fear of introducing a topic, which was better left untouched.

She sat quietly as Dooley guided the heavy automobile through the mountainous terrain. For some time they had been in country that was unfamiliar to her, so the trip was anything but boring. As she watched the mountains slowly give way to flatlands, she found herself dwelling on the situation she now found herself in and wondered why she was so discontent.

She was married to a good man, much better than she deserved. One who had committed wrongs simply because of his affection for her. And in trying to right those wrongs had found him in more trouble. Even now, without knowing what really transpired between her and Jake he was willing to do far more for her and her family than she deserved. Then, why was she not happy with her lot in life, she wondered?

Ida Mae did not want to admit, even to herself, the cause of her restlessness, but in reality she knew it was Jake. He was so different from the man to whom she was committed to spending the rest of her life.

Unlike Dooley, who was somewhat dull and possessed a limited sense of humor, content to deal with little situations as they happened, Jake was exciting, full of energy and always anxious to make things happen. Also unlike Dooley, who was happy to live in his own little world surrounded with all that was familiar to him, Jake was ambitious and wanted to see as much of the world as his years would allow.

More and more Ida Mae was finding herself desiring to live the style of life to which Jake was accustomed rather than that which best suited her new husband.

She did not know how long she had been daydreaming but she was bounced back into reality by the appearance of a large blue and white roadside sign that read, 'Welcome to North Carolina.'

"Got to get some fuel," Dooley said as he pulled his Mercury to a stop in front of an Esso gasoline pump.

Mary Ellen awoke for the first time since shortly after their departure.

"Got a Johnny house?" Ida Mae asked the attendant as her bare feet stepped onto the hot burning clay that surrounded the pumps.

"Around back," he directed.

Ida Mae and her mother took advantage of the facilities as the attendant filled the car with gas, checked the oil, cleaned the windshield and performed any other service that might cause a customer to revisit his establishment.

"How much longer to Winston-Salem?" Dooley asked.

"Most part of an hour if you drive the limit, thirty minutes if you drive like most young fellers your age do."

Dooley gave the attendant the necessary amount of cash and pulled back onto the highway.

"In about an hour, we will be able to visit John Robert," Mary Ellen commented.

"And Jake." Again Ida Mae had allowed her speech to outrun her thinking.

Dooley made no comment, but the look he gave Ida Mae made her turn red with embarrassment.

Thinking it better to say nothing than to apologize, she offered no further comment. As they approached the city limits of Winston, the traffic became heavier. Dooley's driving required his full attention so Ida Mae had good reason to remain silent.

She felt a sense of relief when at last they reached their destination. As they pulled into the parking lot they could see Ira standing near the front entrance. It was late in the afternoon and she knew Dooley would not tarry. It was still some time until visiting hours and he'd promised to be at work Monday morning so he would have to rely on her father for a report on the patient's condition.

"John Robert is improving much faster than the other young fellow," Ira told him, "but the doctors are hopeful that he too will recover."

After hearing the news, Dooley insisted he must leave for the drive back home. He promised Ida Mae he would stop for a bite to eat and gave her a quick kiss on the cheek, more for the sake of appearance than to show affection, she reckoned.

Ida Mae watched as Dooley's Mercury became lost in traffic. When he was well out of sight, she turned to her father and asked, "How are John Robert and Jake really doing?"

"Your brother is doing much better than we expected. His right leg is broken and he has several stitches on the side of his head. The doctor says he may be released in another two or three days."

"And Jake."

"Not so good," was her father's reply. "Let's go get something to eat. It's still some time until visiting hours. There is a nice little restaurant a few block down the street and I'm sure you ladies must be starved."

"Not until you tell me about Jake," Ida Mae insisted.

Ira directed her and her mother to a nearby bench on the hospital lawn. "I'm afraid your friend Jake is not doing well at all," he began. "He too, has a broken leg, minor injuries to his lower back and the left side of his head. His most serious injury is the broken ribs and a punctured lung, caused by the impact with the steering wheel I suppose."

"Was he driving?"

"Yes."

"But Jake is an excellent driver, so I've been told," she quickly added. "What caused him to wreck?"

"It seems they were traveling at a high rate of speed and turned onto a narrow road. They rounded a curve and encountered loose gravel that had been washed onto the pavement by a pouring rain the night before. When the car hit the gravel it went into a skid and slid sideways striking the end of a bridge. Anyway, that's how John Robert remembers it."

"Why were they driving so fast?"

"They were being chased by the deputies here in the county."

"What does Jake say about the accident?" she asked.

"Not a word, in fact he hasn't spoken or moved as much as an eyelid. The doctors are bewildered. The agree his injuries do not appear to be that severe but he has not responded to any medication."

Ida Mae was grateful to be sitting down. She felt her knees weaken and she felt as if she were going to be sick. She found it difficult to hide her emotions but she dare not let her parents know how deeply she cared for the young man about whom they were speaking.

"This way," Ira said as he waved to a taxi on a nearby street.

"The Corner Café," he said to the driver as he helped the two ladies into the back seat.

Ida Mae sat near the door and looked out the window at the many different types of business places they were passing.

"Stop!" she cried out as they drove past a garage that had several wrecked automobiles sitting along one side. "Go back to that garage we just passed," she instructed the driver.

The cabbie made a U-turn and did as he was told. He pulled to the curb in front of the garage and stopped the taxi. Ida Mae got out and slowly walked to a crumpled pile of glass and twisted metal that had once been Jake's shiny new Oldsmobile. Crimson red stains on the front seat and dash left little doubt someone had been at least critically injured. The trunk lid was partially opened. Ida Mae forced it upright enough to see the remains of broken fruits jars were still inside. The smell of alcohol and small portions of clear liquid still in the bottom of some of the containers made her aware that the accident had occurred before their cargo was delivered.

She closed the trunk lid as much as was possible and started to walk away when something in the rear floorboard caught her attention. It was the case containing Jake's pool cue. She reached through the broken side glass and retrieved it.

Oddly enough, the case was undamaged. She returned to the taxi and asked the driver to take them on to the restaurant.

Once inside, Ira ordered the daily special for each of them. Ida Mae sipped her cold glass of ice tea but hardly touched her food. When they were finished her daddy ordered two burgers, fries, and two coffees to go.

"Maybe for later tonight," Ida Mae thought, but she did not question what he had done. She did think it strange, however, when they left without paying for their food. It was not until later she learned the owner of the restaurant was a member of the church that was providing them with lodging, compliments of a contact of Reverend Kyle.

She also learned the real reason her father ordered food to go. When they got back to the hospital, Ira carried the food to a small waiting room just inside the main entrance. He gave it to a weary, middle-aged couple that was seated side-by-side on a small sofa.

It was not until her father introduced the couple as Mr. and Mrs. Hurd, the parents of the young man who was in the accident with John Robert, that Ida Mae noticed a crutch leaning against the wall near where they were seated.

"Neither have left the hospital since the day following the accident," Ira added. "The hospital has provided a place for them to bathe and change their clothing and I bring their food each time I go to the Café."

"For which we are eternally grateful," Mr. Hurd said as he reached for his crutch and stood up to shake hands with Ida Mae and her mother.

"We've heard our son speak of you often," Mrs. Hurd added, "and you are as pretty as he said you were."

The remaining time before visiting hours was spent in conversation with Jake's parents but no mention was made of the accident or why the two boys were in North Carolina.

At last the moment for which everyone was waiting arrived.

Ida Mae told Jake's parents she would first go visit her brother but that she would be by to see their son right away.

She and her mother followed her daddy down a long hallway to a pair of double doors where several other people stood waiting. Unaware of why they were waiting, she watched the single dial on what appeared to be half a clock with ill-arranged numbers above the doors in front of them.

The dial moved clockwise until it reached the number ten, stopped, and began to reverse itself. It moved all the way back to the number one at which time the doors in front of them opened, revealing a small cubical about half the size of one of the corn cribs back on Baxter's farm.

Everyone began to crowd inside, as if they were trying to hide from something. A moment later, the doors closed and some of the people including her daddy began pushing numbers on the wall.

Without warning the cubicle began to move, as did the dial above the doors. She grabbed Ira by the arm and let out a squeal, as if she was afraid of what might happen next. When it reached the number three, the doors opened and her parents stepped into another hallway. "This is our floor," he stated as Ida Mae leaped from the cubical for fear of being left behind.

"Is that contraption what they call an elevator?" she asked, as the doors closed once again, silencing the giggles of those who stayed inside.

"That's right," Ira answered, trying as best he could to conceal his own smile.

Just a short distance from the elevator was the open door to John Robert's room. Ida Mae felt relieved when she saw him sitting on the side of his bed. He had a thick sandwich in one hand and a Pepsi-Cola in the other. An empty food tray was on a small table nearby.

Upon seeing his mother and sister for the first time since his accident, he quickly laid the food aside and gave each of them a big hug.

His right leg was encased in a cumbersome white cast and something resembling a two-inch long zipper decorated the shaved area above his left ear.

"I see they are feeding you quite well, big brother," was Ida Mae's first comment.

"Oh no, this is not hospital food, I finished it off earlier. What you see here was smuggled in by one of the nurses. I sure hope she doesn't get caught. She could get fired."

"So how much longer will you be putting this lady's job in jeopardy?" Mary Ellen wanted to know.

"Just a couple more days. The doctor is going to take these stitches out tomorrow," he said, pointing to the shaved area on the side of his head.

"I will be discharged the day after. Jake may have to stay a day or so longer. He's doing fine but I guess his head is not as hard as mine. We are not allowed to visit other patients but I will go by and chat with him for a while as soon as I am released."

Neither Ida Mae nor her parents made any comment. It was evident that her brother had been spared the true nature of Jake's condition.

"About time you get back home, winter is coming on and there's lots of work to be done on the farm before the snow starts flying," his sister joked.

She lingered another half-hour, trying to cheer up her brother while concealing the anxiety that was about to overtake her.

"I think I'll leave you and Mother alone for a while and have Daddy show me around this place."

"That may take awhile, but make sure you find time to see Jake," John Robert told her.

When she and her father left the room, Ira knew exactly where it was she wanted to go. "Jake's room is two floors up," he told her. "Do you want to take the elevator or would you rather take the stairs?"

"Why, the elevator of course," she smiled.

When they stepped from the elevator on the fifth floor the smell of ether filled the air. A sign directly in front of them read, 'Intensive Care Unit, Quiet Please." In a chair to her left just outside his son's room sat Mr. Hurd. One visitor at a time, five-minutes only was posted on the door.

Ida Mae stepped to where Mr. Hurd was sitting and placed one hand upon his shoulder. She said nothing as she patiently waited until Jake's mother exited the room.

"You may go in now," Mr. Hurd told her.

Ida Mae slipped quietly into the dimly lit room and what she saw made cold chills run up and down her spine. The ghostly white form that lay before her scarcely resembled the handsome man she knew. Tubes connected to bottles containing clear liquid were attached to each arm. White bandaging encircled the head of his motionless body. A nurse, clad in white, sat in one corner.

Ida Mae stepped to the side of Jake's bed and took his hand in hers.

"Jake, it's Ida Mae," she whispered. She waited for a moment, as if she expected him to answer as the tears streamed from her face and fell onto the sheets. "Jake, it's Ida Mae," she repeated in a voice that was more audible, but still there was no response.

"I'm afraid he can't hear you, dear," the nurse spoke in a soft sympathetic voice.

"But he will get better, won't he?" Ida Mae was pleading for some reassurance that Jake would recover.

The nurse took her by the arm and gently led her from the bed. "I shouldn't be telling you this but I feel I must. Physically, the doctors' think he could recover, they are confident they can treat the injuries to his body.

"It's what dwells in his subconscious mind they fear has erased his will to live. I believe if he is to get well, it will take nothing short of a miracle. I must ask you to leave now, and please don't tell anyone what I told you about your friends condition. Perhaps, you will come back tomorrow."

"I certainly shall," Ida Mae assured her.

She stepped outside the room and followed her father down the hallway. As she suspected, he did not go to the elevator.

Instead, he took her to a small vacant waiting room reserved for family member of the critically ill.

"Let's sit a while and give you time to collect your thoughts," he suggested.

"John Robert and I had a lot of time to visit this week," he said, when she at last quit crying.

"He told me why he and his friend Jake were here in North Carolina and why the law was chasing them. He also told me about more of the underhanded schemes Mike Fletcher is involved in.

"I realize now that you and the Deacon would not have gotten married had you not been with child. I also know that you have grown very fond of Jake. I am not telling you these things to criticize; I have made enough mistakes of my own but please don't do something that you may regret for the rest of your life.

"One more thing, the things John Robert told me were in confidence, and I would never betray that confidence, but I assure you that I will do whatever it takes to free you from Fletchers' clutches."

Ida Mae was both relieved and embarrassed. She started to express her gratitude, but her daddy interrupted.

"Better get back to your brother's room," he said. "Visiting hours will soon be over."

She and her father walked hand-in-hand back to the elevator and made their way to where her mother was waiting.

"How was Jake?" her brother asked when she re-entered his room.

"Just as you said, more hardheaded than you," she answered.

"Visiting hours are now ending," came a voice over the loudspeaker.

Relieved there was no time for further conversation, she kissed her brothers forehead and told him she would be back the next day.

When the threesome exited the hospital they were reminded of the season.

Darkness had overtaken the city and the warmth of the sun had given way to the chill of a mid-autumn evening.

They made their way down the long walk, lined on either side with late-blooming multi-colored geraniums, to a street bustling with traffic.

Ira waved his arm high in the air and a moment later a yellow cab pulled to the curb. "Four twenty-one Chestnut Street," he instructed the driver.

Ida Mae and her mother sat quietly in the back seat as the driver skillfully maneuvered his automobile through heavy traffic. Ira was up front pretending to be interested in the score of some basketball game being broadcast on the radio. In a little while, two-story homes with manicured lawns and beautiful flower gardens replaced the tall buildings housing the many business establishments.

It was in front of one of these homes that the driver brought his taxi to a halt. Streetlights made the number four twenty-one clearly visible.

"This is where I have been staying at night since I've been here in North Carolina," Ira explained. "The lady who owns this home lives by herself and she so graciously allows families who have patients in the hospital to use the upstairs."

Ira gave the cabbie a pair of dollar bills and led Ida Mae and her mother onto the porch of the dwelling. He extracted a key from his pocket and unlocked the door. As they stepped inside a stocky, gray-haired lady greeted them.

"Thought you would be in bed by now, Sarah," Ira commented.

"Not until I was introduced to the Missus and your daughter. Remember, you told me they were coming today. I wasn't about to turn in until I gave them a proper welcome."

"Mrs. Johnson, this is my wife, Mary Ellen, and my oldest daughter Ida Mae."

"Need I remind you again, it's Sarah, not Mrs. Johnson," the lady stated in a somewhat scolding manner.

"We will go on upstairs so you can get your rest," Ira told her.

"Not until you and these ladies come into the parlor for some refreshments," she insisted.

They followed their hostess into a large room just off the main entrance. The aroma of burning wood and the warmth it provided was indeed welcome. Shadows created by the flames danced on the ceiling.

The illumination from the fireplace and a small lamp provided the only lighting. Enough to make visible a plate of home-made cookies, a pitcher, which they would discover was filled with steaming hot chocolate, and a huge bowl of popcorn had been carefully placed on a table in front of a rose colored sofa. Three of four matching chairs were the only other furnishings. Bookcases piled with letters ran the full length of two walls.

"You have a beautiful place, and so well kept," Mary Ellen commented.

"Not bad for an eighty-year-old, I suppose.

Sarah listened as Ira told her about how much John Robert was improving. She then repeated the story she told Ira upon his arrival. How she and her late husband, who was from a rather well-to-do family, had built their home shortly after they were married.

How they planned to have a large family and would be able to provide ample room for each of their offspring. About how the Big

War began and her handsome young husband was shipped off to battle. She described how he was wounded shortly after arriving in Germany, and after days in an army facility was sent back to the hospital here in their own city.

"A month later, he passed away," she sighed. She also explained that during his stay in the hospital, she encountered many families who found it hard to find lodging while helping to nurture their sick and wounded back to health.

"It was then, I decided that providing shelter for some of those families would prevent me from living a life of loneliness."

"But why will you take no pay?" Ira questioned.

"These are letters of appreciation," Sara said, pointing to the stacks of envelopes in the bookcases. "I find they provide me with ample compensation."

"What a wonderful gift to humanity," Mary Ellen stated, as she used her handkerchief to dab the corners of her eyes.

Sarah arose and, with a poker, carefully rearranged the dying remaining pieces of burning firewood.

"Now that I have relayed to you kind folks the story of my life, I believe I shall bid you goodnight. Please turn out the lamp before you go to bed."

Ira and Mary Ellen waited until Sarah entered a room adjacent to where they were sitting and closed the door behind her.

"I think we should call it a day, too." Ira told Ida Mae. "Your mother and I will be in the first room to your right at the top of the stairs. Your room is the one directly across the hall."

Ida Mae did not get up right away. She curled her legs underneath her body and sunk deeper into the large armchair in which she was sitting. She watched the tiny sparks from the crackling firewood fall onto the hearth and fade into nothingness. She rested her head on the on the back of the chair and prayed silently.

"Thank you for making John Robert better and, please God, send my friend Jake that miracle."

"Wake up, Dear, it's almost daybreak and you wouldn't want your breakfast to get cold now would you?"

It was the kind gentle voice of Sarah who was beckoning her to arise and face the challenges of a new day.

"I'm sorry. I should have gone upstairs, but I guess I was more tired than I realized."

"No need to apologize, young lady. You are not the first to fall asleep by this fire. Come eat a hearty breakfast and take yourself a hot bath, that always make things look brighter."

And right she was. Ida Mae ate a hearty breakfast, famished by going without food the previous day, took the hot bath Sarah had suggested and found she did feel much better. As were her parents, she was ready to leave in plenty of time to get to the hospital for the morning visiting hours. Their hostess had already summoned a taxi, which was waiting as they exited her beautiful old home.

John Robert was standing in the doorway to his room when she and her parents arrived. He had a crutch under each arm but the stitches in his head were now gone. He was clean-shaven and the hospital shirt he was wearing the day before had been replaced with street clothes. The smile on his face told them he was to be the bearer of good news.

"I will be discharged in the morning," he greeted them. "I can go talk with Jake for a while and if Reverend Kyle will come get us we can be home before dark."

Sad expressions told him that all was not well. "What's wrong," he wanted to know.

"Let's go for a walk,' Ida Mae suggested.

Her brother hobbled along beside her to a small waiting room at the far end of the hallway. She waited until he was seated and as comfortable as the cumbersome cast would allow before she spoke.

"Jake will not be able to talk to you," she began. "He is much worse than you know. In fact, he may not survive, and it's entirely my fault," she sobbed.

"Why didn't someone tell me?" he asked, unable to conceal the anger he felt.

"It's against hospital policy. We didn't want to say anything that might hinder your recovery."

"So tell me now," he insisted.

Ida Mae spent the next hour bringing her brother up to date on all the happenings since his accident. "We can't go home and leave Jake," John Robert told her. "Talk to Mrs. Johnson and see if we can stay with her until he is recovered. Mother and Daddy can go home tomorrow, and rest assured, we will deal with Fletcher later," he added.

"I must take you back to your room now and go upstairs." Ida Mae told him.

She walked her brother back to where her parents were waiting and hurried to spend the remaining time with Jake. She slipped quietly into his room and found him as he had been the day before. A different nurse occupied the chair that sat in the corner of the room.

"Has there been any change?" Ida Mae asked.

"None at all," she whispered.

Ida Mae stepped to the side of Jake's bed and began gently stroking his hand. "This is Ida Mae," she told him. "I'll be here until you are well again." She said nothing more but stayed by his bedside until the loudspeakers in the hallway informed all visitors it was time to leave.

When visiting hours were over, Ida Mae insisted they go back to Sarah's. She also requested her parents allow her to talk to Sarah alone, so upon their arrival Ira and Mary Ellen went directly to their room.

In the dining room, Ida Mae found Sarah sitting at the table. In front of her lay two letters.

"More expressions of appreciation?" Ida Mae asked, as she took the chair across from Mrs. Johnson.

"Yes, dear," Sarah answered. "I sometimes receive half-dozen a week, which is far more than I deserve."

"I'm sure your kindness warrants many more, which brings me to why I am here," Ida Mae told her. "My brother will be released from the hospital tomorrow and my parents will be leaving, but he and I would very much like to stay here with you until our friend Jake is well. I'm sure my daddy has told you about Jake," she added.

"Indeed he has, and indeed you may," Sarah smiled. "I have the highest regard for your father and you and your brother will be quite welcome here."

Ida Mae placed her hands on her frail shoulders and kissed her on the top of her head. "I know why those bookcases are so filled with letters," she told her.

She made her way up to her parent's room to tell Ira and Mary Ellen. Her mother was less than pleased that she was not going back home to her husband but said little to discourage her from staying.

Ida Mae was so excited, she could hardly wait to tell John Robert. She was in his room five minutes ahead of her parents when evening visiting hours began, relaying the good news.

"I guess we won't be going home tomorrow after all," he said.

"Will we stay here until Jake is better?" she asked.

"I will for certain, I guess what you do depends on Dooley."

"We're both staying, I'm going on up to his room now. Mother and Daddy will be along any minute."

Ida Mae took the elevator up to the third floor. She entered Jake's dimly lit room and stood for a moment to get her bearings. Suddenly, she realized the nurse who had always been present was not in the room.

She listened nervously for any sound that might assure her some form of life still existed, but there was nothing but deafening silence. Panic-stricken she moved to the side of Jake's bed, afraid of what she would find.

She laid her hand on his chest. His beating heart brought tears to her eyes.

"Family?" The nurse, who had been sitting with Jake the day before, asked as she entered the room.

"Just someone special," she stammered. "Please tell me he is doing better today."

"I'm afraid not," she answered.

The worried expression on Ida Mae's face told her that her patient must be very special to this lady.

"Why don't I go for another cup of coffee," she said, as she slid a chair up to the side of Jake's bed. "If you need me, just pull this cord and a light in the nurses lounge will alert me."

"Thanks," Ida Mae smiled.

She sat beside Jake's bed, gently stroking his hand and pleading with him to find the strength to live. She also began pouring out her innermost feelings, saying things she would not have had the courage to say, were he able to hear. She told him how she enjoyed their trip to Kentucky, and how she wished she could go with him to all the other places he had told her about.

About how she was tired of being poor and tired of watching her parents struggle to make a meager living on the farm. How she was ashamed of herself for not feeling the way she should toward Dooley, and that she had to find the courage to tell him their marriage was a mistake. How she envied Fletcher's lifestyle, and that she would do anything to break the hold he had on her. She also told him how she wished he had come into her life before she had gotten involved with someone else.

She was not aware of how rapidly time had passed until the nurse came back into the room and told her visiting hours would soon be over.

Ida Mae stood up and used the sleeves of her dress to dry her eyes. She kissed Jake's hand and thanked the nurse for allowing her to visit with him alone. "I must spend the remaining time with my brother," she said.

She stepped to the door and was about to let herself out when a voice as clear as church bells on a cold winter morning filled the air.

"Please don't go.

"Jake!" Ida Mae yelled.

"Please don't go," he repeated, as both she and the nurse rushed to the side of his bed, staring at each other with a look of disbelief.

"Am I in a hospital?" he asked.

"Yes, but you are doing great," the nurse assured him.

"Then, why does my head feel the size of a watermelon?"

"Because you have the best nurses on duty and it's given you the big-head," Ida Mae smiled.

Visiting hours are over came the familiar voice on the loud speaker.

"Not for you," the nurse told Ida Mae as she led her a few feet from the bed. "I have prayed for a miracle for your young friend, but I never imagined it would arrive with blonde hair. I am going for the doctor and I will send someone down to first floor to give Mr. Hurd's parents and your family the good news."

CHAPTER TWENTY-FOUR

A DIFFICULT DECISION

The day following Jake's miracle, John Robert was released from the hospital. Reverend Kyle came to Winston-Salem to take Ira and Mary Ellen back to the farm in Virginia and Jake's parents left for their home a couple of days later.

Ida Mae and her brother began their month long stay with Sarah and the friendship that grew between the two ladies was one that would forever remain embroidered on the pages of the young ladies fondest memories.

Both Jake's health and Ida Mae's affection for him grew stronger daily. Neither she nor John Robert missed a single opportunity to visit him, but when her brother was not at the hospital he spent his time touring the city. He would get a taxi and travel to an unfamiliar site and then hobble from place to place until time to return.

Ida Mae, on the other hand, spent every available minute with Sarah. She would rush to help Sarah with her daily chores so she could set in front of the fireplace and listen to the silver-haired lady recall the experience of her many years. She learned how her only means of survival thru the depressions years was the small gifts she received from families whom she had allowed to share her home.

How she had fallen in love with a widower next door but that he lost his life in a fire that burned his home to the ground a week before they were to be wed. She learned that Sarah was the last remaining member of her family and that she feared no one else in the city would extend the hospitality she had shown once she was gone.

Ida Mae became so engrossed in the stories Sarah relayed to her she would creep into her room when she returned from the hospital at night. If she was still awake, Sarah would prop herself up on pillows and the two would talk until well past midnight.

As Jake grew stronger the day they would have to go home drew nearer. A day Ida Mae dreaded. She had not allowed herself to think about how she would face Dooley. He had only called her twice and neither time had he asked her to come home, so she knew facing him was not going be easy.

She was also torn between seeing her family and having to leave the kind old lady she had grown to love.

Finally the day she both hoped for and dreaded arrived. When she and John Robert entered Jake's room, he was fully dressed, sitting in a wheelchair, ready to go home, days earlier than she had expected.

"Surprised you didn't I Pretty Lady? We're going home today," he smiled.

"But how will we get there?" she asked.

"My brother, Billy, will pick us up at the home where you have been staying at noon."

"Then, what are we waiting for?" the over-anxious John Robert wanted to know as he started gathering Jake's few belongings

They went directly to Sarah's and the next hour Ida Mae spent telling her and Jake good things about each other.

At preciously twelve o'clock a car horn blew. No one had to be told it was their transportation back home.

John Robert and Jake's brother rolled Jake's wheelchair to the car and helped him into the back seat. Ida Mae lingered as long as she could. When at last it was time to go, she threw her arms around Sarah and wept as if her heart would break.

"I hope someday I can extend to others the kindness you have shown to my family. I love you, and I will be back," she promised.

"I know you will," Sarah smiled.

She watched from the front door until all were inside.

"Just a minute," she called as the car started to move. She picked up the case that had been leaning by the door since the day of Ida Mae's arrival, and walked feebly to the awaiting vehicle. "I believe this is yours, young man," she said as she reached the case through an open window.

Jake took the case and opened the secret compartment in one end.

"The case is mine but this is yours," he said, while placing several crisp hundred dollar-bills in Sarah's aged wrinkled hand.

"God Bless all of you, and you will be back Ida Mae," was the last words they heard as the car drove away.

Ida Mae sat in the back seat with Jake and tried to make him as comfortable as she could. The doctor told him the trip would not be easy and gave him a strong pain pill to be taken if needed. Less than an hour into the trip, they had to stop for a drink so he could swallow the pill. Twenty minutes later, he was in a deep sleep with his head resting on Ida Mae's lap.

As the miles rolled by, she sat quietly listening to Billy and John Robert. She watched as the rolling hills of North Carolina give way to the multi-colored foliage on the mountains of Virginia. What a difference a short time can make, she thought, remembering the greenery of a few weeks earlier. Not just to the mountains but also to those who live in their shadows.

The beautiful foliage and the fallen leaves being blown from the highway by rapidly moving vehicles reminded her of the fast approaching winter. And, for the first time since she left home, she started dreading the long winter days she would have to spend alone in her tiny apartment. She dreaded the nights with Dooley, the man she was married to but did not love. Most of all, she was going to miss seeing Jake.

"Something has got to change," she heard herself say aloud.

"Beg your pardon, Sis?"

"Oh nothing, just wishful thinking."

"Do you want to stop at your apartment?" John Robert asked, as their hometown came into view.

"No, take me to the farm!" Ida Mae stated so emphatically it almost sounded as if it was a command.

Ida Mae saw their Mercury parked near the station where Dooley worked, but Dooley was not in sight. A short time later, Billy stopped his car near the gate leading to the Baxter farm and Jake was aroused for the first time since the pain pill put him under. He struggled to a sitting position so Ida Mae could open the gate. As she started to get back into the car she heard one of the twins sing out, "They're home." By the time they reached the house, everyone including Granny, was standing outside to greet them.

John Robert was the first to get out of the car. He started to reach for his crutches but quickly decided that would not be necessary. The twins were standing, one on either side insisting they help him. He placed an arm on each of their shoulders and limped through the yard, up the steps, and onto the front porch.

After a few words of appreciation for Billy, the other family members joined him, everyone except Ida Mae. She stood by the car holding Jake's hand, unable to conceal the tears streaming down her face.

"I never could have made it without you," he told her. "You will come visit me, won't you?"

"Even if I have to walk," she said, looking up at her brother.

"We'll be there tomorrow," John Robert assured him.

"Then take me home so I can rest," he told Billy, and they slowly drove away.

"Will you really take me to visit Jake tomorrow?" she asked, when everyone else had gone inside.

"Sure I will, but you will have to drive. And, this evening I'm taking you to see Dooley."

"Might as well get it over with," she agreed.

The remainder of the afternoon was spent telling Granny, Mary Sue, and the twins about their time away. The questions didn't stop until Mary Ellen announced the evening meal was ready.

After they had eaten and Ida Mae determined she could no longer postpone facing Dooley. She asked John Robert to help her drive to their apartment.

Following her brother's instructions, she handled his Chevrolet much better than she did the last time he had given her a driving lesson. She drove into town with little difficulty and was pleased to see Dooley was still at work. She pulled in front of the station and waited until he came outside.

"Hello, Dooley," was all she could think to say.

"Hello," he answered with not much enthusiasm. "When did you get back into town?"

"A little while ago, I'm on my way to the apartment. Will you be getting off work soon?"

"Right away. Glad you are getting better, John Robert."

"I'll see you there?" she asked.

Dooley shook his head.

Ida Mae parked in front of the restaurant, a short distance from their apartment and helped her brother go inside. She then walked to the apartment to wait for Dooley. When she unlocked the door what she saw was not at all what she expected. Everything was as it had been when she was last there. The two coffee cups on the table she knew were the ones she and Dooley drank from after John Robert's accident, so she knew no one had been living there. She sat at the table and waited for Dooley to arrive.

She did not have long to wait for a moment later she heard him open the door. He did not speak but sat at the table across from her. She waited for him to say something, anything, but he still did not say a word.

When she could stand it no longer, she said, "I'm sorry Dooley, but getting married was a mistake."

"I know," was his only comment.

She felt troubled, but she also felt relieved. "Where have you been staying?" she asked.

"Hanging out at Willie's place until closing time, then I go to my parents home."

"I'm so sorry for all the trouble I've caused you Dooley, but we could never be happy living as man and wife."

"I'm sorry too, Ida Mae, but I think it would be better if you move back to the farm."

"I'll get my things tomorrow while you are at work," she said, as she got up and walked to the door. "I will always have fond memories of you, Deacon," and she closed the door behind her and walked back to the restaurant to where John Robert was waiting.

"How did it go?" he asked.

"Just wonderful," was her reply. "Now let's go home."

A week later Ida Mae received notice that Dooley had their marriage annulled.

CHAPTER TWENTY-FIVE

A BOUNTIFUL HARVEST

The next morning, Ida Mae went to the apartment, packed only her clothing, and moved back to the farm. By mid-afternoon, she and John Robert were on their way to visit Jake. They drove several miles into Buchanan County looking for a large mailbox on the side of the road bearing the name 'Hurd.'

"This is it," her brother said when the mailbox came into view. Ida Mae was traveling too fast to turn into their driveway but she turned anyway, almost running the car over an embankment. After recovering, she saw Jake sitting on the porch of his parent's home and became so excited she almost ran into their gate.

She helped John Robert with his crutches and they walked to where Jake was sitting.

"Hi, Pretty Lady," he greeted her. "I didn't know you could drive."

"She can't, didn't you notice?" John Robert said as he took a seat near Jake.

"I'm so glad you came," Mrs. Hurd said as she joined them. "Jake has been sitting in that wheelchair all day looking for you. Maybe now he will get up and try to walk. The doctor told us that if he doesn't exercise every day his back injury could cause him to be crippled for the rest of his life."

"Then we will exercise, starting right now, won't we Jake?"

"But it hurts to bad," he protested.

"It would hurt me much worse to see you a cripple," she said as she and his mother lifted his weakened body out of the wheelchair. They supported him and he half-dragged his broken leg from one end of the porch to the other. It only took a few trips until he was totally exhausted.

"Enough for today, but we'll do it all over again tomorrow," Ida Mae told him.

They visited for a short while longer before leaving Jake to some much needed rest. Both Ida Mae and John Robert made the forty-mile round trip on a daily basic for the next two weeks. By then John Robert's cast had been removed and Ida Mae had mastered the skill of operating a vehicle.

Having fully recovered, John Robert went back to helping with the farm chores but Ida Mae continued to visit Jake every day. Although his recovery was slow, he showed improvement with each visit. Ida Mae would help him with his exercises and then they would visit until late in the evening. She would then drive home, hoping to find a letter from Sarah who was now writing her almost every day.

Sarah was keeping her informed about the goings on in the city and about her guests who would stay for a day or two and then they were gone. She told her that she missed their late night visits and confessed she grew lonely at times. She often told Ida Mae she was exactly like the daughter she wished she could have had. She never failed to ask about Jake and John Robert and her letters always ended the same way, "I LOVE YOU, and please come see me again."

Sarah's letters never went unanswered and Ida Mae did long to go visit, but her every day routine and the lack of finances prevented her from doing so. With each letter she promised Sarah she would see her in the summer.

Fall grew into winter and then spring. Jake was almost better, disregarding the stiff right leg that would remain with him for the rest of his life. Ira was now Baxter's Chief Deputy, and John Robert was taking care of the farm.

Fletcher was still making big bucks in the bootlegging business and was even heard sometimes bragging about how he could outwit the law. It was a fact he had avoided getting caught by Sheriff Baxter or any of his men. By using different cars, different drivers, and various routes through the county, he was able to outsmart them. It was rumored he made some of the runs himself just to show his men he could get away with it. He had virtually created a monopoly in Buchanan County and parts of Eastern Kentucky. He used blackmail tactics to force as many of the whiskey makers as he could to sell to no one but him. The others he managed to have arrested by local law enforcement, or he would hire men to destroy their stills, which sometimes included inflicting bodily harm on the owners.

Ida Mae did as much as she could to help on the farm. Now that her daddy was almost always busy with the legal activities in the county, her brother welcomed all the help she could give. She made her daily visits across the mountain to visit Jake, which left no time for anything else. She never went into town, and she even quit attending church on Sunday. She did not want to face Dooley, and most of all she did not want to be questioned by any of the local gossip seekers.

Dooley, she learned, had resigned his position as deacon, but was still caretaker of the church's funds. She was also told that he spent every free minute practicing nine-ball down at the local pool hall, and that some of the local players would declare he was now better than Jake.

By mid-spring Jake was as fully recovered, as he would ever be. His daily exercises were no longer necessary and the pains that once seemed almost unbearable were becoming less severe. But because his leg made it difficult for him to drive, their deep affection for each other kept her going to visit every day. She had grown to love Jake more than she could have ever loved Dooley, but that was a secret she only shared with Sarah. In fact, she had shared all her secrets with Sarah, both during the late hours they spent together while Jake was in the hospital and in her letters since she came home. She had no regrets about confiding in Sarah, for she always seemed to understand. The only advice I can give you she wrote, when she learned about the annulment, was go find some one else. If you fail to do so you will grow old smothered in a world of loneliness as I have done.

Maybe she was looking for someone else and maybe she was lonely and needed someone to settle down and spend her life with, and maybe that was why Jake's comment rendered such a devastating blow.

It was late one evening in June, during her daily visit, that Jake made his heart-breaking announcement. "You have to stop coming to see me Ida Mae," he said.

"But why?" she asked.

"Because I am well now, as well as I can ever be thanks to you, and you have to think about getting on with your life."

"But you are my life Jake, don't you know that? I want to marry you someday."

"That can never be, Ida Mae. As much as I love you, that can never be. I have no way of supporting you, or myself for that matter. The sawmills are practically at a standstill. I'm not able to be much help at either of daddy's stills, and the meager amount Fletcher pays for his whiskey is barely enough to keep our body and souls together. Besides, I'm sure that income will end someday, when either he or Fletcher gets caught."

That was the first time Jake had told her he loved her, and were the most beautiful words she ever heard. Then to give her so many reasons why they could not share their lives together was more than she could bear.

"I love you too, Jake, and you don't have to worry about supporting me. I know I can find work. A lot of girls I know have jobs."

"You are young and beautiful and that's why you need to find someone who can afford to buy you pretty things and take you to pretty places. Someone who can give you all life has to offer. I'm sorry I didn't have the courage to tell you weeks ago, but I hung on to the false hope that I might fully recover."

Angry and hurt, Ida Mae got in her car and headed for home.

He was stealing her dream of spending the rest of her life with him. She was angry because he thought material things would mean more to her than their living together as man and wife.

"I'll write Sarah as soon as I get home and ask her what I should do," she thought.

She realized she hadn't received a letter from Sarah in over a week.

"The thing I won't do is go back to visit Jake, at least for a while," she determined. "If he cares for me as much as he has led me to believe he will come visit me."

That decision and many others were discarded by the time she had driven back to the farm.

Rejected and disappointed was the best description for Ida Mae by the time she got back home. She needed something to put her mind in the mode of positive thinking and she thought it had arrived in the letter that was waiting for her. But she was to find that too would only tend to darken her day. She knew at first glance it was not Sarah's handwriting. She felt her hands begin to tremble and she read.

Ida Mae,
Your friend Sarah has suffered a severe heart attack.
She is growing very weak and requests you come at once.
Sincerely,
Gladys Watson
5th Floor Nurse.

The postmark indicated the letter had been mailed three days earlier.

"When can we leave?" she asked as she handed the letter to John Robert.

"First thing in the morning," he said, without hesitation.

Shortly after daybreak they were on their way to North Carolina. They arrived at the hospital shortly after the beginning of morning visiting hours and wasted no time getting up to the fifth floor. "We're no strangers to this place," she told John Robert as they made their way to the nurse's station.

"Can you give us directions to Sarah Johnson's room?" Ida Mae asked.

"You must be Ida Mae Hale."

"That's right."

"I'm sorry to have to tell you this, but Sarah departed this life shortly after mid-night."

"Oh no!" Ida Mae cried.

"I'm Gladys Watson, and I know how you feel," the lady said. "Sarah was our Angel of Mercy and a friend to all those who needed help. She used to visit the hospital often but we hadn't seen her for the last year, her heart being so bad and all."

"Not once, during the weeks I spent with her did she mention any medical problems," Ida Mae confessed.

"She spoke of you often during her last hours and she asked that I give you this."

The nurse handed her a key that they both immediately recognized as being the front door key to her home. Attached with a string was a note that read: Call David Brown, at 312 17th Street.

"Thank you," Ida Mae said and she and John Robert made their way back to the parking lot.

"What do we do now?" she asked.

"We go to her home and then we call this David Brown. I think that's what she wanted."

They drove the familiar streets to Sarah's home. Several newspapers, encircled with rubber bands, were scattered on the lawn. The mailbox beside her front door was almost filled to capacity.

Ida Mae unlocked the door and stepped inside. A feeling of guilt gripped her. "I should have come visit her, John Robert. It was so little for her to ask in return for all she did for us."

"I wonder where she is now," he asked.

"In Heaven, of course," was her quick response.

"I mean her body."

"I have no idea. Maybe Mr. Brown can tell us."

John Robert found a phone directory beside Sarah's favorite chair. Among several David Brown listings he found one with the address, 312 17th Street. He dialed the number and after several rings a ladies voice came on the line. "David Brown, attorney at law. How may we help you?"

"He's a lawyer," John Robert said, reaching the phone to Ida Mae.

"My name is Ida Mae Hale, a friend of Sarah Johnson's. She passed away last night and she left instructions for me to call this number."

"One moment please, Ms. Hale."

A moment later, a man's voice came on the line. Ida Mae repeated what she had told the lady who answered the phone and asked if he knew which funeral home had Sarah's body.

"Yes, I do. Where are you calling from?" he inquired.

"Sarah's home."

"Marvelous, I was just about to leave my office. I'll be there in fifteen minutes and I'll give you all the details."

She hung up the phone and both she and her brother went to the porch to wait for Mr. Brown. An advertising circular protruding from the mailbox caught her attention. She pulled the circular from the box and with it came two letters, both postmarked in other states. More letters of appreciation they agreed.

"Wonder what will become of all those letters now that she's gone?" Ida Mae asked.

"I guess we will never know," John Robert answered, just as a large black Cadillac pulled to the curb. An elderly gentleman got out of the car and came to the porch.

"I'm David Brown, Ida Mae. You look exactly as Sarah described you."

"That's right sir. This is my brother, John Robert. I'm sorry we were unable to get here before Sarah passed away. She was the kindest, most generous person I have ever known. We became very close during my stay here and I grew to love her as much as if she were family."

"The feeling was mutual, I assure you. I could have told you this on the phone but I wanted to meet you in person. Sarah's body is at Conrad Funeral Home on the outskirts of the city. The viewing will be tomorrow night and the funeral is at 11:00 o'clock Friday. I am to be one of the pallbearers so I can take the two you to the viewing, and to the funeral if you would like."

"Thank you very much, but I don't know where we will be staying."

"Oh! You must stay right here. I can assure you, as her attorney, that is what Sarah would want."

"Then we will see you tomorrow evening, Sir."

The next morning both Ida Mae and John Robert slept late. Just before noon they drove into the city to purchase flowers for Sarah. They also had to buy clothing to wear to the wake and funeral. Nothing expensive, mind you, for John Robert's funds were limited and Ida Mae was flat broke, just something suitable for the occasion. They ate a late lunch at one of the cheapest restaurants in the city and went back to Sarah's place to get dressed and wait for Mr. Brown.

"Do you have enough money for food and gas to get us back home?" Ida Mae asked.

"Just barely, but we will need to leave immediately after the funeral," he told her.

They were about to sit on the porch and wait for the attorney when they saw his Cadillac coming down the street. They got in the back seat and listened to Mr. Brown talk about the many wonderful things Sarah did for families who had friends or loved ones in the hospital. Most of them, like her, could not have afforded to stay anywhere in the city had it not been for Sarah.

As they were about to leave the city, Mr. Brown turned his car into the parking lot of Conrad Funeral Home. Two well-dressed gentlemen met them at the main entrance, and one of them directed them to the chapel containing Sarah's remains. A plain, closed, oak coffin, surrounded by dozens of floral arrangements, each a symbol of the many lives she had touched, sat in front of the pulpit.

"Sarah made her funeral arrangement a long time ago," Mr. Brown told them. "She lived a simple life and she wanted to be put away in the same manner. Since she has no family I would like for you to join me in greeting those who come to pay their last respects."

"Certainly," Ida Mae told him.

They both stood near the head of the coffin and spoke to the hundreds of mourners who filed by. They stayed until the last visitor was gone and the funeral director dimmed the lights in the chapel. Mr. Brown drove them back to Sarah's and as they started to get out of his car he laid his hand on Ida Mae's shoulder. "Thank you Mrs. Hale, I'm sure Sarah was looking down on you tonight and I'm sure she is grateful."

"It is I who am grateful," she said as she got out of the car and followed John Robert inside.

The next morning the chapel was filled to capacity, again the coffin remained closed and the funeral was very short. The casket was hauled a short distance out of the city to a cemetery beside a small county church. Again few words were spoken and as John Robert led her to Mr. Brown's vehicle, Ida Mae could see the coffin being slowly lowered into the ground.

"Exactly as she would have wanted," Mr. Brown said once they were on their way.

They drove back to Sarah's place and as they got out of the car Ida Mae asked the attorney if he would mind to stay long enough for them to change. "I will give you the key and then we must be on our way."

"May I come in," he asked. "There is something I need to discuss with you."

"Please do."

The lawyer opened the trunk of his car and took a briefcase from inside. He followed them into the house and went straight to the kitchen. He placed the briefcase on one end of the table, extracted some legal looking document, and asked her to have a seat.

"I could have mentioned this yesterday, but I felt it would not have been proper until Sarah was laid to rest. Knowing how fond Sarah was of you, I am pleased to inform you that you are the soul heir to all that she owned."

Ida Mae stared at the attorney in disbelief. "You mean this home is mine," she stammered.

"And all her personnel property, which means all its contents. Sarah did not trust banks but she had no cash anyway, I'm afraid. I sometimes wonder how she ever got by. There are no unpaid debts; even my fee has been taken care of, so everything you see here now belongs to you. Provided you can stay in town until Monday so I can have the will probated, of course."

"We can, can't we John Robert?"

Her brother, who was also almost in shock, gave an affirmative nod.

"Then, I must go, I have one other appointment. I will see you at the courthouse at 9:00 o'clock Monday morning. I'm sure you will have no trouble finding it."

John Robert was the first to settle down enough to speak. "Well Sis, what do you have to say?"

'What can I say? Except I am so ashamed for not coming to visit Sarah."

"I'm starved. Do you mind if I go through your cupboards to find something to eat?"

"Not at all, I'll help you," she said and the two of them started opening doors displaying enough food to last a month.

"Why don't you go into the rest of the house and see what else I own while I fix us something to eat. And, get the mail from outside and open it, if you will please."

Cooking meals in Sarah's kitchen was not new to Ida Mae. She collected the necessary cookware, selected enough food for their dinner and in a short time was almost ready to put everything on the table, when John Robert came running into the kitchen.

"You're not going to believe this," he declared, handing her several greenbacks of various denominations.

"Where did all this cash come from? I thought you were almost as broke as I am."

"From these," he said, holding up four or five envelopes he had taken from the mailbox. "There is over fifty dollars here. Each envelope contained a letter thanking Sarah for some past deed and each contained at least one piece of currency."

"Mr. Brown wondered how Sarah got by. Well, I guess now we know."

Suddenly she remembered all those envelopes piled on bookcase shelves in the sitting room. "Let's eat," she told him, "and then I have something else for us do."

They finished their meal and Ida Mae hurriedly washed the dishes. John Robert dried each piece and put them in their proper place. "Now let's go to the sitting room," she said to him.

She took a handful of envelopes, many with postmarks twenty years old, from one of the shelves and began looking inside. More than half contained greenbacks, some only had a dollar or two while others had larger amounts. There was no time to read all the letters; she would do that later. They each opened the letters and wrote the amount they contained on the back of the envelope. The money was placed in a stack on the coffee table and the letter put back in the proper envelope and back on the shelf. As more and more letters were opened, the stacks of money became more plentiful. Sometime late into the night the last letter was examined, put back on the shelf and several thousand dollars were neatly stacked in front of them.

"How does it feel to be rich and single?" John Robert asked.

"I'd rather be rich and married and that's just what I'll be when we get back home," she smiled.

"What are we going to do now?"

"Why don't you count this money? I'm going to take a hot bath and go to bed."

Near mid-night there was a knock on her bedroom door. "Good night, Sis. I just wanted to let you know you have a little more than twenty-eight thousand in cash, minus whatever it costs to take me out to dinner tomorrow."

The next day was Sunday and no business could be transacted, so the couple spent much of the day taking inventory of Ida Mae's newly acquired possessions. Late in the afternoon she did treat herself and John Robert to a steak dinner at one of the cities finest eating establishments. They stayed out late, just cruising the city, and Ida Mae was glad. It would only be a few hours until she could meet Lawyer Brown at the courthouse, deposit most of her cash in one of the local banks, and then go home to share the news of her good fortune with the other members of her family.

And that's exactly what she did. By dinner time the next day, all she set out to do had been done. The business at the courthouse had been taken care of.

She had a twenty-five thousand dollar checking account in her name, more than three thousand in her purse, as the Baxter farm was coming into view.

Everyone in the Duncan family was gathered around the dinner table when Ida Mae and John Robert walked into the house.

"Welcome home, weary travelers," Granny greeted them. "Grab a plate and tell us all about your trip."

"Well, I guess you could say it was a trip we will always remember," Ida Mae began.

"You can say that again," John Robert interrupted.

Ida Mae kicked him under the table and the look on her face was hint enough to let him know to keep quiet and let her finish.

"As I was saying," she went on, "the trip was one we will always remember. We got to the hospital just hours after Sarah passed away. And, even though we were not able to see her before she died, we were not going to leave until she was laid to rest. There were more flowers than I had ever seen, and more people than I could count came to pay their last respects."

"More than came to stare at Brother Taylor?" Kevin wanted to know.

"More than came to stare at Brother Taylor," Ida Mae smiled.

"You grew really fond of her, didn't you?" Mary Ellen commented.

"And you will never guess how much she loved Ida Mae," John Robert interjected.

One more swift kick told him to keep quiet.

"We could have come home a couple days ago, but I wanted to look at all the pretty things they have in those big stores in the city," she continued.

"I shore would like to go to one of them big stores and buy me one of them fancy Daisy BB guns," Kevin said. "They shoot further than them slingshots."

"Me too," Kervin chimed, "but I bet they don't shoot no better than my slingshot."

"What would you buy, Mary Sue?"

"A new red dress and a pair of black high heels," she answered without having to think for a moment.

"Mother, what about you and Granny?"

"Since we are wishing for all these things, we aint never going to get, I'd like to have me a new rocking chair with one of them things that sets in front to put my old tired feet up on," Granny told her.

"I'd be happy with a new washing machine," Mary Ellen added. "Ever since your daddy left his police whistle in the pocket of his britches and I tried to run them through the wringers, they aint been doing just right."

"What about you Daddy, what would you wish for?"

Ira thought for a moment before he answered. "I guess the thing that would make me most happy would be to catch Mike Fletcher with a big load of moonshine. Then I could put him behind bars and make fun of him like he has been doing the Sheriff and all us deputies for the last while.

"Thought I had one of his boys a few nights ago, but that big black souped-up Kaiser he was driving left me so fast I thought my engine had died. Heard they were going to make a big haul this weekend too. I reckon they will be furnishing liquid refreshments for all the folks at that fiddler's convention coming up the Fourth of July. The Sheriff got word they would be coming through the county this weekend, but he don't know how many will be making the run, or which roads they will use. If I could catch one of them it would make me happier than buying anything them big city stores has got on their shelves."

" Since we are all wishing, I might as well wish for a new round of tires for my old Chevrolet. Ida Mae has made so many trips to see Jake, the ones I got are as slick as a peeled onion."

"Speaking of Jake, has anyone heard from him?" Ida Mae asked. No one had.

"I'll go see him tomorrow, if my big brother will let me use the car, and all the tires still have air in them," she smiled.

After they had finished eating she and John Robert went to get their belongings out of the car.

"When are you going to tell them?" he asked.

"Right away, but not until you and I have gone shopping."
"You're all right Sis," he smiled.

Chapter Twenty-Six

WE'LL FIND A WAY

da Mae could hardly wait until the next day to go see Jake. Not seeing him was easier when they were miles apart, but to be so close was a different matter.

She didn't care that he had asked her not to come again. She knew he loved her, and she had to make him understand that if they both really wanted, they could find a way to have a life together.

She also knew she would have to do it without him knowing about what Sarah had left her. To even suggest they start a life together with only her possessions would be an insult to his pride.

It was just before noon when she decided she could wait no longer. She drove the twenty miles in a state of total frustration. It had been almost a week since their last contact and she didn't know whether Jake would be glad to see her, or be upset because she came. It did not take long for her to decide, it was not the latter.

When she turned into his driveway he greeted her with a smile. He was working under the hood of a huge black automobile and some young fellow, she did not recognize, was behind the wheel revving the engine as fast as it would run.

As she pulled her car up along side the black automobile, Jake immediately signaled the other fellow to turn off the ignition.

"Sounds like an airplane and looks almost as big," Ida Mae said.

"And will move almost as fast since Jake's got her all tuned up. She's got a 226-cid six-cylinder Continental L-head engine, built-up rear suspension, plenty of space in the trunk, and will outrun anything brave enough to challenge. Who knows, Saturday afternoon she may get put to the test."

"What kind of car is it, anyway?" she asked.

"Why, it's a Kaiser, young lady. You must be Jake's sister."

The wheels in Ida Mae's head started to spin. A big, black souped-up Kaiser — this had to be the car her daddy described just last night.

"I believe we agreed on twenty bucks," Jake said, as he slammed the hood and walked to where Ida Mae was standing.

"And worth every penny if you ask me," the stranger smiled. "May get put to the test Saturday afternoon." Ida Mae was rapidly putting the pieces together.

The stranger gave Jake the twenty-dollars and goosed the engine. He drove to the end of the driveway and then took off like he had been shot out of a cannon.

"Who was that?" Ida Mae asked.

"One of Fletcher's redneck associates. Fletcher told him I was a pretty good mechanic, and that I could get that hot rod running properly. I guess he figured I needed the money. But forget about that dude; just tell me that you missed me as much as I did you. And, if I ever tell you not to come visit me again, you should have me committed."

She threw her arms around him and gave him a long passionate kiss. It was not until she released her embrace that she noticed his father sitting on the front porch.

"It's unusual to see your daddy home this time of day," she commented. "Is something wrong?"

"You might say that. Fletcher found out Daddy sold a gallon or two to one of his competitors and told him he would take his business somewhere else. That night someone destroyed both of Daddy's stills. Just another way of eliminating the competition, I suppose. But I have some good news," he continued.

"The insurance company paid all my hospital bills and I have already received a check for the value of my car. I took a part-time job at the Piggly Wiggly stocking the shelves at night.

"I made Mother and Daddy take most of the insurance money, but I did keep a few hundred so we could get married," he grinned. "Do you still think you could put up with a country boy, with a slight limp, for the rest of your life?"

"Yes! Yes! Yes!" She squealed, and not caring that Jake's mother and daddy were both now on the porch, grabbed him and gave him another long passionate kiss.

"Now get in," she told him.

"Where are we going?"

"To tell Mother and Daddy, of course, and there is something else I want to tell Daddy. And I would like for us to go back to Winston-Salem on our honeymoon. It's such a beautiful place and there is something I want to show you."

"Whatever you want sweetheart," he smiled.

On the way to the farm, she told Jake about the death of Sarah and that she and John Robert had gone to North Carolina to attend her funeral. She would tell him the rest of the story about Sarah, but she chose not to do it today.

When they pulled up to the gate at her parent's home, her daddy was the first one she seen. He had a hammer and a few nails in one hand and a newly sawed piece of lumber in the other.

"Hi Daddy, Jake and I are getting married," she called out.

Her voice must have echoed through the entire house, for a moment later everyone in the family was outside.

"When is the big day?" Mary Ellen wanted to know.

"I was thinking the Fourth of July would be just right," Jake answered. What do you think, Ida Mae?"

"I think the Fourth of July would be perfect," she smiled.

"That's just a week away, we won't have time to plan the wedding," Mary Ellen protested.

"Oh no, Mother, we want to keep it simple, just Jake's parents and all of us, and a preacher if we can find one. I'm sure Reverend Kyle would not want to do the honors."

She left Jake's side and led her daddy a few feet away.

"That Kaiser you were telling us about last night will be coming through the county late Saturday afternoon. I'm not sure who will be driving, but I'm sure they will take the easiest route because they will have a full load."

"That would be Route 80. Are you sure your information is correct?"

"I'm positive, Daddy."

Ira laid the hammer, nails, and piece of lumber on the end of the porch and started toward his car. "I'm going to go tell the sheriff right this minute," he said.

"We're leaving, too," she told him. "Jake and I have to get a blood test, and then I'll take him back home. John Robert and I have some errands to run tomorrow and we have to get an early start."

The next morning she and her brother left the farm shortly after sunrise, and it was well past suppertime when they returned. Everyone except Ira, who was off somewhere with the sheriff, was gathered on the porch discussing the upcoming wedding. When John Robert's Chevrolet pulled through the gate near the end of the lane, it got everyone's attention. A small canvas covered trailer was attached to the rear bumper, and a new green 98 Oldsmobile, being driven by Ida Mae, was following close behind.

By the time they got to the house, everyone except Granny, was standing at the gate to find out what was going on.

It did not take long for John Robert to satisfy their curiosity. He loosened the canvas, rolled it back, and revealed a brand new washing machine. A smile appeared on Mary Ellen's face and when he unveiled a rocker and matching footstool, Granny stood to attention.

Without giving any of them time to ask questions, Ida Mae reached into the back seat and handed each of the twins the Daisy BB guns they'd wished for. "And, this is for you, little sister," she said as she gave Mary Sue a package containing a low-cut red dress and a pair of shiny black high heel shoes. "John Robert's new tires are in the trunk. He will have to mount them later."

"Where did all these things come from?" Mary Ellen wanted to know.

"Don't worry, Mother, everything's paid for," John Robert assured her. "Ida Mae bought them."

"Who died and left you wealthy?" Granny asked.

"A kind, sweet, humble lady by the name of Sarah, but if any of you tell Jake, I promise I will take everything back."

"The new car is for her and Jake," John Robert told them. "We are hiding it behind the barn until after the wedding."

"If anyone breathes a word of this, I will take everything back," she repeated. "I just hope I can help Daddy get what he wanted," she sighed.

Ida Mae saw very little of her daddy for the next two days. He and the other officers were busy planning how to stop the moonshine run planned for the weekend. They were determined that if the big Kaiser entered the county, it was not going to get through.

By noon Saturday, Ira was as tense as a rattlesnake coiled to strike. He could hardly wait to go on duty. As soon as he finished lunch, he dressed in his uniform and was ready to go.

"Got to top off the tank. We may be in for a long chase before this day is over," he said as he went out the door.

Ida Mae followed him until he got into his car.

"I hope you can catch them, so you can put Fletcher out of business, but most of all I want you back home safe. You be real careful, Daddy."

"You bet. I got a wedding to go to next week remember? Thanks for the tip." He winked and drove off.

Ira drove to his designated position near the county line.

After backing his car into an unused logging road, he placed a few small tree branches he'd cut against the front grille and waited.

He, like the other deputies, was as well hidden as he could be, and hoped he would be the one to make the arrest. They had withstood Fletcher's humiliation long enough and each of them wanted to be the one to shut Fletcher's business down. No one knew if more than one vehicle would be involved, or exactly which route they would use, so Sheriff Baxter was on the move. He drove from place to place; ready to rush to wherever he was needed as soon as the call came on his two-way.

Ira watched every vehicle that passed until after sunset. He had about decided his daughter had misunderstood what she had heard, when out of nowhere, the big black Kaiser roared past.

It was not exceeding the speed limit, however, and he could not see well enough to tell who was driving.

He could, however, tell the rear bumper was closer to the pavement than was normal for that make and model. When the Kaiser was far enough past that Ira could leave his hiding place and not be detected, he pulled onto the highway. He picked up the mike to his two-way and alerted the other officers that he had the suspect in sight. "We're on Route 80, heading down the mountain and he hasn't seen me yet."

"Ten-four," came the sheriff's voice loud and clear. "Use no lights, no siren, and don't crowd him. Stay as far as you can behind, but keep him in sight! I'm about 20 miles out on Route 19, but I'm headed your way. Let him get through town if you can and we will set up a roadblock just before he reaches the Blackford Bridge on the Clinch. All units, leave your positions and we'll have a welcome party waiting at the river."

"Better step on it. He knows I'm back here," Ira said, as the Kaiser started putting more and more real estate between the two vehicles.

"Stay on his tail," Baxter came back. "I just turned onto Route 80 and I've got a State Trooper right behind me. Guess he's been listening to our radio. We'll try to beat the Kaiser to the river."

"We're coming into Honaker now and we're flat out."

"Pray there is no one in the streets and push him as hard as you can. How close are you?"

"If I was any closer, I'd be riding with him," Ira's voice came back amidst the sound of screeching tires and the wail of his siren.

"Good job," Baxter answered. "We will be on the west end of the bridge in two minutes."

"That won't be soon enough. This sucker is flying."

"Make it a minute and a half," came a strange voice.

"Who's that?" Ira asked hurriedly.

"Trooper Jim, but my friends call me Big Country. I just showed the sheriff my taillights. Back off when you get near the bridge, we wouldn't want both of you to try to run over us."

"Thanks, Trooper," Baxter said.

Ira was too busy to respond.

The trooper drove onto the east end of the bridge just as the Kaiser came into view. Ira was close behind but he began to fall back. The trooper locked up all four wheels and went sliding to the other end, blocking one of the two lanes. A second later the sheriff came sliding up beside him, blocking the only way of escape. "We got him," he sang out.

Tires began to squeal and the heavy automobile went into a tail-spin.

"Run," the Sheriff cried out, when it was evident the driver had lost control.

Somehow the car missed the end of the bridge and plunged into the rushing water below.

"That's Fletcher," sheriff Baxter yelled to Ira as his cruiser slid to a stop. "Run down-river in case he makes it out and tries to run. The trooper and I will watch both banks from up here."

Ira jumped down the embankment and ran about a hundred yards downstream. He sat down on a large sycamore log, took a plug of Brown Mule from his hip pocket and cut a small chew from one corner. Two or three minutes later, he heard Fletcher yell from the middle of the river.

"Help! I can't swim."

Ira waited for a moment, while looking at the other officers on the bridge. When he was sure the call for help had been muffled by the rapid flowing water he replied, "I can't e-i-t-h-e-r!"

He sat back down on the log, cut a larger chew from the plug, and pretended to be watching the river. Fletcher was nowhere in sight.

* * *

The next day, about a mile downstream, a search party pulled Fletcher's mangled, bloated body out of the water.

When Ida Mae heard the news, she was absolutely ecstatic. She was at last free from the hold Fletcher had on her. And, she was determined to never put herself in a position that would allow anyone else to blackmail her. After all, life had afforded her a new start. She was out of a relationship that should never have taken place to begin with.

She was now better off financially than she could have ever dreamed, and was soon going to marry the man she really loved. She did not even mind that Fletcher's funeral was to be on the same day as her wedding; no one in her family would want to see him off anyway.

The evening before the big day, Ira, Mary Ellen, Mary Sue, John Robert, Ida Mae and Jake was sitting on the porch of the Duncan home enjoying the coolness of the evening. The twins, as usual, were in the front yard target practicing, and Granny was somewhere around back.

A large blackbird flew into the maple tree near the corner of the yard and perched on the end of a limb. Kervin cocked his BB and looked at Jake. "You ain't no preacher are you?" When Jake shook his head, indicating that he wasn't, Kervin pulled the trigger. The bird fell to the ground.

"Oh," Granny yelled, as if she had seen and was alarmed at what had just happened.

"Guess I've put it off long enough," Ira said smiling. He picked up the hammer, nails, and the piece of lumber he'd placed on the porch a few days earlier and started toward the Johnny house.

"Let's you and I drive down town Jake," John Robert suggested, "I need to get some tires mounted if you and Ida Mae are driving my car to North Carolina."

Kevin started to snicker, but the look his big sister gave him silenced him at once.

Jake looked at Ida Mae as if he was asking for permission.

"Go ahead," she smiled." It might be your last night out for a while."

"I'll have your brother take me home."

Twenty minutes later, they were setting in front of the new Texaco Station in the middle of town. John Robert told the attendant what he needed and was informed it would be at least an hour and half before he could have him back on the road.

"What are we going to do for an hour and a half?" Jake wanted to know.

"I hear you are a pretty good pool shot," John Robert answered. Let's stroll over to Willie's place and I'll let you give me a lesson or two."

"Sounds like a great idea. I haven't had a stick in my hand in months."

They walked the short distance to the pool hall and to their surprise the street in front of the place was full. Two or three of the automobiles they noticed had out of state license plates. "Guy's come home for the holiday," Jake suggested, as they rounded the corner and stepped through the back entrance.

Neither of them could ever remember Willie's Place drawing such a crowd. The room was filled wall to wall but all the action seemed to be centered at one table.

"What's going on?" Jake asked someone who was standing near the back of the smoke-filled room.

"Big game going on," he answered. "One of the local boys challenged some guy from out of town and they have been going at it for three or hours all ready. High stakes too, mind you, but I think the local boy is about ready to bite the dust. That's his lady friend over there and she doesn't seem to be happy at the moment."

Jake and John Robert moved a step or two closer, to see what was happening.

"Oh, boy," Jake said.

"That's Dooley," John Robert whispered.

"I know, and the other fellow is a friend of mine from up North. He grew up in Buchanan County and he taught me everything I know about the game of pool. He is probably the best shot in Chicago and maybe the whole state of Illinois. Who is the pregnant woman sitting near the end of the table with the cigar box in her hand?"

"Oh, that's a gal who lives just out of town, one who has quite a reputation too, I might add. I'd heard she and Dooley had been keeping company but I had no idea it had gone this far."

They watched as Dooley asked the woman to give him another fifty dollars.

She handed him a few greenbacks and with a bit of sarcasm in her voice she stated, "I guess you know that's all there is." Five minutes later the game was over. The lady threw the cigar box on the table and started toward the exit. Dooley laid his cue stick on the table, hung his head, and followed her outside.

Within a week, Dooley's parents had sold their home. Mr. Hale wrote a check to replace the funds his son had taken, and the Hale family, along with Dooley's lady, left town. They would leave no forwarding address.

Chapter Twenty-Seven

A DAY FILLED WITH SURPRISES

July Fourth began as Ida Mae hoped it would. There was a beautiful sunrise and not a cloud in the sky. Not only was it the Fourth of July, it was the day she was to become Mrs. Jacob Hurd. It would be a simple country wedding; both she and Jake wanted it that way.

No floral arrangements, no expensive clothes, no wedding march, and no fancy reception after. In fact, she hardly knew the preacher. He was some young fellow who had just become pastor at one of the neighboring churches, but Ida Mae didn't mind. At one o'clock, she and Jake would exchange vows on the front porch of her parent's home nestled in the foothills of the mountains she had grown to love and then they would be off to start a life together.

She would miss life on the farm no doubt, but thanks to Sarah, she would be able to come visit often. And, knowing her family was doing much better financially made leaving easier. The income from Ira's new job was allowing them to have things they once just dreamed about.

Ira still worked a few hours on the farm each week but most of his time was taken up with legal matters. The responsibility of running the farm had been given to John Robert and he was doing an outstanding job. The sheriff was so impressed with his capability he came to the farm almost every evening just to talk to him.

A new Ford tractor and several pieces of machinery were now being used to do the work once done by a team of horses, which made life on the farm much easier for all her family. The weather could not have been better and the fields were yielding bumper crops; all of this made Ida Mae's leaving much less painful. And thanks to her, next week they would be getting a telephone, which meant she could talk to them as often as she liked.

The entire family was out of bed early, but little out of the ordinary was taking place. They were going about doing their daily chores but the feeling of anxiety was very apparent. The twins were more anxious than anyone else. They were more excited about Jake finding out about the new car than they were about their big sister getting married.

As the one o'clock hour grew closer, Ida Mae became more nervous. She was the only one who had made any preparations for the upcoming event. It was half past the noon hour and her mother; Mary Sue and Granny were still busy in the kitchen. John Robert was sitting on the porch, dressed in a pair of overalls, and the twins were off somewhere with their BB guns.

She had no idea about the whereabouts of her daddy. She put on the same dress she was wearing the first night she met Jake and went onto the porch. She sat in the chair closest John Robert and started staring down over the fields. "Something has happened, Jake and his parents should have been here by now, and where is Daddy?"

"I guess Daddy's forgot but it don't matter, appears like old Jake has changed his mind. By the way, if he don't show up can I have that new Olds?"

"Ah, quit teasing, John Robert. What time is it?"

"He's got plenty of time, it just ten 'til one, and I really would like to have a new car."

Ida Mae was about to make a comment when her attention was drawn to a long line of traffic coming toward the farm. There must have been at least twenty vehicles and the sheriff was leading the parade. Her daddy was the last in line. When the sheriff turned into the lane his flashing lights came on. He started blasting his car horn and all the other drivers followed suit. Children in the back of some pickups were ringing cowbells and they were all yelling, 'Here Comes The Groom.'

A moment later, the vehicles were parked in front of the gate. Ira, Jake, and someone she did not know got out of Ira's car and came up the steps. Jake took Ida Mae's hand and led her to the edge of the porch. She stood speechless as people, most of whom she did not know, got out of their vehicles and gathered in the front yard.

The stranger who had arrived with Jake and her daddy raised his hand. The crowd grew silent, as he took a small booklet from his inside jacket pocket.

"Dearly beloved, we are gathered here today to join this couple in the bonds of Holy Matrimony," he began. Five minutes later he was pronouncing them man and wife.

Suddenly the cowbells started ringing again and firecrackers were being exploded all over the place. Men started unloading tables from the back of pickup trucks and placing them end-to-end in the shade of the huge maple tree. Ladies began taking container after container of food from the trunks of cars and soon the tables were filled. Mary Sue carefully carried a small cake from inside and placed it in the center of one of the tables. The cake had white frosting and a miniature bride and groom and a message that read, "Together Forever." Ice chests filled with soft drinks were placed near the gate and someone yelled, "Let the festivities begin!"

The next two hours were filled with eating, drinking, opening gifts, and making introductions. Many of the guests were friends of hers and the others were Jake's friends or members of his family.

It was near mid-afternoon when Jake stood at the top of the steps with his new bride by his side.

"It's time for us to leave," he told their guests, "and I want to thank each of you for coming. Ida Mae had no hint of any of this, but unlike myself, I knew how much she likes surprises."

"I want to thank you too," Ida Mae added. "I'll have a surprise for him some day and I promise all of you will be there. Now, would you mind to go get the car, John Robert?"

"Not at all," he said. He left the porch and started toward the barn where he had parked his old Chevrolet. A moment later he pulled the shiny new Oldsmobile up to the gate. He got out, walked up the steps to where Jake was standing and handed him the keys. Jake took the keys and stared at the Olds but was unable to utter a word.

"I promised all of you would be there," Ida Mae smiled.

"Don't ask me to explain, Jake. I'll do that on the way to North Carolina," she whispered. "And it changes gears by itself, so you can drive," she added.

Jake could hardly wait to learn about how Ida Mae had purchased the car. Little did he know what other news his new bride had in store.

She told him about the long talks she and Sarah had had in her room late at night. About all the people Sarah had befriended and how their gifts of appreciation had been her only source of income since the death of her husband. How Sarah had left everything she owned, which amounted to a small fortune to her and now it belonged to both of them.

"Enough for us to live on until I can find a good honest job?" Jake asked.

"I'm sure, but you won't want to be looking for work for a few days," she smiled.

They talked about Sarah and of starting their life together as the miles rolled by. Shortly before sundown they reached the outskirts of the city. Jake remembered exactly where to go and a few minutes later they pulled in front of the home where they would live for many years to come.

"I remember the first time I came here with Daddy," she told Jake as they stepped onto the porch of their new home. "Sarah opened her home to us and treated us as she would her own family. I don't know what any of us would have done without her," she added.

"I guess there will never be another Sarah," Jake said, as he unlocked the door and carried his new bride over the threshold.

The young couple spent the new few days doing nothing but enjoying each other. Just after dark about a week after they arrived, they were sitting on the front porch having an after dinner cup of coffee. A taxi pulled to the curb and an elderly white haired man and woman got out of the car. Hand in hand they slowly moved to where the couple was sitting.

"May we help you?" Jake asked.

"Our son is critically ill and has been sent to the hospital here in your city," the lady answered. "Our funds are very limited and someone told us the lady who lives here might give us free lodging, but I guess we must have come to the wrong place."

Without a moments hesitation Ida Mae sprang to her feet. "You most surely are at the right place," she said.

"You are most kind," the lady said. "Our suitcases are still in the taxi."

"I'll get them," Jake volunteered.

He headed toward the cab as Ida Mae held the door, allowing the couple to enter.

"My name is Viola and this is my husband Henry; and you just have to be Sarah," the lady said as the door closed behind them.

The End

Ida Mae's
Moonshine, Money & Misery

James Campbell

Printed in the United States
37301LVS00003B/61-162